THE
ACCIDENTAL JIBE
AND
OTHER STORIES

THE
ACCIDENTAL JIBE
AND
OTHER STORIES

BARBARA WOLFENDEN

authorHOUSE®

AuthorHouse™ LLC
1663 Liberty Drive
Bloomington, IN 47403
www.authorhouse.com
Phone: 1-800-839-8640

Published by AuthorHouse   08/04/2014

ISBN: 978-1-4969-2747-7 (sc)
ISBN: 978-1-4969-2746-0 (e)

Library of Congress Control Number: 2014912746

To Martin

THE ACCIDENTAL JIBE

The weather promised a wonderful day on *Edelweiss*. While Chris bailed out the dinghy, Jennifer readied the boat. She took a deep breath. Let's see - remove the sail cover and stow it and the wheel cover below, turn the power switch to ALL and flip on the instrumentation; bring up the flag, winch handles, cushions, GPS, boat key and the hand-held radio to the cockpit; press the glow plug button for thirty seconds and THEN push the start button. (Make sure the rev arrow points to the 10).

After three months of sailing, she was getting the hang of it.

They left the mooring in Marion, Massachusetts, and sailed across Buzzard's Bay to Tashmoo, a quiet lake tucked into the southern coast of Martha's Vineyard. They picked up a mooring and ate lunch. Jennifer called to Chris who was below getting his swim mask.

"I'm signed up for the piloting course in the Fall, as you suggested." He emerged from the cabin wearing his snorkel mask.

"That's good – you'll learn a lot." His voice was nasal and pinched from behind the mask. "Those Power Squadron instructors know what they're talking about. Oh, the SEO asked me to teach Piloting this fall."

What's the SEO?"

Chris turned from the swim ladder to face her. "How many times do I have to tell you? Squadron Education Officer." Chris continued in his Donald Duck voice, "Oh, Damn. I forgot to bring the squadron manual for you. I'll give it to you tonight."

Jennifer had not opened last week's present, *Galley Recipes*. She wasn't sure about having this much involvement in this boating thing, never dreaming sailing was going to be so much work. Or dangerous. Like taking down the main sail while they were in a billowing sea. You had to really hang on.

One thing was really starting to bother her: Chris' attitude on the boat. That morning she had tied the dinghy to the stern before they set off, yet Chris called out almost immediately "If I can't count on you to tie the dinghy properly then I can't trust you to do other things right." Later he went: "Dear, you mean you want to go to the head, not to the bathroom." "No, Dear, that's not the halyard line. I asked you to loosen the jib line." He actually got uptight over silly stuff. "No, it's not the floor, it's called the sole." "That's not a rope, it's a sheet." She usually didn't know what he was talking about. Why did he insist on calling everything by its special name as if he were playing pirate or something?

Chris dived into the water while Jennifer fell back on her pillow in the cockpit. She glanced up at the mast, a majestic, towering presence. She smiled. She'd prepared the mainsail for hoisting that morning all by herself. She had unhooked the halyard (that was the rope you pulled to raise the sail), and then re-hooked it to the sail. She'd squatted, the suckers on her boat shoes gripping the surface like frog's feet. Sweat ran into her eyes, smarting. She pinched the shackle's shiny prongs to free its metal pin. Then, clutching the shackle in a death grip and holding on to the mast with her free hand, ever so carefully she'd led it over to the metal-rimmed hole in the sail – Oh yes, that was called the cringle – and pinched the prongs again to insert it. She'd concentrated fiercely. It would be unforgivable to let the shackle out of her hands. Chris had warned her that if she let go, the halyard might fly up and lodge at the top of the mast, more than forty feet in the air. And then what would happen? She had no idea but Chris had said NEVER let it go. She frowned. Chris had not praised her yet for today's work.

He was certainly not perfect but she wanted to hang on to him if she could. They'd met at a party given by some of her friends, each fifty-something woman bringing an eligible male for the others to meet. Jennifer'd brought a divorced geek friend from work. She hated these get-togethers but she had to admit she wanted a husband or at least a steady man in her life since being single off and on since her divorce several years earlier. She was tired of living alone. If she didn't find someone, would she become a Lulu Kruse? Now there's a case in point. Back in Michigan when Jennifer was growing up, Lulu Kruse was the dependable church lady. Crispy gray perm, age spots and boobs down to here, Lulu had never married and until recently, had cared for her ailing mother until the old lady finally died. Lulu was always shuffling around in the church kitchen refilling the coffee urns, putting out cream and sugar and washing the pots after weddings while everybody else had fun. Jennifer shuddered. She did not want to live in that kind of hell.

At the party that night, Jennifer had noticed the cute redheaded man standing over by a picture on the wall. Pale white skin with a dusting of freckles, just enough wrinkles to show he had character, and good strong shoulders, too. While her own skin was the color of warm toffee (a universal brown woman she liked to call herself), Jennifer liked the scrubbed, bleached quality of natural redheads with their cold white-lashed eyes. She walked over. The picture he was examining was an etching of an old man holding a small bouquet in his hand. She said in a quiet voice, her best German accent, *"Schneeblumen."*

He turned, surprised. *"Ya, Schneeblumen."*

"Sprichts du Deutsch?"

"Ja wohl."

They eyed each other for a split second, then he gave a little chuckle. "Not really. I studied German for four years in college but that doesn't mean I could order a *Wienerschnitzel* if my life depended on it."

She laughed. "I spent a summer at the Goethe Institut in Rottenburg ob der Tauber." She exaggerated her "r's" gutturally, authoritatively, like a Nazi commandant in a movie. "Hi, I'm Jennifer."

"Kwrissssss." Equally guttural. They both laughed and shook hands. Chris had clean, strong dry hands. They turned back to the etching.

"Did you travel around Germany when you were over there?" His voice was soft, with a sexy little rasp to it.

"Just a little. Got an overdose of *Grammatik* at the school – God, those declensions - but it was a wonderful experience."

Chris smiled. "Hey, you're out of wine. I'll get you another. White? By the way," he called over his shoulder, "Summer's coming. Do you by any chance sail? I have a 28-foot sailboat."

An image opened up in her mind. Orange bikini, snowy pitcher of daiquiris, aquamarine sea. "No, but I'd love to learn… " She showed her teeth in a broad smile.

Jennifer shifted her back on the pillow under the mast. Chris never gave her credit for getting things right but oh boy was he prepared to jump on her if she mixed up one single little thing. She sighed. She'd earn his respect if it killed her. She dozed, dreamily replaying last night's lovemaking - the touch of his lips on her neck; the pressure of his freckled hands on her body, the shuddering climax. She had to give him credit – he was a good lover. Chris surfaced at the swim ladder in an explosion of spray. She jumped up to give him a hand and as she teetered on the top step of the ladder, he pulled her into the water. She bobbed around with him for awhile, her arms around his neck, buoyed by the salty water.

When it was time to get back to the narrow channel of water called Woods Hole, predictably Chris became Chris Hyde. "Okay, now we're going to come about. Pull on the jibsheet when I say, 'Helms alee.' No, no, no! You've got the sheet wound the wrong way. God when are you ever going to learn? Okay, now pull. Put your back into it. Harder! Use the winch handle if you can't get it." She'd developed a tough hide. She'd just take deep breaths and let the harsh talk roll off her. He was so sweet when they were on dry land. For some reason, Lulu Kruse kept coming into her head today. Lulu wearing a cotton housedress with an apron! Lulu dropping off a Christmas present of jelly cookies for her parents, the gap in her front teeth proclaiming her poverty. Jennifer pushed Lulu out of her thoughts, allowing in a more pleasant, if wistful one. Maybe Chris would get tired of sailing.

They rode a strong current going through the Hole. It would not have been so bad except that massive power boats with names like *Big Bottom Girls* and *Easy Terms* roared past them kicking up big wakes that caused *Edelweiss* to pitch and yaw. Chris had said there was too much weight in the hull for *Edelweiss* ever to capsize but Jennifer wondered. Chris was at the helm barking orders and demanding information while Jennifer tried to identify the bobbing white numbers on the buoys as they flew past, her binoculars braced atop the hatchway slider. "What number is that?" "I can't see it yet!" "We'll get a little closer... okay now what number is it?" The white numbers on the red nuns and green cans faded and refocused before her eyes, sliding out of view just as she thought she had them in her sights. Placid cormorants sunned and preened on jagged piles of rocks as they flew by, holding their black wings outstretched in the sun. Jennifer imagined what it would be like to be trapped in a semi-submerged boat repeatedly crashing, smashing, against those rocks.

Sometimes her imagination went a little wild. The more she sailed, the more she learned about all the things that could go wrong. Chris once told her that boating was "hours and hours of boredom punctuated by moments of sheer terror." It was true. Just last weekend a fog had come up suddenly and they'd circled a buoy in this very Hole to wait out the hazard. She'd held back her terror as she heard the thrum of motors and had smelled fuel as invisible boats slid by.

They passed the last rock in the Hole and then, keeping the big entrance buoy to their left, they emerged into Buzzard's Bay. The sea here was utterly calm. No rushing currents, no preening cormorants, no rocks. The sun felt warm again. Chris killed the engine and set the sails humming in the perfect twelve-knot breeze. "I need some cotter pins for that starboard turnbuckle. Think you can handle the boat alone? I'll be a couple of minutes." Chris would have to move cushions, sleeping bags, blankets, pillows, and duffels just to get at the spares box.

"Absolutely." Jennifer planted her feet and noted the course on the compass. Three-sixty degrees, due North. She checked the knot meter: they were sailing at five knots. The telltales, short pieces of yarn attached to the sails, were flying straight out, a good sign. She began to relax. At least they'd made it through the Hole. At one point, going past Eel Pond, she'd stifled a scream when a green can rushed toward them in the churning water. Of course it was the boat that had done the rushing, not the can, but perspective could get out of whack in an instant when you're on the water. Chris had avoided a collision, but it was a close call. She hadn't dared complain, but she thought he could have given that buoy a wider berth. No matter. She was safe now. She stretched her face to the sun. With the wind at their backs, they'd be home well in time for the usual gorgeous sunset, where she'd sit in the cockpit with Chris, beer in hand, watching the sun go down. She loved the end of the day when the water looked like it was spread with a blanket of nickels all melted together, when the surface would then turn to orange to pink and back to gray as the sun disappeared.

She remembered one more thing. Have to make sure there's nothing behind us. She craned around to check the sea. A mere forty feet behind them, full sails billowing, was a Catalina-360, a heavier and beamier boat than theirs. It was closing in, intent on crashing into them.

"Chris, Chris!" she screamed. "Get up here! Right now. There's a sailboat coming at us!"

She yelled at the boat, "Hey, Hey there!" You're too close!"

The small oval of a female face peered around the voluminous sails, then disappeared.

"Chris!" Get up here! A boat is about to ram us!"

Clinging to the wheel, she twisted around again to see if there was time for the Catalina to change course, but its forward momentum was too great. The Catalina closed to within ten feet from *Edelweiss*, then eight, as Jennifer stood transfixed. *Puff,* their dinghy, was the first to be run down by the juggernaut. Jennifer watched as the big hull touched, gently nudged, and then buried it. *Puff* lifted its bow once in protest, the outboard motor a brave a sentinel for a few seconds, then the dinghy, motor and all, disappeared underwater.

The big anchor came next, gliding in slightly to the left of Jennifer's head. (The main part of the larger boat's hull was still eight feet back since the bows of sailboats are diagonal to the water.) The anchor was mounted on the tip end of the boat's prow, and Jennifer saw the shiny chrome fence that keeps people from falling overboard – what was it called... yes, now she remembered –the bow pulpit. But it was the anchor that captured her full attention, a lethal pronged thing coming ahead of the fifteen thousand pounds of boat. It was a Danforth anchor, she dreamily noted, remembering the drawings in her U.S. Power Squadron Basic Seamanship textbook. *Of the kedge, CQR, plow, mushroom, and Danforth anchors, the Danforth holds best in sandy, grassy bottoms.*

"Chris!"

Chris bounded up the main gangway, frowning. "Holy shit!" He grabbed the wheel from Jennifer, then cupped his hand to his mouth and yelled at the still invisible captain, "You sank my dinghy."

How could he worry about the dinghy when *Edelweiss* itself was about to be rammed? The anchor, riding its bow pulpit as if with pride, floated forward across the cockpit and touched the thick rope of the mainsheet with a lover's probe. It stopped, as if awaiting further instructions. The two boats traveled in synch, enmeshed in some terrible mating ritual over the light chop of Buzzard's Bay, the larger Catalina high in the water hovering over the smaller boat. The anchor would tangle in the mainsheet if it moved an inch right or left.

Water sluicing under the boat was the only sound as Jennifer waited for the Catalina to crush them. Would their demise be quiet, leaving just a few bubbles to mark the event?

Chris yelled again about the dinghy.

Jennifer came out of her trance. First she wanted to kill Chris. It was his fault that they were about to die and all he cared about was the damn dinghy. But she saw something she could do. She stepped up to where the anchor was fondling the mainsheet and, making sure her fingers didn't get caught in the crevices of the triple-looped-and-pullied lines, freed the right prong from the mainsheet. Immediately, as if the Catalina had been waiting for permission, it began to back up, pulling its anchor gently back across the cockpit. It passed by Jennifer's head, whisked across the transom and then was gone. Christ' dinghy popped up out of the water like a fried donut in hot oil. Then, as if realizing all it had suffered from its dunking, the waterlogged little boat settled low, a half-submerged coffin dragging behind *Edelweiss*. When the Catalina was fifty feet behind, it stopped and people began to take down the sails.

A man appeared to be giving orders to two women. As Chris and Jennifer stood watching, the man stood on the cockpit seat, stripped off his clothes down to his boxers, dived into the water, and swam toward them with even, powerful strokes. Chris released the mainsail. Freed, the boom moved sideways with a contented clanking, away from the cockpit. Their forward motion thus slowed, Chris cranked in the forward jib sail with ferocious speed and soon, *Edelweiss* stopped moving altogether. The stranger caught up and clung to the *Puff's* transom. He was slightly older than Chris with a craggy, square-jawed face. "We're so sorry. I went below and my niece just wasn't watching when we came out of the Hole. The least I can do is get your dinghy back." Treading water, he rocked the dinghy to and fro with powerful thrusts, throwing out water with each jerk. The muscles of his shoulders gleamed in the sun.

Jennifer ran below to bring up towels, thinking hypothermia while Chris rummaged in the locker for his mechanical water pump. Pulling *Puff* close, he went down the swim ladder, jumped in and began extracting the water with forceful pulls on the handle - hiss, gurgle, hiss, gurgle. The water in the boat started flowing into the sea through the plastic hosing. The square-jawed man hauled himself into the dinghy with a single powerful heave.

"We're sorry. We were going wing-and-wing and you know how the sails block the forward view? No excuse, but that's what happened."

Jennifer waited for Chris to admonish the man. Chris said, "Hey, no sweat. Nobody was hurt." The man shook water from his hair, "Here, let me," taking the pump from Chris. A torrent of water flew from the boat. The water went "hiss-gurgle, hiss-gurgle, hiss-gurgle" at warp speed. Jennifer watched his muscles at work.

"Where you headed?"

"Marion."

"We are too. When we get in, I'll take the dinghy motor and get it flushed. I'll get it back to you by next weekend."

"That's great. Works fine with me. No harm done." Chris had never been more magnanimous, more forgiving.

The two men finished emptying the dinghy of water and climbed into the cockpit. They shook hands all around.

"Here, take this towel – you're going to freeze," Jennifer said.

The stranger flashed a brilliant smile, put the towel around his shoulders and sat back. "Sorry to have frightened you," he said.

"Would you like something to drink? Hot tea?" asked Jennifer.

"No, thanks. I'm going back. Just taking a short rest."

She studied him as he and Chris chatted about the properties of the Yanmar diesel engine. The man was a head taller than Chris and not quite handsome with bushy black eyebrows. Jennifer noticed his prehensile toes, his high-arched feet and straight, slender ankles. Nice body. Probably non-judgmental, too.

The man stood up.

"I'll be on my way. I'll pick up your motor when we get into the harbor and we'll get it repaired and back to you. And I'm so sorry this happened."

"No harm done," Chris repeated. The man paused on the top rung of the swim ladder for an instant, then dived. Jennifer and Chris watched him power back to the Catalina with even strokes.

It was over. Jennifer slumped against the seat, waiting for Chris to congratulate her for her quick thinking in disentangling the anchor.

Chris frowned. "Oh, Jennifer." Then he sighed. "Jennifer, Jennifer." He drew himself up. "Boy, we were lucky he was the one who came up behind us."

"What? What are you talking about?"

"If it was a different sailor, we'd have been in deep shit."

Jennifer stared. "Why are you giving credit to Tarzan when I was the one who got the ropes untangled?"

"The word is 'lines', not 'ropes'." Chris spoke with great patience, as if to a child.

"But."

"And as far as that entanglement is concerned, it wasn't all that bad. We could have released the main and let the sheet pay out – no big deal."

"But."

"And if I've told you once, I've told you a hundred times, you have to keep your eyes all over the ocean – not just in front of you."

Jennifer took a deep breath. "I *had* been watching. That's how I knew the boat was coming up from behind."

"If you'd seen it in time, you could have avoided that boat." Chris gave her a disparaging look. "I leave you for one minute and you almost get us killed."

Jennifer moved as far away from Chris as she could get without going overboard. She had learned another new thing today: space was finite on a boat. She would be confined with Chris until they reached land. She was too angry to speak. She would let Mr. Perfect get their direction, let him set the sails, let him take the helm. She would become a passenger and would not say a word. Not one word.

Chris grabbed the binoculars, stood up on the cockpit seat, and began to scan the horizon. Jennifer wondered how many hours more did they have together? Let's see, maybe three hours to Marion, and then a half hour to get the boat shipshape, (oh yes, she'd have to haul up the buckets of seawater and scrub down the topside. Mr. Perfect wouldn't skip that step) and then another hour and a half to drive home. Three, a half, plus one and a half, that's five more bloody hours. She was dying

11

to get off the boat. She would sleep alone tonight. If there was one unalterable, indisputable, incontrovertible truth at that moment, this little prick would not be in her bed tonight.

She sat behind the wheel and watched Chris scan the horizon. The wind had come up, ruffling his red hair. It began to nudge the main sail that hung limp over the water like a big white wing. The wing trembled, preparing for flight, and began to move, dragging the boom with it, moving toward where Chris stood. The boom, a ten-foot, fifty-pound hunk of white-painted aluminum, was starting on a potentially dangerous trajectory for anyone standing in its path.

You need to be wary of the boom. Never stand up on
the seat when the wind is shifting. You can be hit by
the boom in what is called an accidental jibe.

She started to warn Chris, to call out. Then she stopped. Mr. Perfect should be following his own advice by paying attention, she thought primly, just like I should have been paying attention when the Catalina came up behind us. Jennifer noted with satisfaction that Chris had forgotten to re-apply sunscreen after his swim and his arms were the color of boiled shrimp. His back was burned, too, The boom gathered momentum in the breeze and was now heading straight at him. Too late she recalled the stories of men whose heads had split like melons by the terrible force of an accidental jibe. She held her breath. The boom caught Chris at the shoulder and swept him overboard. There was a light thud, and then a splash.

Jennifer noted the surprise in Chris' face as the boat glided away from him, the "o" of his mouth growing smaller. She felt giddy. The jibe might have killed him. But he was alive. He'd be okay. She tossed a cushion overboard. She'd have to save him, of course. It was deeply gratifying to see his head grow smaller in the deep green water. She heard his muffled shouting – typical of him to try to control things when he was so powerless. The confidence of the male ego – was there no limit?

She'd have to turn the boat around by herself. She took a couple of deep breaths and checked the sea. The Catalina, a blob of white in the distance, was the only boat in sight but too far away to be any help. If there was any time to stay focused, she told herself, now was it. First, control the boat. She steered *Edelweiss* into the wind and it stopped. The jib was still furled, thank God.

Only one sail to deal with. She locked the steering wheel and released the main sail. The big white tenting collapsed around the boom. Jennifer grabbed the sail ties and managed to tie the center section of sail to the boom. Just to keep it from flapping around. She kept glancing back at Chris, far behind now, a dot. The little prick was trying to swim. She winched the boom tight. No more mischief from you, she thought, as she bent into the task. Then she burst into tears. "He's all right! Thank you, God, for not letting me kill him!"

She returned to the cockpit. What if the engine didn't start? Her fingers shaking, she pressed in on the switch that turned on the glow plugs. Thirty seconds. One, two, three, four,… she hurried the count, her heart beating fast, then turned the key. It caught. She pushed the lever forward, goosed the throttle, and steered the boat around, steering toward the speck in the sea that was Chris. When she got close, she threw out the Lifesling™, remembering the lesson on Crew Overboard Rescue.

Do not get close to the victim with the motor running. Circle the victim
to draw the trailing line in toward the victim until contact is made.

She killed the engine and looked at him. He could bring himself in, she was thinking, but in the end, she saw she had to help him get up the ladder.

He was pale and wheezing. His shirt and shorts stuck to his skin and rivulets of water ran along the pimpled white flesh of his arms and legs. Jennifer picked up one of the big towels the Tarzan man hadn't used and rubbed him briskly around the shoulders.

"What the hell happened?"

"I guess we had an accidental jibe."

Chris's lips were blue, his face pinched, and the yellow strap of the binoculars around his neck looked incongruously cheerful. He stared at the boom.

She said, gesturing lightly, joking, "I incapacitated it. It can't hurt us any more," she said, paraphrasing a great Tom Hanks line from *The Money Pit*. Chris didn't smile. "Chris, are you all right?"

Chris toweled his hair. "Didn't you see it coming?"

"Didn't I see what coming?"

"The jibe!" he yelled.

What to say? Tell the truth and save her soul, or lie and keep him? A whole script unfurled in Jennifer's head. She'd lose him if she told the truth. She imagined what it would be like to be alone again, to face more singles parties in those hotel meeting rooms filled with losers as hordes of predatory women courted them. She could continue trolling for an eligible man, continue being a predator herself even though she knew there were no eligible men out there. Except Chris. Would she end up sitting alone in a room with a flickering television watching reruns of "Family Feud?" Would she become like Lulu?

Better to lie.

Chris waited, dangerously still.

"I'm glad you have stopped shaking. Would you like some cocoa?"

"Did you see it coming?"

"What?"

"The jibe! The boom!" he exploded again.

Could she live with herself if she didn't admit that she'd held her tongue out of spite? That she'd had a lapse of common sense, of responsibility, of maturity? Could she face herself in the mirror every day knowing she'd lied to Chris? It might not be so hard. She'd had so many fantasies being Chris' steady girl, or even wife; attending one of the dozens of parties his yacht club held; she saw cozy Sundays when they could curl up by the fire to read *The New York Times*; she saw the two of them double dating with her married friends who had almost but not quite dropped her since her divorce; she saw dinner parties for six; she saw vacations and movies no longer attended alone but with a respectable male, a partner.

Jennifer took a deep breath.

Chris was staring at her, his sunburned face pinched and deadened by the sunlight.

"Well, yes, actually I did see it coming."

"You saw what was happening and you didn't warn me?"

"That's right."

His eyes widened. She hurried on. "You're always so critical of me, this was one time when you were breaking your own rules about standing on the seat and I just thought well he can notice that boom on his own, or the hell with him. You probably wouldn't have paid attention if I'd said something anyway."

"You could have killed me."

"I'd like to point out that I wasn't the one who started the damn boom moving. I never told you to stand on the seat. I didn't put binoculars to your eyes. I was just a witness to your usual take-charge bullshit. The wind almost killed you, not me."

Chris stood up, eyes narrowed. "You know what I mean. Of course it was the wind, but you saw it. You could have warned me. The person behind the wheel is in charge."

That did it. Jennifer stood up. "Well, you know what you are? You're a pig. A chauvinist pig, a hypocritical chauvinist pig. It's bullshit to say I was in charge. I wasn't in charge. You don't want to admit that sometimes accidents just happen. Sometimes it's not anyone's fault. As they say, shit happens. But no, with you, it always has to be someone's fault, as long as it's not your fault."

"That's ridiculous and you know it.'

"Oh yeah? Well why was it my fault that the Catalina rammed us? Just name one reason it was my fault."

"You should have been watching. You were at the wheel." Chris' voice had weakened.

"I *was* watching! It was because I *was* watching that I alerted you and the truth is, if I hadn't been watching we'd be dead. If you weren't such a self-centered hypocritical little prick, you'd know I saved our lives."

"Oh, so now I'm a prick. Well you're a fucking bitch, that's what you are."

They stared at each other. A large power boat roared past, out of nowhere, kicking up a huge wake that heaved the boat up and sideways. Jennifer lost her balance and Chris put out his hand to catch her and they both crashed hard onto the seat, snapping off the base of the stalk that held the GPS with a sickening "CRKKKK". Jennifer waited for Chris to retrieve the expensive instrument, turn it on, check to see if it worked. And then blame her.

But he merely sat up. Jennifer also sat up. She waited for the reprimand. Then Chris spoke.

"Okay, you made your point. The Catalina wasn't your fault."

"Now you're mocking me."

"No, I mean it."

Chris shifted his weight, Jennifer looked carefully at him. "Yeah, I mean it. I've been a prick. You've been trying hard and I haven't given you any credit. Man, you got the boat turned around. I never thought you'd have it in you."

All of a sudden Jennifer was exhausted, empty, sad. She swiped at her eyes with the back of her hand and looked out at the horizon. Chris was a stranger. A nice man but one she barely knew.

She said in a soft voice, "It was big of you to apologize. I know it wasn't easy."

"I wasn't apologizing." He loomed close to her face. His hair smelled briny and she could see the pores of his porcelain skin and a forest of white eyebrow hairs. She froze. Then he laughed and grabbed her by the shoulders. "Just kidding. No more blaming – at least I'll try not to be such a Captain Queeg. Am I forgiven?"

"I'll think about it." Jennifer turned away, unsmiling. She picked up the GPS. "We can probably fix this, don't you think?"

As they set sail for home, Jennifer pondered. Chris had become a man who had apologized, who had treated her like an adult. It was complicated now and her world had shifted, kaleidoscoped into a new, bigger pattern where her old thinking seemed archaic and stale. Was being Lulu Kruse so terrible a fate? Living alone had its advantages. Lulu seemed pretty happy when she worked in the kitchen. She was loved by everyone in the church. Jennifer may have to be like the woman in *The King and I* – and Lulu even may have had a love of her own. It was possible, Jennifer was thinking, seeing Lulu in a new, more compassionate and understanding light.

She looked over at Chris at the helm, calmly steering, eyes on the telltales. "Hey Captain, we need to get some sun block on you right away."

"It's in the lazarette. And before you get it, pull the traveler to port."

"Chris, okay, I know what the traveler is, but please, no more demands that I get the exact words right, every time, okay? I need a little slack."

Chris looked at her as if thinking over her request. So it was going to be that kind of a deal, she thought. She said, "This is the part where you're supposed to say, 'okay, you got it.'"

Chris smiled. "Okay, you got it." And he tried to continue, "… but…"

"Uh uh uh…" she said, putting her finger to her lips.

And all was quiet on the sail back to Marion.

ONE LOUSY KITTEN

Sheila hurried toward Avis Preferred, dragging her suitcase, cell phone pressed to her ear. She kept her voice calm. "What? A power outage? At Schattswell?" Schattswell Paper Company was her IT client. This latest foul-up could jeopardize her promotion. "Just a minute, Gary, let me think." She stopped and the man walking behind her also on his cell phone bumped into her. Her iPhone went sailing overhead to land on the hot asphalt. She felt like screaming. After the air conditioned airport, the South Florida humidity was a blanket of flannel about to smother her, and she didn't need this.

The man clicked off his own phone and bent to retrieve hers.

"What the hell!" she said, turning, putting the phone back to her ear. "Oh, Hi, Irv." She held up a finger to freeze Irv in his tracks. "Gary? I'm still here. Okay. Get Sanjay, follow the escalation process and I'll call you in thirty minutes." She snapped the phone shut.

"Irv Grandin! What the .... "

Irv laughed. "Sheila! You okay?"

"Of course I'm okay. It was my fault too. Well, not really." They both laughed. "You fly in on Delta?"

"Yeah. How's Beantown? You keeping all those Corporate bean counters off your back?" His teeth were gorgeous - obviously a bleach job - but his jaw with those sculpted dimples was always a turn-on for her. A whiff of expensive aftershave distracted her for a moment.

"Don't bring that up - it's a zoo. The servers just went down at Schattswell. But I've got it covered," she quickly added, to forestall any unwanted advice. They began walking again. "So, how're you doing since your divorce?" she said. "It's over a year now, isn't it?"

"Life is good." Irv spoke with lazy confidence. He came to a sleek black sedan and stopped. "This is me." He turned to her. "Hey, how about a drink, say about 9:00? I'm meeting with Peter but he should be gone then. My room. I've got a suite."

A bead of sweat trickled between Sheila's breasts. Irv was in line for the same promotion she was. Was it wise to see him? Then she remembered she had seniority on him. "Sure, why not?"

"Aaahright! See ya tonight." Irv got into his car and pulled away. Sheila found her car, put her laptop and suitcase into the backseat, then headed onto the freeway, eyes scanning the map while her fingers punched the radio buttons for some country music. She pondered the power outage at her client's facility back in western Massachusetts. This was bad. At the hotel, waiting in the check-in line, she speed-dialed Gary again. "Get the third-level backups to come in. I'll call Jansen to let him know we're on it."

Her room was on the eighteenth floor. From her balcony the ocean view was spectacular: tugboats, sailboats and water ferries crawled, sailed and skittered across the turquoise water. An art deco bridge glowed peach in the setting sun beyond which a narrow wedge of pewter – the ocean - appeared in the distance. Just below, blades of the towering palm trees swayed in the light breeze. She took a deep breath. It would be dark up in Boston now and the only view outside her own house would be the incandescent light from her front window that painted a tiny square of light on the snow. Yipee. No black ice for three whole days.

She'd left that morning with her four-year old sobbing and her husband complaining ("I'm not taking this travel much longer, Sheila. You need to set your priorities straight, get a stable job and stay home").

She was sure she'd bruised her coccyx when she slipped on the black ice getting into the limo – her tail still hurt. Then she'd had a caffeine headache on the plane until that first cup of coffee.

Sheila picked up her phone again and dialed the plant manager at her customer's facility.

"… Jack, yes, we've got it under control. ….. I'll let you know as soon as I hear from my guys that your systems are up."

She helped herself to a tiny bottle of Scotch from the minibar while dialing home, holding the phone against her ear with her shoulder as she twisted off the top. The first swig went down like a healing fire.

"Hi, Rick. Yes, the flight was fine….. I told you about the Spaghettios in the cupboard … Oh good. You found them." Sheila took a close look at her lacquered nails. Could you put Cindy on?"

"Hi Honey! How is Mommy's baby? ….. You're in a play and you get to sing Jingle Bells? That's great! …… Of course I'll be there…" She thought to herself, yeah, if it's not during a program review. Cindy had been a model baby and a contented toddler, and Sheila had loved her fiercely from before she had been born. But after three months at home, Sheila couldn't wait to get back to work. From systems maintenance to Program Manager in five years –one hundred and ninety grand a year, with bonuses on top of that – way more than Rick's eighty-eight thousand at Stoatley Preparatory School – she was pleased with herself. Soon she could afford a nanny.

Rick came back on the line and she frowned. "Okay, okay. I get it. We'll talk when I get back…. Yeah, I gotta go now. Okay, bye."

She changed into white linen slacks and black silk sweater, knowing that her thick gold necklace and bracelet made at statement (the sales clerk's words). Not bad, she said to her mirror. Thank God she didn't have her mother's hips. Thirty-four, perky nose, good boobs, and fair skin. Sheila nurtured her professional image with tailored, expensive clothing. Her hair was a mass of orange curls that she tamed with a black scrunchie. Rick used to call her his Botticcelli Venus early in their marriage. That's when he couldn't keep his hands off her. These days she was too tired for lovemaking. The travel made for tough sledding with her marriage but as she said to Rick, it would only be a little while longer. If she could land the Director's job (which would put her in charge of the other program managers), then they could afford a nanny – AND she could work from home sometimes.

She took another swig from the J & B. The Scotch raked her throat. She punched in some numbers on her phone. "Sanjay, what's the story on the servers? They're up? Way to go, Sanjay! Good going!" Thank God. The Schattswell pulp machines would run tonight and her ass was saved. A few moments later Sheila rode the glass elevator down to the lobby, staring outside at the bay but thinking of her daughter. The sea was now liquid copper.

She ate a hamburger in the hotel café while reading the rest of the *Wall Street Journal* that she had saved from the morning, had a cup of coffee, then dialed her client one more time as soon as she was back in her room. Something nagged at her, something that didn't feel right, but she brushed it off. She turned on the television set and lit a cigarette. She was excited to be in Miami, to mix it up with her male colleagues (she was one of two females in the program management squad of fifteen and cherished the belief that as first hired female for the field work, she had broken the gender barrier at her IT company.)

When she got to Irv's room – she had waited until 9:20 - Peter was still there. Peter, their boss. She helped herself to a J&B on the rocks from Irv's minifridge and wandered out to the balcony while the men huddled around the coffee table. A half hour passed. Sheila came inside once - "Sorry guys! Just coming in for a refresher" – and they'd paid no attention as she scuttled back to the balcony. She sat, her feet on the railing, and gazed out at the liquid moonlight floating on the bay. Sheila was reminded of an illustration in one of Cindy's picture books. *Winken, Blinken and Nod.* In it, three tots in a boat among big silver stars floated in a black sky just like the Miami sky up above. It was a book she'd saved from her own childhood.

Irv came out to the balcony. Peter had gone.

"Hey. What's up with Peter? You're so solemn."

"Nothing." He hesitated, as if he wanted to say something else. She lit a cigarette.

"Com'on. What's up with Peter?"

"Nordron. You know, my new customer. The same bullshit." Another note of hesitation in his voice. Irv wasn't looking at her as he spoke. He continued. "Sorry you had to wait. Oh by the way, Peter told me those numbers I gave you for Schattswell weren't correct. That new financial analyst - you know, Mary Ng? She made a mistake but Peter caught it. I should have checked before giving them to you." A warning bell sounded. Irv continued. "But I have the corrections."

Why was Peter telling Irv about the numbers and not her? Could it be possible that Peter was considering Irv for the promotion? She said, "Why is he talking to you and not me about the Schattswell forecast?" She took a swallow, the ice clicking against her teeth.

"He's going to talk to you tomorrow about all of this."

"Oh." She examined the square white tips of her fingernails. Manicure. Professional Woman. There was only one explanation why Peter would talk to Irv about Schattswell. Irv was taking over Schattswell so that she could be promoted to Director. She gave herself a little hug, smiling and stretched languidly.

"What's funny?"

"I don't know. Was just thinking whether Peter wondered why I dropped by? Do you suppose he thinks we've got something going? Wouldn't that be a hoot?"

"Hell no. He knows we're just buddies."

"Oh. Hmmmm. Well, you know it's not an impossible thought, you turkey."

Irv hitched his front-pleated pants – had to be Brooks Brothers – that rode attractively low on his narrow hips and sat down. He stretched out his long legs on the balcony.

"So did you get Jansen calmed down?" Irv knew Sheila's customer well. After all, she'd been the one who had trained Irv at Schattswell when he was learning the ropes. They'd worked together for nine months in Boston before he got his own account in Houston.

"Yeah, finally. Do you have any idea what that sexist cretin called me the other day?"

"A hotty?"

"No, Irv. I'm serious. He called me 'young lady.' What planet did he come from?"

"Oh, I wouldn't worry about that. Jansen means well." It galled Sheila how easily Jansen and Irv got along. "Are you ready for your presentation tomorrow?" She lit a cigarette and blew a thin stream of smoke past Irv.

"Yeah."

"I can look it over if you'd like a double check."

"No, thanks. I'm all set." Irv put his hands on the rail. Capable hands, well-trimmed nails.

"Say, Irv, are you okay? You're being quiet."

"Oh, no, I'm fine. How's Cindy? Cindy's four now, isn't she?"

"She's fine. Growing up too fast, though."

"It's rough, isn't it? Juggling schedules and all."

"Yeah, tell me about it." Sheila stubbed out her cigarette on the railing, then carried the butt to the wastebasket just inside. Irv said, "Does it bother you? To be a working mother?"

"I hate leaving Cindy. Mommy guilt, you know? She cries when I leave her and then talks baby talk for awhile. They regress you know; I had to promise her a pony this time just to get out the door."

Irv gave an explosive laugh. "Rick give you any grief when you're away?"

"Yeah. We're having some problems."

"Oh?"

"We don't have any time together. He's always ready to play on the weekends and all I want to do is sleep and catch up on my mail; he hates my travel." Sheila thought to herself... and I'm not spending a lot of time with Cindy. "Rick wants me to give up the travel, even my career if necessary. And that makes me mad. He likes me to help him out with his stupid faculty parties. 'Please, Honey, help this biddy or that bozo with the scholarship bake sale.' And I do support him. But no vice versa." Why was she talking so much? Too much booze. She had to be careful, she thought as she took went in for another drink.

"Marriage can be a trap," said Irv when she returned.

"What do you mean?"

"I almost lost my career by spending too much time at home. Eventually I changed jobs, came to Comline and really put in the time. Of course," ... and here he gave a rueful smile, "Patty left me..."

"I am so sorry, Irv, to hear that it had to come down to a choice."

"Don't let it happen to you, Sheila."

"Don't worry. I can handle it." They moved indoors and Irv went to turn on the table lamp. She said, "No, leave it off. It's nice in the dark."

"Okay." Irv settled back in an armchair, she took the couch. There was that cologne of his again, intoxicating. She crossed her legs and rubbed at her eye with care to avoid smearing her mascara. She yawned, beginning to relax.

"Cindy's so sweet. Know what she said to me the other day? She was playing with her Legos and arranging them all neatly, so I said to her, 'You're so fastidious, Honey.' About a half hour later, I'm in the kitchen and she comes up to me with these big eyes and says, 'Mommy, why did you call me hideous?'"

Sheila leaned back. She felt safe. They sat in the silent room, each lost in thought. Then Irv said, "Don't let your marriage wind up like mine did, Sheila. My advice? Get out of the field and go into Corporate; save your marriage."

"You're a fine one to talk. I thought you said marriage was a trap."

"It's different – you're a mom."

"That's just the last thing I need to hear from you at this point, Irv. You know Corporate's a dead end."

"Not really."

She snorted. "What the hell are you saying? Is this Irv Grandin talking? We both hate those little weenies who live off our work, making up rules back home at corporate headquarters in their ivory tower."

"Okay okay. Just one thing, Sheila. Sometimes when things don't always work out exactly the way you want them to, it's not always for the worst. Know what I mean? Sometimes we get what we need, and not what we want."

"Yeah, like the Stones." She and Rick had married on a whim once they knew the baby was on the way. Had she needed a baby? Not really.

"Ya know, sometimes I feel I'm fighting a losing fight," she said.

"Yah, it all gets down to priorities." He sounded sad.

It was late. She downed the last of her drink. Suddenly she felt dizzy. "Irv, I can't get up. Help me." Irv stood up and pulled her up. She staggered a little.

"Bye Bye."

They embraced, old friends, old chums. "Hmmmm." For some reason, she hung on to Irv, slightly swaying. She said, "Irv. Let's not think about work right now."

"Hey there, you've had way too much to drink."

"Don't worry about Rick, if that's what you're worried about. I'm a big girl. I know what I want." She kissed him. "Now give me a real kiss." Pressed close to Irv, her desire extinguished any reservations she might have had. It was just so relaxing to be held by Irv. They stood there, lust swirling around like a thick fog.

"Are you sure you know what you're doing?"

"Why not? No strings. How can that hurt us?"

"Oh, it could. Believe me, it could."

She moved her hands over his body, lost to herself, and Irv scooped her up and carried her into the bedroom, past the big TV, the bar, the suitcase, and the laptop on the desk. He plunked her down onto the queen sized bed. Sheila helped him with his polo shirt, then squiggled out of her clothes. There was no second thought, no decision making: her limbic system was in control. It was his intoxicating scent.

Afterward, Irv slept a little, then woke up with a start.

Sheila was on the balcony, completely naked. She didn't care of anybody could see her. The balmy air with its sea smells wafted over her skin. The tip of her cigarette glowed hot in the breeze. She was pondering the consequences of a long-term affair with Irv. Not what she really wanted but...

"Hey, did I give you a good time?" Irv called from inside. She turned in annoyance. Why did Irv have to act like he owned her sexual experience? After a long pause as she took a drag on her cigarette and said, "Irv, do you ever think that sex can just be sex, without any baggage or guilt or expectations?

"Sure. Why are you asking? You're a real tiger. Come back to bed."

"Why?" she said, unsmiling. She put out her cigarette and walked in to spread herself over his body, hovering and teasing; withholding contact. She'd show him a thing or two.

When it was over she ended up on the bottom after all.

Back in her room Sheila checked the phone service for voice messages. "Mommy, we saw "Little Mermaid" tonight. When are you coming home?" Then Rick's voice, deep and growling, "Yeah, and where the hell are you?" The guilt stabbed but just for a moment. She was so tired. She went into the bathroom, then emerged only to fall asleep in her underwear. In the morning she had no time to go to the fitness center, her hair was a rat's nest, and she felt queasy. God, what had she done?

"White Christmas" was being piped throughout the hotel and as she walked along the carpeting toward the function room. How obnoxious. Christmas music in the hothouse climate of Florida clashing against the chilled air of the hotel. When she was in Bangkok last year at the world-wide meeting, she'd taken a tour of the royal Grand Palace with its gilded spires and rooftops; the chapel of the Emerald Buddha with its mother of pearl, teak, gold and crystal fittings. The gold was brilliant in the hot sunshine. As then, the spell had broken when she heard "Chestnuts Roasting by an Open Fire" streaming from hidden speakers.

She felt disoriented, as if moving in a dream. It was the booze from last night. How much had she drunk? She reached the Bougainvillia Room with its breakfast table full of Danish pastries, yogurt, and fruit. She picked up a porcelain cup of decaf bypassing the foiled-wrapped pats of butter on the table that twinkled gold: offerings in the Wat Pra Keo shrine.

An enormous screen dominated one end of the function room. Each of the twenty places at the conference tables featured pitchers of water, goblets, writing tablets, sharp pencils, and bowls of hard candies. People entered the room like eager children, glad to be in Miami. Irv came in and chortled, "Hey everybody. It snowed in New York last night." A few people cheered. Irv didn't look at Sheila as he sat down next to Peter on the other side of the room. Sheila paused. A soughing from the air conditioning unit gave her the insane momentary fear that there was something alive just outside the door. She settled into her armchair, one of the upholstered kind that had little chrome wheels you can push around with a toe. She moved around and sipped her coffee and thought about Cindy. She'd be in day care by now. Two years ago they'd only been able to afford Mrs. Maundy's Play School held in a decrepit house down the street. With her bonuses, Sheila had been able to move Cindy into Montessori this year.

Peter came in and picked up the mike. "Okay. Anybody get to the beach yet? Raise your hands." Perfunctory chuckles rippled across the room. "I've got good news. Stock options are going out to you next week." A few people went "Yeah!" Sheila knew most of the people in the room from other meetings. They'd flown in from Phoenix, Seattle, Colorado Springs, Detroit, Atlanta. Hard-working guys, one other woman, most up from the ranks like her and they all carried big responsibilities. They kept the computers running for Fortune 100 companies. Out went the lights and Peter started to talk.

"We're making money because a few years ago everybody started yapping about the Internet, right? So I started intellectualizing, okay? The future is fiber optics, Cloud,…"

Five minutes into Peter's kickoff speech Sheila stopped listening. She ran her fingers across the condensation on the metal pitcher and daydreamed about her promotion. She'd earned it. The latest contract renewal at Shattswell was worth another $4 million; she'd definitely earned it. Suddenly it was break time. The lights came up and the group blinked awake. Sheila got up for some coffee when Peter approached her. "We need to talk. How about now?" This was it. Her heart thumped as they headed across the corridor over the thick carpet of sage eel grasses, violet clamshells and mauve lily pads. They sat down on two fat sofas. "Jingle Bell Rock" trickled from a corner speaker.

"Great idea you having the meeting here, Peter"

"Yeah, thanks."

Peter swept his stringy brown hair away from his owlish face. He had a potbelly, thick glasses and to Sheila, an unexpected sweetness, a shy diffidence that was unusual in the rough world of service delivery. Peter ran $972M of annual business. Sheila smiled broadly and Peter leaned forward, his hands clasped, and assumed a thoughtful expression. "Sheila, I'm going to give it to you straight. We're transferring you out of Schattswell and into corporate. We're moving Irv into your job."

The import of his words came slowly, like marbles dropping through one of those Plexiglas toys with the little chutes and holes. One by one, clunk, clunk, clunk.

"Excuse me?" Her question came out as a whisper. "What?"

"We're pulling you out of the field."

Sheila was having difficulty processing Peter's words. She couldn't stop herself and said, "What about the Director's job?"

"What the fuck you talking about? Oh, that. We're bringing in somebody from IBM."

She looked down then lowered her voice and spoke carefully.

"I don't understand, Peter." He looked at her with the same sad eyes that Irv had last night. Why was he the sad one? She was the one getting the shaft.

"We need Irv to manage Schattswell. They love him there - Jansen called me last week."

It was the golf. Irv played golf with Jansen. She knew she should have taken golf lessons last summer. Her anger started rising from her feet, like a cartoon character who turns red. No. Never get emotional. First rule in business. She made sure her voice was still low and in control before she spoke.

"So what would I do in Corporate?"

"Serve as a liaison with the field – write policy and shit like that." Sheila saw her perks going down the drain: the profit sharing, the incentive bonuses, the prestige, the frequent flyer miles. All the goodies circled around and around like bathwater down the drain.

"I don't get it Peter. I set that account up. I did all the legwork, all the selling. And now you're handing it over to Irv?"

Peter ran his hand through his hair. "Hold on. You're taking this personal and it's not. Listen. You'll thrive in Corporate."

"My career is in the field, not in Corporate. I'm good with customers. You know I give 110 percent; they respect me."

"Hey, take it easy. I didn't want to get into this, but what nailed you is this month's forecast. I had to work to keep them from axing you, to tell the truth."

"But I got those numbers from Irv. You remember the problems with the new asset management system during forecast week: that's what I was doing."

"Well, you goofed with your forecast. Somebody has to pay."

He stood up. "I'd hate to lose you, if you're thinking of going to IBM or CA. Don't do it. We'd like you to stay with us. Give it some thought. Let's talk next week when you've had a chance to think this over. Stay through this meeting. I'll need to know if you're leaving the company though." He paused, then looked at her. "Sheila, it's just business."

She returned to the Conference Room. Irv was speaking, his laser light pointing to a moonscape of numbers on the large screen. She hunched, glad to be hiding out in the chilled room. She no longer belonged there. The others mattered, she didn't. Word of her humiliation would spread.

"First column's the quarterly figures for the Southeast. Second column's for the North. Third is Central Plains. Over here's the variance. Fourth column's for the West."

She lost track of time, scorn burning in her throat when various singsong voices called out, "rat hole, rat hole" when the discussion went off the subject. Scorn for her colleagues rose out of the depths of her bitterness. Irv had betrayed her and there he was, so calm, so sure of himself, a winner. He was a stranger to her. A smug, arrogant, son of a bitch. She hated him. Somebody's pager warbled and everybody clutched at their waists as if all were suffering gastrointestinal distress. Then the man two seats down from her left the room, dialing into his cell phone as he walked through the double doors. She hated him too.

Sheila skipped the lunch buffet and had room service brought up. She made it through the afternoon session of small group financial exercises, and at 6:00, joined the group dinner in Miami Beach. They took two water taxis that passed under the art-deco bridge. Tonight it wasn't peach but a shadowy blue. At the restaurant, they feasted on crab leg appetizers, swordfish, filet mignon, Caesar salad, cheesecake, Key Lime pie. She drank Cosmopolitans. She was on her third, with a glass of Pinot Grigio at the ready in front of her plate, when the man next to her started his Rodney Dangerfield act. "I get no respect. My wife thinks I'm a stranger when I come home – but it makes for better sex." People roared. The other woman in the group spoke up. "I travel so much that I only go home on weekends to do the wash and service

the master. (In a singsong) "... do the wash and service the master."
Everybody laughed again.

When she headed toward the women's room, Irv materialized in the
dark corridor. He took her arm and she shook free.

"I wish it hadn't turned out this way," he said.

"Did you plan it all along or did it just fall into your lap?"

"It wasn't me who hurt you."

"Oh, what a crock. This is me you're talking to, Irv."

"It wasn't my fault I got transferred into Schattswell. I was quite
happy with my own account. If you think about it for just a moment,
you'll believe me. Peter made me swear to keep quiet. But I did NOT
set you up."

Sheila gave a harsh laugh. "How can I believe that when you gave
me the bad numbers?"

"I thought they were good."

"Sure you did.

"Hey..."

Sheila's anger took over. "Just one thing. Do you know how damned
patronizing you've been lately? Did you know that? You've got the
morals of a jackass– all that talk about understanding me. You know
something? You make me sick. Now let me get by you." Her voice had
become a snarl. She ducked past him into the door marked "Little
Girls."

That night, on the way back to the hotel, people fell silent, lulled
by the steady chugging of the diesel engines. Sheila sat by herself in the
bow, staring into the inky water. She would never forgive Irv. She'd fix
him. A word to Peter about Irv – that perhaps Irv was not someone to
trust? She knew stuff about Irv. Maybe padding the expense account?
Peter was a family man – but then she paused. Who was she to bring
up a morals charge after last night? A large yacht roiled the water as

it passed them and a few people started to talk softly. "The tab for dinner tonight was more than $3,000." "Way more," someone else said. Okay, it's true, Peter was right that the forecast numbers had been her responsibility, not Irv's. But she'd had Cindy's birthday party that week and the asset tracking process was in shambles taking up all her time so she'd handed Irv's numbers, unchecked, over to Peter, that one time.

Later that night, Sheila sat out on her balcony, alone in the bay with its romantic blue bridge as the moon made its way across the sky. She shifted in her chair, she paced, she smoked, she lounged on the hard metal. She woke with a jerk at 2:00 with a crick in her neck and stumbled into her room to fall into bed where she lay awake the rest of the night.

By Day Three, people were tired of the meeting. Everybody wanted to go home. After lunch, Sheila watched the Rodney Dangerfield man, a nice guy from Cedar Falls named Phil, sneaking scraps from the roast beef station. She followed him out to the patio. He'd found a litter of kittens that napped in the pool side shrubbery. Sheila helped Phil to coax the kittens out. She sat leaning against a palm tree, a couple of kittens on her lap, sunlight in her face. After a while Phil got up. "Come on, Sheila, time to get back." She kept stroking one of the kittens, her eyes closed. "Sheila. You're going to miss the part about compensation." She shifted and the kitten sank its needle claws into her thigh. The pain was delicious.

"Go ahead, Phil, I'm not up to it."

"Peter will notice."

"Fuck Peter. I'm not going." The kitten had a pink suede nose. "You go ahead."

Phil shrugged. "Okay, fine with me." She held the kitten against her cheek and when Phil had left, began to cry into its fur. Cindy had wanted a kitten. "Mommy has to travel too much, Honey, it wouldn't be practical to get a kitten." Soon she was crying openly. A couple basking on the other side of the pool looked over at her. The same ones she'd seen in the lobby last night with their maps and cameras. A passing waitress slowed, disappeared inside, and returned with a man in a blazer. He knelt and said in a careful voice, "Can I help you, Ma'am?" Sheila clutched the kitten and said, "I don't think so, but thank you," between sobs. She said, "All Cindy ever asked for was one lousy kitten. What do you think of that? One lousy kitten."

The man lowered his voice. "Would you like to go to your room?" No, she wanted to stay in the sun. She said, "Yes, thank you." The man helped her stand up and she carefully placed the kitten in the shade of the palm tree. "I think I can make it to the elevator. I'm sorry." She shuffled off like an invalid. In her room, Sheila noted her Donna Karan slacks and her Adrienne Vittadini sandals; she fingered the diamond and sapphire ring she had bought herself on the business trip to Brazil last year. Her Rolex was also a gift to herself. She packed.

She ran into Irv one more time. It was at the airport. She'd run all the way to the gate, her laptop bumping hard against her hip with every step, just as the boarding gate closed. No, it was against policy to open it even if it was just seconds closed; they couldn't let her on the plane. She returned to the Club Lounge and made arrangements for the next flight with a cheerful young blonde who checked her lounge privileges. Sheila sank into a puffy chair. That's when she saw him. Irv was sitting with Peter and two others at a table nearby. Peter spotted her and motioned. Irv's face had the same sad smile he'd had last night on his face. She wanted to slap him. Here was her chance. She'd fix him. She picked up her suitcase and laptop and moved to the group.

"Hi guys!" she said brightly." She put her things by a chair. "What's the matter, Irv? You don't look so hot." Irv said, "I'm perfectly fine, Sheila."

"You know, Peter, Irv's quite a guy. Were you aware of that? Let me tell you about Irv." Her voice had a high, nasty tone she didn't like. The men looked at her, suddenly somber, the fun over. Tired middle-aged kids with five o'clock shadows dressed in golf shirts and khaki pants. The table held their drinks and a bowl of peanuts.

"Sit down, Sheila," one of the men said. "And tell us about Irv." He winked at the other man.

"Thanks, I appreciate it." She settled in. "About Irv." She popped a peanut in her mouth. What about Irv? She swallowed hard and realized that she would never make it in this world. She didn't belong here. She didn't even want to be here. She'd been playing a game and had lost in the final round. Was it really sexism that had done her in? For the first time, she felt the question a valid one, one to ponder later, at home, over time. She looked around with a new sensation, almost one of compassion.

"Well, I'd say Irv's a damned good guy who works too hard. He's someone you always want on your team, especially if you're a woman."

"Irv, she's got you mixed up with someone else." Chuckles all around.

"Oh, I'll bet she's just saying that so I'll buy her a drink."

As the talk turned to other subjects, Sheila's attention drifted. She saw that the men around her lived for the life on the road; they had little family life and liked it that way. She wasn't like them. She was a mother and she loved her child. And she realized she loved her husband, too. Her guilt rose up like a tsunami as she remembered last night; she would have to live with the memory for the rest of her life. How could she have sunk so low? She took a handful of peanuts as the men chatted about the Red Sox.

She was going home. She thought of Cindy's serious little face looking up at her, big eyes so full of trust. She would soon be walking into the house with the prospect of waking up tomorrow with Cindy's little body climbing into bed with her and Rick. And she wouldn't have to plan her next trip. She'd have more time. Maybe a Corporate weenie could earn respect. She had the contacts and experience after all. Corporate work would have dependable hours and a decent salary. She could do this. In fact, she decided to make up her past to Rick if it killed her. She could bake cookies for his projects with the best of the others.

And the first thing on her agenda was to adopt a kitten. They'd go to the shelter and Cindy could pick it out. Sheila sat back. It was time to come in from the cold. She came back to life, looked around at the men and smiled.

"Hey, what do you have to do to get a drink around here?"

VIENNA

It is March, 1938 and Hitler is arriving in Vienna like an Easter gift carried in with an extravagant parade. A young woman stands in front of the magnificent Opera building, scanning the crowd, ignoring the hoopla. She has straight dark hair, a plain, inquisitive face and a lanky boyish figure. She is chic in a suit of gray wool with big shoulders, pink silk blouse, black gloves, boxy hat and thick-heeled pumps. She looks in the direction of the street when a loud cheer goes up.

"Heil Hitler!" "Wunderbar!" "Fantastisch, ya?" The middle-aged man standing next to her displays a mouthful of large yellow teeth. A convoy of tanks whine and clank into view; their snouts point toward heaven and their undersized wheels push iron walking-belts around and around over the ancient cobblestones. The tanks grind past neat rows of policemen.

The young woman squints into the sun. She's thinking about Stefan. He has caught her by purest coincidence just as she was ready to leaving her house. Her father has stopped her at the door.

"Dorothea. What are you doing? Why would you meet that man Stefan after his vile behavior? And he's never been right for you."

"It'll be okay, Vati. I think of Stefan as an old friend now, it's all in the past. We'll go for a coffee, that's all." Her father took a step toward her.

"Vati. I need to see him. I'll be okay." And she has fled.

Stefan. After all this time. The crowds are not something she has expected when they agreed to meet at the Opera; it took her forever to get here. He's probably trapped in traffic. Dorothea takes out a small gold compact and freshens her lipstick. She takes off one of her gloves and looking into the mirror, licks her forefinger, then catches a strand of hair with a twisting motion to put it into place. There. What a bore, all this noise, this pomp. She sees her expression in the mirror and with a thrill that taps the bones of her spine up and down like a marimba paddle, imagines Stefan again. She snaps shut the compact. Why would Stefan call me after such a long time? He wasn't coming back, he had made it clear long ago that he wasn't interested in me, so why would he call me now?

*   *   *

The last day she had seen Stefan started in the Vienna Woods two years earlier; just a group of friends on an impromptu hike before they would leave the cocoon of family and school for a future that stretch out like a German *Autobahn,* exciting and endless with possibility. Those days Dorothea nursed a secret passion for her long time friend Stefan who in turn, had been in love with Renate, a small, dark-haired, curvy and intense girl who looked just like Stefan's late mother right down to the dimple in her cheek.

Dorothea would have sacrificed everything for Stefan's love. She'd known so on that carefree spring day as the tram clickety-clacked through the countryside. That last year Dorothea would listen to music on the radio and transform her unwitting friend into her lover. She'd loll on her bed searching passing memories for clues to the mystery of Stefan, examining details of his clothes, his hands, and his smile and pretending the love songs on her radio were written about her and Stefan. She thought of the times when Stefan and she had shared confidences. She thought of the adorable speck of blood on his chin the time he'd cut himself shaving. She tracked Stefan like a bloodhound for signs, any at all, of hope.

For Austrians, the Vienna Woods is a romantically pleasurable idyll, no longer the menacing place of bears and wolves, outlaws and hermits of folklore. Most Viennese consider the Woods a treasured locale for romantic rambles. That long-ago day, Dorothea and her friends met at the tram station, then entered the woods full of high spirits. Dorothea rejoiced in Stefan's proximity as the seven young people slouched along the shadowy paths in the spring sunshine, the light filtering through the trees making the forest feel enchanted. The little group wandered, they ate their picnic lunch, they wandered some more. When it was time to leave, everybody headed for the tram except Dorothea and Stefan, who sat down on a bench beneath a beech tree, lost in conversation. Stefan played the story of his unrequited love again and again as Dorothea listened, indifferent to the rest of their friends. Once Stefan paused to call out, "Yeah, we'll see you. Bye bye."

Dorothea said, "You'll find someone else just as nice. She just isn't ready for you, Stefan."

"D'ya think so? If only I thought that was true."

"Hey you guys, you coming with us?" The last of their friends called to them.

Dorothea said, "It's okay if we go back, Stefan, now that everybody else is going."

Stefan shouted, "Why don't we all have dinner in Baden? … No? Okay, Dorothea'll go with me. See you! *Wiedersehen.*"

He turned back to Dorothea, "That's okay with you, isn't it?"

She nodded, liking the authority in his voice. Stefan sat back and put his arms behind his head.

"Enough about my tale of woe. Say, you never told me about your job with Chanel. Will you be going to Paris at all? Or better, to *Köln,* so you can visit me some time?"

"I'm going to Paris some day but I sure hope we can meet before then."

They found at a small restaurant near the tram station. Over dinner Stefan talked about his upcoming job at the architectural firm in Köln. Once he grimaced and left the table, but Dorothea brushed aside any doubts of his health and felt it would be rude to ask if he were sick. After dinner he suggested they go to the Café Splendide back in Vienna for a *Schnapps,* and once there, they drank down a shot of the strong liqueur then proceeded to order a bottle of *Gewürtstraminer.* Soon their evening took on a warm and boozy glow. The string quartet started to play "*Wien, Wien, Nur Du Allein,*" and they both sang, "Vienna, Vienna, you alone…" One of the violins played a flat note and Stefan made a funny face. Dorothea laughed too loud. "Did you hear that? Oy veh."

Suddenly everything was hilarious and a woman in a navy suit at the table next to them glared at them. Stefan jumped to his feet, bowed and clicked his heels. "*Entschuldigen Sie, Gnädige Frau.* "I'm so sorry." They sat at their table in dignity until Stefan exploded with laughter. The escort of the woman in the suit, a small bald man in pin stripes, said not quite under his breath "*Judenschwein,*" "Jewish pigs," as he lit a cigarette.

"Let's dance, Stefan," said Dorothea. "Those people don't deserve our contempt. Let's not let them ruin our day for us." He sat back down. "Okay, okay. I won't stoop to their level. No, sir, just because they're Jew haters. After all Vienna's full of 'em these days. …." They danced without speaking and the small string ensemble stuck up "Thanks for the Memory." Stefan said, "Good song…. Memory. . I wonder what it'll be like in Köln, when I start my job next week….. Ah!" Stefan winced.

Dorothea said, "What's wrong, Stefan? You look pale."

"Nothing, just there a terrific pain that comes and goes. It made me sick a bit ago it hit so hard."

Dorothea's heart clenched. "Nothing! That sounds serious, Stefan."

"I'll see the doc this week, I promise. Now let's have some fun. Where were we?" He gently pushed at her waist and Dorothea pirouetted under his arm then back again. "Ah, that was good. It won't be long before we'll be in the real world, you as a big-shot buyer for Chanel and me, a big-shot architect. And you know something? You're going to be a great buyer! The best." He swept her around in a fast spin.

They slowed again and gazing over Stefan's shoulder, Dorothea noticed a beautiful woman just coming out of the powder room, wearing a hat with red feathers that trailed behind like a lure. She is so self-possessed, so unlike Dorothea in her yellow blouse with the amber pin on her narrow chest. Dorothea wonders what it is like to be so attractive.

As they danced, Dorothea started feeling the full effects of the wine. She asked in a lazy voice, "So do you think you'll come back some time to Vienna?

Of course, Thea. And I'll call you when I come to visit Papa."

"Stefan, I'm sorry it didn't work out for you and Renate but I'm glad we're together tonight." Dorothea shifted closer to Stefan as they danced, enjoying the scratch of his whiskers against her cheek.

"I have to admit she doesn't love me, and after all I did for her, all those pastries and trips to the cinema. Can't understand it – I'm such a catch." He gave her a big smile." "You know something? Look at me, you."

He took her chin in his hand. "You're nicer than Renate. You've always been nicer than Renate." He traced a line across her forehead with his index finger. "In fact, you're quite a dish, you know…."

She giggled. "That's the wine talking."

"No, no, no, no, no. I mean it."

When the music ended, Stefan walked her to their table past the table of the navy-suited woman and the pinstriped man. Stefan deliberately bumped against the man's chair as he passed. The man said "Hey, watch it."

Stefan sat down, ignoring the man and took a big gulp of wine. "Thea? Now where were we? Oh, I was telling you you're a dish, and you are, you know, in your own way, quite a lovely woman."

"Sure. And what about Renate? Aren't you still in love with her?"

"Renate is something I can't have. Yeah, I guess I love her but she doesn't want me." Stefan sat back in his chair with a scowl on his face which shifted to puzzlement. "Why do you care about Renate and me anyway?" He looked at Thea. She tried not to slur her words, "Because I care about you, Stefan."

"Well, I care about you, Dorothea," Stefan said, and he leaned over their little table and kissed her.

Before she could stop herself she said, "I love you, Stefan....." And, brushing away a lifetime of warnings and dire consequences to girls who walk on the wild side, she continued, "Stefan, let's make love tonight, before you go away."

"Thea, what are you saying? You're a good girl, I mean, you haven't, well, you know what I mean…"

"Oh Stefan, let's not talk nonsense. All my life I've been good. I'm tired of being good…. Good, bad, what does all that mean?"

The conversations at the other tables, the chattering and the clanking sounds from the kitchen, all receded like the last scene in an art film when the picture shrinks down to a pinprick before disappearing. Dorothea and Stefan were alone in the restaurant eyes locked. Stefan stretched across the table and they kissed again.

They looked at each other.

"Check!"

They left the Café and walked down the street. Stefan found a small hotel and stared down the skeptical night clerk. When they were in the room, Dorothea shivered and crossed her arms. The double bed seemed to be the only furniture in the room, a looming thing she tried to avoid looking at but which tugged at her attention like a monster in disguise. The bed was covered in worn green chenille, like an old bathrobe, not with the silk and goose down bedding she was used to. She watched Stefan cross over to the opposite side of the bed and click on a bedside table lamp, turning the room orange and cozy. Stefan spent a moment looking out the window before closing the flimsy drapes against the glare of the streetlights.

"*Schatzi.*" He crossed the room to where she stood and put his arms around her gently, like a swan folding large wings around her body. He held her for a long time until she stopped shivering and moved her head from its hiding place under his neck to find his mouth. They kissed.

The next morning Stefan dropped Dorothea off at home to face her father, a furious man who berated both of them, ordered Stefan out and embraced Dorothea in tears of sorrow. She wote to Stefan and started her new job managing a small *parfümerie* that she hoped would lead to a job in Paris one day. She wrote Stefan again, and then again, and went to work every day in a state of suspended animation, her emotions put on a shelf and out of reach. That she received no letter in return became a self-fulfilling prophecy for her, confirming her worst suspicions. After many weeks of waiting, she gave up hope.

*　　*　　*

The well-dressed young woman continues to scan the crowds. On the street pass the German tanks, then the infantry. An elite platoon of soldiers struts into view, legs stiff and toes pointed like dancers. A

Pathé Movietone camera stationed by the curb whirrs as an American newsman scribbles on his pad. The footage will be rushed to the U.S. and shown next week in theaters in "Time Marches On." The yellow-toothed man jostles Dorothea in his excitement, and she checks her watch then looks away from the procession, searching the mass of people spread out around her.

A man in a coat of Loden green, wearing a red tie, fights against the crowd, moving upstream from the direction of *Albertinaplatz*. He is European with a touch of Slav, handsome with thick wavy hair, wire-rimmed glasses, big nose and wide mouth. With as much courtesy as possible in the circus atmosphere of the moment, he pushes and shoves and manages to reach Dorothea's side. He waits until she sees him.

"Stefan!"

"Dorothea!"

"You caught me by surprise!"

"Let me look at you! You're looking wonderful, elegant as ever!"

He kisses her cheek.

"You look well, Stefan. I thought we'd miss each other – this crowd, this scene, I didn't realize!"

"Yes, the Little *Führer* – here in our city. I say the hell with him. And the Nazi swine in our country – they forget they're Austrians too! What happened to red, white, red forever?"

"That's what my father says. He has kept the Austrian flag flying from our window but I don't know for how long it will be possible. I didn't realize this horrid spectacle would come by on this day of all days. I want to keep on working for Chanel and I'm going to whether my father likes it or not. He thinks we should leave the country but I think this so-called takeover will all be over in a few months. I don't know what the fuss is all about."

"Well, he's right, you know….," Stefan says. "Let's get out of here away from the crowd."

They find a café on a side street and order espressos.

"Dorothea. You do look wonderful… Just the same perky nose, bright eyes. You've filled out a bit."

"Well, I'm still me, aren't I? You look well. How's your father?"

"He's fine. He moved to Köln to be near me…"

"How do you like your job?" She asks, and they talk for awhile when Stefan interrupts himself. "But let's not talk about architecture." He takes her hand. "You know I haven't forgotten our last night together. You wore purple. I could never forget that night."

They can hear the band playing a strident march, the bass drummers hammering. From their little table, they see the trumpeters blaring as the crowd claps in time to the music. The flag bearers arrive, ten rows of men in ten columns each. The camera records the red banners with black-stitched swastikas that flap sluggishly as they pass. The thick blood-colored cloth will be seen in the movie theaters as gray since Technicolor™ is still a new phenomenon.

Dorothea whispers to Stefan, "Of course I remember that night. I was wearing yellow, though, not purple; it was the blouse Tante Annie sent me from Prague. I wore it with the amber brooch. Yes. It was a wonderful evening." She removes her hand from Stefan's grip.

"Why didn't you write to me or call? I thought I'd never see you again after you left for Köln. "

The crowd roars. Hitler's motorcade is passing. The Yank newspaperman at the Opera House pushes back his hat and writes, "The shouts are coming from the depths of Austria's long-frustrated thirst for past glory."

She continues. "I don't have a lot of time…. I need to get back soon…." She wants to get away now, afraid she might cry.

A new cheer signals Himmler's black Mercedes gliding into view just behind Hitler, Himmler standing in the rear seat compartment of the convertible. Next to him a big woman in a flower-print silk dress is waving. A small fox winds around her neck, its black eyes bright, its mouth arranged so that it is biting its own tail. Himmler has his right arm in the classic Nazi salute. As he passes the crowd, his glasses refract the sun like two oval beacons that flash then die out.

Stefan takes Dorothea's hand in his and waits for the shouting to subside.

"Yes, my sweet, what were you saying?"

"When you left last year you never wrote. Why? Why didn't you contact me?"

"I want to talk about that, Dorothea. That's why I'm here."

Dorothea says, "You never wrote to me. I could only draw one conclusion: you'd changed your mind about us."

Stefan pulls out a white handkerchief from his breast pocket and wipes his forehead. "This noise – too many people. It's too loud here, don't you think?" He's sweating. He leans in close his eyes grave behind his wire-rimmed glasses. He's grown up, she thinks. She smells coconut pomade in his hair and peppermint on his breath. And a whiff of garlic. Dinner with a woman? His lover? She is jealous, then angry. She hates him. She straightens her posture.

He presses. "Thea. Listen to me and then judge me. But hear me out. I became very sick just after I left Vienna. Remember that night when I had to leave you for a while in the Café Splendide? I heard voices, voices that were telling me to do terrible things, things I could never do. First the voices went away but then after I got to Köln I thought I'd end up in an asylum.... You can't possibly understand – it's been hell. And I couldn't write to you because you would have come and I couldn't let you see me like that. I was out of my head. Please just believe me when I say I've lived in hell hoping you'd wait for me."

She's thinking Liar. "Oh, Stefan, Stefan, I can't believe what I'm hearing! You talk about hell!" She turns away.

"They finally found a medicine that keeps the demons quiet, and now I'm strong enough. To come back to you."

Stefan's chin shows the blue-on-white skin of a close shave. He describes the hospital ward with nurses and syringes, pill bottles, injections, nights of sweating and and loneliness.

"Oh Stefan. You were sick!... But... Stefan...."

"Thea, before you say anything more I have to tell you that there was another reason I didn't write to you. Everything that happened that night after the Café Splendide and the hotel, well I thought we needed some time to think things over. So, when I got sick, it was really just convenient not to write to you. I'm sorry if I hurt you."

Dorothea looks at Stefan. "Well thanks a lot. One thing I have to say about you, Stefan is I have to give you credit for honesty, now that it is safe for you." She gives a little snort. The crowds continue to cheer. Some people nearby shout *Heil Hitler*, arms raised in salute.

She continues, "So why are you here in Vienna and why did you call? Do you think the time has come to talk? It's now convenient for you and I'm supposed to understand?"

"Yes."

"I'm trying, but it's difficult." She looks down at her purse, then back at him. "I need to know at least one thing: are you really okay now since you left the hospital? Are you all right, are you cured?"

"Yes, Dearest, I can be my old self with my medicine." He pats at his chest. "And I want to be with you. In fact, I want you to come to America and live with me, never leave me again, marry me." Stefan's eyes are shining.

49

"America? What do you mean?" she says.

"You have no idea what's going on in Germany. First they took away leadership posts from Jews, now they are treating the Jews as if they're animals. Some of the papers – I can't even describe the pictures - horns, drooling, big noses. Jews are in danger in Germany. We must get to America if we can. If not, I have an aunt in Buenos Aires who will help us. *Schatzi*, you and your father are in real danger here." He paused.

"What's wrong, *Schatzi*?"

A pain starts up in her chest, as if a doctor is pulling stitches out of a wound.

"Oh Stefan. I'm sorry. For you and for me. It's not just the Nazis."

"What do you mean?"

She began to cry. "I'm trying to say it's too late, Stefan. It's too late for us."

Stefan reaches into his inside coat pocket and puts a cigarette in his mouth. He digs in again and pulls out a lighter which he flicks toward the cigarette, drawing deeply, producing a bright orange glow before turning his head to exhale noisily. He slides the lighter into his pocket. He looks at Dorothea. "What do you mean, too late?"

"Stefan, listen. After my hundredth letter went unanswered I had to believe you'd found someone else; that you really didn't care. I had no right….. after all, it was only one night and then you went away. It was horrible… I missed you and finally I thought of you as dead, as if you had died. It was easier that way. After that, I almost didn't make it, with only my work to keep me going." She gives a rueful laugh, her eyes glistening. She waves her hand. "It hurts my throat to talk. Give me just a minute."

She is thinking of the man she met a few months ago at her cousin's wedding, his name is Kurt and he's a good man, older than she, a banker from Bratislava. Also Jewish, Kurt has asked her to marry him. He has a child from a previous marriage. I'm fond of Kurt, she thinks, and I can't let Stefan hurt me again. It cost me too much.

And then she smiles ruefully to herself. Kurt will be a fine father for little Georg. She studies Stefan. How much little Georg resembles Stefan with his thick curly hair and dark eyes. Stefan watches her, his eyes large and vulnerable behind his glasses. I once loved those eyes; I loved this man so much, it hurts to think about it. This man now offers me everything I ever wanted, at last. She sinks into memories of their night in the hotel on the lumpy bed in the small hotel near the Café Splendide. No. She has promised Kurt, and she will keep her promise. To brace herself, she summons up the memory of waiting to hear from Stefan, of anxious searching through the daily stack of letters and bills and announcements, of bitter disappointment and dashed hopes and humiliation.

"It's too late for us, Stefan. It's too late for us. I'm sorry."

"Am I right? It's another man."

"Yes."

Stefan's face changes. He looks at Dorothea, as if searching for the lie in Dorothea's words. He throws down his cigarette and crushes it with exaggerated swiveling motions of his shoe.

"Thea, I feel like a fool. No, don't say anything." Stefan stands and pulls at his coat. "Let's not make this more of a farce than it is already. But before I go, tell me one thing."

He pulls her toward him. His gloved hands burn her arms through the layers of wool and silk at the points where he touches her. Thea closes her eyes. She wants to have her life move ahead by several years, to have this time be gone, finished. Her heart has frozen over, like the Danube in the winter, thick and opaque and impenetrable.

"Are you happy?" he asks. She nods once, her tears leaking onto her cheeks. He looks at her one last time, stands and pushes back his chair. She watches him walk away from all the noise, all the pomp; from her.

Back in front of the Opera house they are now shouting in unison, in a roar that blots out the world, *"Heil Hitler, Heil Hitler."*

Just a Cup of Coffee

Big Red is getting ready for work. She's in Room 4511, Business Level, where she always stays during her monthly trips to New York. She's finished spraying her hair – a thick mane she dyes cordovan red - and is applying her lipliner. She hears the shot, a sound that rises over the muttering wind that has moved in overnight and has been making a racket since dawn. Gale force, the TV says. She is focused on her lips, paying no attention to the whining and whooshing. Then she straightens, frowns. On the forty-fifth level you never hear anything, especially outside the window. Yes, you'd hear the click of a latch down the hall, or the whisper of an Instant Checkout receipt sliding under the door in the early morning darkness, but that's all. She has to investigate so she puts down her lip liner and makes a mental note to remember to fill in the lines before leaving for the office. (Once she'd forgotten, and halfway through the morning her ghastly puppet's mouth, white lips inside a bright red outline, leered at her from the mirror of the Women's Room. She'd been mortified. And nobody in the office had mentioned it to her.) She moves her six-foot frame toward the window, trailing a scent of Coco in the closed air. Her talc-coated thighs whish-whish under her nylon half slip. A nice big girl, her mother calls her.

She kneels on the small boudoir chair in front of the window, a small fussy piece of furniture out of a *film noir* in which the bad girl, revolver in hand who's clad in satin nightgown and rabbit-fur mules, waits to confront the gumshoe. The cushion engulfs her knee. She leans forward and cranes. At first she sees nothing out of the ordinary, and then, across the courtyard, it all makes sense. A window is open - perhaps the room is being aired by the maid - and the floor-length drapes heavy and sad like old theater curtains have been sucked outside the building and are flailing in the strong wind. Every time they slap against the concrete they make the gunshot sound.

She pads back to her bathroom for a bottle of nail polish and sits down on the bed to do her toes. Burnt Coral - a beautiful color with just a tinge of frost they've sold her at her last make up session at Macy's. She hoists up one shapely, large size eleven foot and plants her toes on the bedside table. The wind continues to moan and slam the drapes as she strokes careful lines of enamel. That open window is dangerous. She wonders how it would feel to free-fall from Business Level. She thinks of the poor souls who jumped from the Twin Trade Towers on 9/11; of the people in the world who have jumped or fallen from bridges or from airplanes; of the suicides at Grand Canyon that the Ranger said number two or three a year. The newspapers are full of stories of people falling. Are they conscious once airborne or does that mechanism kick in that they say happens to prey animals in Africa, when the fangs sink into their flesh and the animals know they will die, yet a blessed narcosis sets in so that they don't really feel anything?

The phone rings. Who could that be? She picks it up and a soft masculine voice speaks.

"Hello. Are you the pretty lady I took to the Sheraton Hotel last night? The one with the red hair?"

Oh God, it is the cab driver from Afghanistan. She never should have given him her card. Their conversation had been so pleasant, though, on the drive in from Newark. He genuinely seemed nice, educated, well-spoken, and she had enjoyed showing him that some Americans understood Afghanistan, at least a little about it. He'd been a teacher in Kandahar. Now she isn't so sure she wants to meet him, no, not at all. What had she been thinking of, giving him her card? The truth was she'd been drunk. She had seen in this man a gentle, safe person (sexy too with his accented English) and had been so lonely after her whole day at the office back in Boston. And it had been six months since she'd broken up with Earl and she'd had no luck with Match. com. It was her size that always turned men off. Or there were men who liked big women but who were all wrong for her: wrong grammar, wrong hygiene, wrong education. This man seemed clean, relatively good-looking, and nice.

She straightens her backbone and grips the phone tightly.

"Hi. Yes, I am the red-headed woman."

"This is Kamar. You gave me your card last night, remember? I thought you'd like to talk with me." After two quick vodkas on the rocks on the shuttle, Big Red hardly remembers getting to her hotel.

"Well, actually, Kamar, I am kind of busy right now. I am getting ready to go to work. Aren't you driving your cab today?"

"No, I don't start until noon."

"Well, Kamar, I really can't talk. I'm sorry but I have to go. Bye."

She hangs up before he can answer.

She walks along Eighth Avenue down to Thirty-third with plenty of time for a coffee and a donut before class. Soon she is speaking to a roomful of young men who sit around a table in a darkened conference room. She is thirty-eight years old and her face flushes easily beneath her schoolmarm glasses. She wears a burnt orange linen and polyester suit whose big jacket, short skirt with cream colored blouse, could be almost stylish if only she wore opaque panty hose. But no, there are those massive marble legs that end in big feet wearing (of all things in New York City) ballet flats. Soft, tan suede flimsy flexible sandals, a grown-up version of the shoes made of leather flaps and elastic bands.

White triangles of her feet show that marble skin again. And everyone in New York dresses in black or gray except Big Red.

Big Red is teaching the class how to manage the customers' assets – the personal computers, the laptops, the network printers. The students know how to install, boot, diagnose, repair, replace and maintain the equipment. But they don't know how to do the reporting on new software. "It's very important to report any updates, because why?" No one speaks as she looks around the room. "Because we need to keep track of our inventory." Big Red's voice sometimes takes on the tone her mother uses when she takes her cocktail on a Sunday afternoon and holds court with Big Red, her sister and her mother's friend's teenager daughter, who always join the family for drinks after church.

Her students are a United Nations of nationalities. There are: a Japanese woman, a couple of men from Trinidad and Haiti, a Frenchman, and several Americans. A third generation Indian-Guayanese man has Tourette's syndrome and emits an unearthly chirp every few minutes during the entire presentation.

"Ghaap" "Ghaap"

"What's that sound?" asks Big Red.

"It's me. I have Tourette's syndrome."

The silence in the room is worse than any sound. It takes her a moment to understand what the Guayanese man has said. But without missing a beat she turns back to her laptop to start the presentation. Nobody looks to the back of the room where Tourette's is sitting.

"Ghaap"

When the overhead portion is finished, the lights come on.

"So don't forget, you have to upgrade memory, and you have to track the seat code."

"I want to ask you about the 'sit' code,' ask one young Chinese man in a crisp blue pin-striped suit.

His English is difficult to follow but Big Red strives to listen. She supplies a lengthy detailed answer while the rest of the class sits stiff, bored.

To the right of the Chinese man sits an African American man with a baby face, shaved head, gorgeous clothing. He wears a three-piece suit with a teal blue-striped shirt. He has taken off his jacket to reveal a satin-backed vest that excites Big Red. Of course it's not the vest – it's his smile, his charisma. She is drawn to him. She takes in his oxblood shoes, the perfect color accent to the charcoal and blue of his outfit that makes his walnut hued skin glow. A dime-sized gold earring glints from one ear. When they all leave for a coffee break, his head has a little crease near the neck, pointing to the place where his primitive brain site, the medulla, meets the higher-purposed cerebellum. Big Red approaches him at the coffee urn with a winning smile.

"So, where are you from?"

"I was born in Jamaica but now I live here." The man stirs his coffee with a stick and tosses it into the wastebasket.

"You don't have much of an accent." She smiles broadly, encouragingly.

"No, I was around my American cousins all the time and besides, I used to come to New York every summer."

Before she could say anything else, the man says, "Excuse me," and turns to talk to one of the young secretaries waiting to get coffee. Big Red takes her coffee back to the conference room, sits down. She takes a sip. Oh well. He seemed nice but of course, he'd be more interested in a young secretary.

If only she hadn't lost Mark the Masher. He had loved her large breasts. She'd discovered she was in love with him the night they went to Tanglewood, the summer home of the Boston Symphony Orchestra. The people scattered about on the lawn had stowed the candles and wine, the brie and olives, the cold chicken, taboule salad and grapes, and had settled down on the blankets. She had snuggled with Mark against a tree, and he wrapped his arms and legs around her keeping her tight and safe. At that moment, looking up at the starry sky, with "Pathetique" swirling around them, she'd almost cried, so perfect was her joy. Then things went badly. Back at the motel she'd been so ready to make love. She'd danced out of the bathroom. "Honey, what do you think about my new panties?" The Masher hadn't answered. He was sitting on the bed, absorbed in Jay Leno. She sat down and put her hand on the zipper of his Wranglers. "Hey, Handsome," she said. "Here I am."

Leno said, "And then Bush goes to the B'nai Brith meeting..." The audience was laughing and Mark snorted. She distinctly remembers this part. She had pulled at his zipper and he slapped away her hand absently, his eyes still on the TV.

"You're not serious about watching TV, are you?"

And he'd said, "As a matter of fact, yes, I am. You know we don't always have to have sex every time we get together."

She could take the rejection if he hadn't delivered it so coldly. His face looked like something carved in granite, his eyes pellets of b.b. shot. She'd lain in the dark all night, her hurt possessing her body like an incubus until the birds began to warble and she finally slept.

No, she had not had good luck with men.

In the classroom a man named "Angel" with the face of a Michelangelo David, approaches. His features hint of Aztec ancestry, and his purposeful gaze from large movie-star eyes is pacific and stoical. She sees his ring. Probably two babies at home and a wildcat wife.

"Okay, let's get back to work. Is everybody here?"

The class resumes. A few more slides, a few more admonitions, no questions, and then it's over for the day.

"Remember, we're not tracking things like drivers or Rhumba software," says Big Red. "Now don't forget to please fill out the sheet at the end of your training package and send it to me so you can be registered."

The young men file out of the room. A few shake hands with Big Red as she gathers up her laptop. She closes the door and within minutes the conference room is quiet, the air dead. A few stapled stacks of white copy paper lie at one end of the long table next to an empty Dunkin' Donuts coffee cup with a crumpled napkin in it. Otherwise the surface is bare. The fluorescent lights hum and emit a stale light that washes everything sickly grey.

Big Red walks back to her hotel room. The night is balmy; the moist wind blows her hair into a frizz. Around the corner of her hotel, she enters her favorite take-out food shop and takes a tray. So many delicacies to choose from. She never can settle on just one entree, but instead she piles on wings, noodles, chicken with cashews, spare ribs, (a tiny amount of vegetables to salve her conscience), pineapple chunks, sushi, pork fried rice, and a large chocolate cupcake.

She opens a bottle of wine from the minibar and settles on the hotel bed in front of the TV to watch "Saving Private Ryan." She sees herself reflected in the large screen as she takes a mouthful of rice. The body of a soldier hit by the Germans flips into the air; Tom Hanks is stumbling through the beach amidst the wreckage of the assault on D-Day. She sips her wine and watches her own face - a ghostly backdrop to the bloody carnage.

Time for a walk around the block. She's restless so she puts on her sneakers and leaves the hotel. Kamar flits into her memory as she turns left on West 65th. There was something needy about Kamar. Why does she pick up men who need to be rescued.

She's worked miracles with unhappy guys all her adult life; saving souls had been her true calling. She'd sit there in the restaurant (or bar, coffee shop, shopping mall, Starbucks) and they'd talk. She'd ask helpful questions, always keeping it light, always focusing on how to make the guy feel good about himself. One voice in her head would go, This guy's a loser. What are you doing with him? While the other would go, Give the guy the benefit of the doubt. You never know. Her hope sprang up again and again like a trick birthday candle. She believed that if she gave enough love they'd have to give it back. Sex, of course, was part of the path to love. She was willing to give anything if it led her to the prince beneath the frog's skin.

The night has little moonlight on Sixth Avenue yet there is enough light to see how few pedestrians remain. Only taxis, always taxis, true residents of the city.

Impotence could make a man feel worthless. Big Red let her mind drift for a moment, thinking of that sticky lump of gristle and loose skin that sometimes went on strike at a critical moment. Whenever that happened on a date with someone, someone with whom she had carefully built rapport, instead of being disappointed or angry like some women, she'd say, "Let's see what we can do;" or "You know, it's great for me just to be with you." She'd apply lavish amounts of praise and forgiveness along with some well-placed pressure with her hand and tongue. "Let's try this ... does that feel good? I LOVE to touch you. Let's slow down a little. I have an idea." And on and on it went, until either she'd cooked up a nice erection for them both to enjoy or they'd end up in an overlong, awkward hugging session.

The wind accelerated again, chuffing and whooshing in a sudden burst.

Big Red never expected real love after what she had gone through with Paint Guy from over in Marlborough, the time she'd gone into the

Sears store and fallen head over heels for that liar. Not to mention her ex-husband and the fact that he'd gone out and gotten himself a trophy wife after all she'd done to bolster *his* self-esteem.

Her Ex had introduced her to pot.

"I don't feel anything. Are you sure this is good pot?"

"Yes, it's good but you don't call it pot - it's weed." He spoke in a constrained, singsong voice. He took another drag. "You may need to try it a few times before it does anything for you." His voice was abnormally high and his words came out constricted, as if he were in pain.

Frankie Vallee and the Four Seasons were on the radio. "Oh, I love that song," she said, "Whatever happened to that group?" Her Ex closed his eyes, his arm around her neck, his hand massaging her breast. "Sh-sh-sh" he said. "Just lay back."

"Shouldn't it be lie back?' she asked, the thought out of her mouth before she could stop it. There you go again, said one of the voices in her brain. Stop it. Okay. He doesn't have your level of education, but education isn't all that counts in this world. Give him a chance. She'd settled back into the pillow, sleepy and contented. Her mind drifted; she felt she was flowing on a river. She could stay this way forever. Eventually the music on the radio veered back into her consciousness and she heard, "… Sweet surrender, what a night…" The very same song, after such a long stretch of time! She had laughed out loud, then rolled over in a rush of exuberance. "Hey, stop that! You're gonna crush me!"

She'd tried hard to be a good wife. But then had come the text message. She couldn't help notice it since his cell was just lying there on the table as she was finishing up the dishes. He was in the bathroom when it chirped. It was from "Sally Wilton," the female half of a couple they played canasta with. It read: Mark's traveling come on over baby.

Big Red took it in with a thirty-second delay, the full impact passing through a filter before reaching her brain. When it hit, she forgot that she had planned to be the one to do the leaving when the time came, not the other way around. The pain numbed her like an injection. Then her Ex was by her side, hugging her, saying I'm sorry I'm sorry. They stood, foreheads touching, in the kitchen next to the butcher block table, a shaft of light streaming through the dirty window. She felt that if she didn't move, if she stayed perfectly still there in the kitchen, that what she'd heard would not be real, that she'd imagined it all, that her husband really loved her. She remembered looking past his shoulder and seeing, as if for the first time, the pair of salt and pepper pigs, genuine Occupied Japan, she had given him. They looked cheap and worthless. Inside a voice was screaming, what's wrong with me? Weren't we going to have children?

Big Red nears the corner on 49ᵗʰ street holding her bag of food when Kamar appears at her side. He takes her elbow and speaks softly. "Hello there. I was looking for you."

Oh God. What to do? Big Red says, "Kamar, what are you doing here?"

"I thought we had something together. You were so nice to me on the cab ride. I'm lonely. You're lonely too. Am I right? We can talk." Hi voice is sweet and soft, like an overripe mango.

Big Red struggles to recover from her surprise. She looks around. The street is empty. A small fear struggles against a sick compulsion to be with this man. "Kamar, Kamar, it's nice to see you but really, I can't see you."

"Why not, because I have dark skin? Are you like all Americans? Afraid of dark skin?"

"No, no, it's not that at all."

His eyes fill with thick tears. "What is it then?"

Now what can she do? Big Red's Achilles heel of compassion is always getting in the way and she has come to realize that her compassion is a cover. What does she want? She almost never takes the honest route to go for what she wants when the feelings of others are at stake.

She comes up with the one thing that she hopes will make him back off, that won't hurt his feelings. With her voice quavering then settling on an unnatural register, she says, "Kamar it's nothing like that. It's just that I have a boyfriend, back home. I don't want to betray him."

"Then why were you so nice to me?"

"I don't know!"

Kamar steps away. She is confused. Where is her head? Why did she come on to this guy, a stranger, when she has no intention of messing with her mixed up emotions. She's played too many games and this is just another one. He may be dangerous and yet, probably not. He's watching her now.

She stops moving, thinking, planning. She's tired, emotionally shut down, like a tormented, prodded animal who simply stops moving. She stands still on that New York corner, the taxis and other street traffic moving, while she exits the stage. It's as if she were playing a game of statue back home in Michigan thirty years ago in her neighbor's backyard when she still had her life ahead of her. How she had loved that moment when the kids had all been twirled and released and had to stay frozen in strange, twisted postures: a hand on an ankle, a goofy expression, a leg in the air.

Kamar breaks into her reverie. "Why don't we go have a cup of coffee? I'd like to know you better." He smiles.

"What?" Big Red slowly looks at Kamar.

"I don't think you have a boyfriend. I think you are afraid of me. Or maybe afraid of yourself. Why don't we just sit down, have a cup of coffee and talk?"

Big Red takes in Kamar's clean smell, his shy smile, the winsome way in which he looks at her. He is dressed in khakis and a long-sleeved cotton shirt, just like an American. His black hair shines, slicked back. He has excellent teeth. She looks at her watch.

"Well, there is a coffee shop in the hotel here. We might just as well talk. But I do have to get up early."

Kamar steps back politely, as if to say, you lead the way. Big Red likes that. And it's a curious thing. This moment is new for her; no sex, no games, no fantasies. Just a cup of coffee.

"Mommy, can I watch TV?"

Big Red looks down at the mocha-skinned five-year-old with the limpid eyes.

"Just until Daddy gets home, Peanut."

"Okay," and the boy runs away.

Big Red smiles. Could she be any happier, she wonders, waiting for the arrival of Kamar.

THE RUNAWAY CANISTER

Evgenie thought she was going to die that day. They were just outside of Newport Harbor aboard Joe's 32-foot sailboat, *Osprey*, and she was fighting to remain on board as the two boats kept parting and crashing together. Between each collision, the boats backed off from each other, opening up a view of snot-green water. Each time the steel-rimmed edges closed like the blades of some monstrous scissors, Evgenie saw herself falling in to be cut in two at the waist.

The day had begun peacefully enough. She and Joe had left Cuttyhunk, Massachusetts, the last little island in the string of Elizabeths in Vineyard Sound. It was the second day into their cruising vacation. It would take them about five hours to get to Newport. Their friends on big *Sarabande*, Hank and Carolyn, quickly passed them, flying past the green and red buoys that dotted the entrance to Cuttyhunk. *Osprey* had just reached Rhode Island Sound when the trouble began. Evgenie and Joe were trying to keep *Sarabande* in sight but visibility was not good; there was fog in the distance; and worse, there was little wind to fill the sails. It would be a dull crossing. With the mainsail hoisted, little *Osprey* power-sailed at six knots to *Sarabande's* seven.

Sarabande had long disappeared into the fog when Evgenie, who was at the wheel, noticed that their speed kept dropping. With the engine still churning, they slowed, then stopped moving all together, dead in the water. Wisps of black smoke from the engine compartment confirmed the bad news. The transmission had gone; probably a leak. She shut down the engine and they floated in the silent gray of the morning, alone at sea. It was one of those moments. Something goes wrong and you're out in the middle of nowhere and thoughts of a good meal on terra firma flitter away..

In the quiet of the moment, Evgenie, thirty-nine, divorced, and a novice reminded herself that Joe, forty-two, also divorced, was an excellent sailor. He'd get them out of this predicament.

Joe radioed to Hank and soon *Sarabande* turned around; their friends insisted on coming back to help. Hank thought he might be able to diagnose the problem. While waiting, Joe fussed around with the engine below, pulling out transmission fluid along with his toolbox. When *Sarabande* arrived, Evgenie took the dinghy to pick up Hank across the fifty feet of ocean between the boats, rowing against a surprisingly strong current. Hank climbed aboard and as the men worked below, Hank's wife, Carolyn, drove *Sarabande* around and around the area. Joe called up from below. "Turn on the engine." After a few seconds of valiant sputters, the engine failed to catch. No dice, it was a leak, too big to fix; the damage had been done. Evgenie rowed Hank back to his boat, her adrenalin seeping away to be replaced by a nattering dread. How were they going to get to shore and into a marina? There went their plans for a nice dinner in Newport.

Evgeny rowed back to *Osprey*. She cleated the dinghy and stood up on the dinghy seat. She clutched at the metal stanchions and the lower half of her body rode the dinghy up and down like a bucking bronco. She had felt confident she could board from the rear and too late remembered from the Sail course: "Boats of different sizes will rise and fall at different rates, especially in choppy seas." *Osprey* was going up and the little dinghy she stood in was going down, presenting a logistical challenge. She hadn't been aware of the increasing swells in the water until it was too late. But she had to get back on board. She concentrated. When *Osprey* slewed and the dinghy rose, she grabbed the lifeline and hoisted her left foot up and over. Her right foot refused to follow and she clung, tossing up and down like a bug on a bouncing ball. Then with a tremendous effort, she forced her body over the lifeline and collapsed on the cockpit seat.

Joe came up from below. He said, "We could be towed to Jamestown for $1,300 minus my $300 insurance coverage. There's no point in trying to sail back to Cuttyhunk which has no boatyard. Besides we have no wind." Evgenie had an idea. "What about the Rhode Island coast?" she asked.

"There's no convenient harbor along the Rhode Island coast and how would we get there anyway?" Just then *Sarabande* radioed. They would tow them to Newport. "… Roger that. Oh, God, you are a lifesaver, Hank. We'll accept….. Over." Joe turned to Evgenie. "They'll tow us. Okay?" He turned back to the radio. "Thanks, Hank. Over."

Hank said, "Roger that. No problem, Buddy. We'll throw you the line. Out."

Elaborate preparations ensued.

Being towed requires that someone be at the wheel. Joe and Evgenie passed the next several hours engaged in steering through increasingly agitated waters. Between shifts at the wheel, Evgenie lost herself in a half-doze to the soporific lull of the wide and empty sea. Joe dozed too. They passed Old Cock Island then Chicken and Hen Rocks, and soon the mansions of Newport hove into view. The entry to Narragansset Bay is a wide thoroughfare and on that Sunday afternoon it was full of weekend boat traffic churning the waters. For a reason Evgenie didn't understand, Hank dropped the towline, leaving *Osprey* adrift a half mile out of the harbor. Left to its own devices, *Osprey* began to bob about. Joe got on the radio. TowBoatUS couldn't get to them for an hour, and since it was too deep to anchor at one hundred ten feet, he radioed Hank for ideas. Hank had an idea. "Listen. I'll bring you in but instead of towing you as before - because it might be dangerous with so much traffic - I'll bring you in alongside us. I'd like to try this harbor-friendly thing I learned at a seminar two weeks ago. We tie together side by side." Listening to the conversation, Evgenie felt a tickle of worry. Side by side? *Sarabande* was several tons heavier and ten feet longer than *Osprey*. Joe said, "I'll get back to you, Hank." "Roger that," said Hank over the radio. (Evgeny thought the guys played at being military with all their "Roger thats" when they got on the radios.)

Boats roared past and she spoke up.

"I'm not so sure, Joe. Couldn't the shrouds and masts clash if we were tied next to them?"

"It could happen… but Hank knows this stuff better than I."

"But I have read that boats of differing weights ride at different cycles."

"Oh, I'm not so sure that would be a problem with us. I say let's try it. Could be fun."

They were ready. *Sarabande* moved away from them, turned around, and like a bull ready to charge, it made its first pass, coming at them with what Evgenie thought was excessive speed. Joe and Evgenie waited to catch the lines. They closed in, coils of line flew out, lines uncoiled, and everything landed in the water. Hank turned Sarabande around in a wide half circle and started back toward them, coils again at the ready. "This is a bad idea," shouted Evgenie, too late, as the big boat roared toward them again and the lines came flying. This time the couple caught the lines but for some reason Carolyn shrieked across the water, "Drop the lines. Drop the lines!" They did and off went *Sarabande* preparing to come at them again. "I don't want to do this any more. This is not right. Let's think of something else."

Joe said "Oh, you're just a scaredy cat. Let's give it another try."

Sarabande returned and again the lines flew. This time they were caught and cleated fore and aft. That's when the trouble began. *Osprey* started rocking, gently at first, jerking toward *Sarabande*. The boats parted a few feet, then came back together because they were tied together bow and stern. The masts and shrouds of each boat started to hit each other. It occurred to Evgenie how much higher in the water *Sarabande* was than *Osprey* - at least four feet more of freeboard. At each clash, *Osprey* seemed to disappear under the bigger boat. The big boat kept jerking *Osprey* toward it. Collide, drift apart, jerk back to collide, drift apart, jerk back. Each cycle was worse, masts tilting at greater and greater angles, surfaces becoming steeper. Big bully *Sarabande* was going to wreck *Osprey*.

Evgenie was clinging to the hand rail. She shifted her weight and her foot slipped at the same time she lost her hold. She heard exposed wood splintering as she started to slide toward the abyss.

She forgot any orders the men may have been shouting. She dropped down on all fours like a maddened spider running for its life, and scrabbled forward to untie the line, to free *Osprey*. Everybody had the same idea and within a few seconds, the two sloops floated away from each other to drift untethered in the greasy water.

Sarabande towed them into the harbor in the traditional way – bow to stern – and dropped the line prematurely, forcing them to drift to their mooring. The two couples barely spoke to each other the rest of the day.

*   *   *

Several hours later, Hank and Carolyn had gone into town for dinner, while Evgenie and Joe found themselves safely tied to a substantial mooring in the Jamestown harbor. They had drunk double scotches, eaten a dinner of canned warmed-up Dinty Moore Beef Stew, savoring it as if it were the finest of cuisines, and they now sat stuporous in the cockpit, wineglasses in hand, looking dully at each other. Joe and Evgeny hardly noticed the gorgeous sunset that spread tangerine and silver across the bay, nor the evening air that blew warm, nor the fact that harbor traffic had quieted to a whisper.

Joe took a sip of his wine (their best Malbec having been brought out for the occasion of thanksgiving.) They had dropped the topic of their recent near-disaster and Evgenie had said, hoping to save the day on a friendly note said, "Tell me again what the winners won in our race last week? Those Beverly Yacht Club sailors are serious about racing, aren't they?" She stretched one leg onto the cushion. "It's just a sport but you'd think they were in it for their lives." Joe said, "They race for the trophies. And for the prestige. And yes, it is a serious sport." He paused. Then continued. "We might even have had a chance....."

"What? What chance?" Evgenie asked.

"Well, since you ask, in last week's race, if you only hadn't let the jib line go so early we'd have had better turns. You have to hang on as the boat swings around until the sail catches the wind on the opposite side and starts to move away. Only then do you let it go so you don't lose precious momentum."

Evgenie shifted the cushion at her back and said, "I know I know. I'm sorry we lost the damn race. I'm still learning, you know."

"Yes, Evie, but how many times do I have to tell you these things? With *Osprey* we had a chance at taking the trophy this year. And all you had to do was hang on longer. I just don't know...." He continued. "I don't know how many times I've told you. If Hank had been available, I would have used him as crew..." His voice had taken on a certain nasally whine that Evgenie had become used to but had never liked. Something snapped.

"Well, that's just wonderful. What am I, chopped liver?" As if on automatic, her voice kept going. "I've been practicing with you for the last five weekends, all day long, on reaching the starting line, on coming about, on adjusting the sails and blah blah blah. And you wish you had asked Hank to crew. Oh, I forgot. I'll bet you did and he wasn't available. So you were stuck with me. Why was this race so important to you? And you have the nerve to criticize my sailing after you made the half-wit decision today that almost took my life."

Joe put his cup on the center table. "Aren't you being a little dramatic? Took your life?... You didn't almost lose your life. The boats were being damaged but you didn't almost lose your life." Evgenie took a deep breath, puffing out and straightening up, ready to retaliate. Joe continued as if he didn't see her, "Yes, it was a dumb move to tie them together, but we survived, didn't we? God you are so…"

Plunk. They both heard it.

The gas tank for the grill on the stern rail had fallen into the water. It was the cooking gas container – they had used it that night to heat up the Dinty Moore. Of course, the canister was replaceable. They'd get another one perhaps tomorrow, or the next week.

They sat there, unable to let go of their quarrel. Evgenie was secretly pleased that the canister fell because Joe would have to spend more money, but then she remembered that for Joe, nothing was too expensive for *Osprey*. Joe stood up and walked over to the stern. He pointed. "Look. It was the canister, all right. There it is. We might be able to get it." The canister was floating in the still water, just a few feet away from the boat.

"Are you serious? You mean get in the dinghy?" She shot him a dirty look.

Joe pulled the dinghy from the midship cleat to the stern and jumped into it. He kept an eye on the canister as Evgenie slowly fetched the boathook and climbed down the swim ladder. The canister was now making a leisurely getaway between two nearby boats that rested quietly in the harbor.

"You row, since you always have to be in charge," said Evgenie, as she uncoiled the dinghy painter and sat. Joe said, "Oh, for Pete's sake, there you go again – can't you give it a rest?....."

She saw it first. "There it is, hiding behind that big mooring buoy. Go slow."

"I see it. You don't have to try to control everything."

"I've got the boat hook ready," said Evgenie, between gritted teeth.

Joe nudged the dinghy and she leaned out, extending the boat hook. But when she touched it, the canister skidded away and headed toward a big Catalina further into the harbor. The chase was on, and they went after the canister again, Joe working the oars with precision. They drew close, and again she reached out with the boat hook. Again the canister skidded away, playing catch-me-if-you can. The couple kept an eye on it and paused to re-calibrate their strategy. Evgenie said "If I hold this closer to the end, I can handle it better….." Then she had a thought. "You know what? I think we're setting up a little wavelet that keeps pushing the can just out of our reach."

"You're right. I'll try to slide the dinghy in toward it this time without setting up a wavelet." She noticed he had used her word "wavelet" in his reply. Was he mocking her?

The canister lurked in the shadow of a big Grady White, snuggled up against the hull. Evgenie reached out, snagged it, but at the last minute, dropped it.

"Shit. I'm sorry."

"Oh, don't worry, we'll get that little bastard. Look over there. I think its going toward that Catalina again."

Joe rowed quietly. On the harbor's horizon glimmered a line of lights, mostly white, interspersed with soft, glowing orbs of red, blue and green. The lights were the only way to distinguish the sky from the shore. A police siren broke the silence from far away. A boat radio squawked from a nearby yacht. Just as suddenly, the noises stopped. Joe guided the dinghy past a large trawler in silence. A hand from the lighted inner cabin of the trawler reached up to close the curtains.

"Oops – too close," whispered Joe.

They drifted past."

"Okay, I see the little bugger…. slowly slowly," he said.

Silence, then, "I got it. I got it this time, Joe."

Evgenie scooped the canister close to the boat with the hook, then grabbed it and dropped it into the middle of the boat.

"Great going," said Joe. They kept their voices low because people might be sleeping in the neighboring vessels. "Wow," whispered Evgenie. "We did it…." She paused and said. "This was fun. I'm almost sorry we caught it."

"Yeah, I know what you mean. I feel the same way."

It was completely dark when they turned around and rowed silently back to *Osprey*. Evgenie caught hold of the swim ladder at the stern and wrapped the painter around the cleat. They climbed aboard, tied the dinghy and collapsed in the cockpit.

"Whew! Another glass of wine?"

"Sure!... This is the part of sailing I like the best, " Evgenie said.

She settled back into the cushions as Joe poured the wine.

She said, "You know, I've been focusing on the scary moments in the boat, and sometimes forget the good times. Not only the chase for the canister – that was a blast! - but just the quiet of the moment here in the harbor, the cozy atmosphere away from the noisy world. And you know what else? In case you don't think I like sailing, I do. I like the sound of the water swooshing under the gunnels. And I like the froth. And the greenness of the water. And the feel of the wind on my face. And I like being outside in the sun. And I like being with you even if you're a Captain Hook sometimes."

"Me too, Baby." Joe said, taking her hand. "Sorry if I yelled at you. You'll get it right – all you need is more experience."

"Yeah." she said, taking a sip of wine and wondering if she had the courage to stick with this thing she had going with Joe. Sailing was part of the deal.

He said, "And by the way, I'd much rather have you as racing crew than Hank. He's got no sense at all. And you're better at the wheel any day. Better than me, even."

The sweet breeze caressed Evgeny's face as she moved into Joe's arms.

On Glennie's Wedding Day

The wedding party stood motionless, young faces rapt, frozen in time, a Renaissance tapestry minus the unicorn. Father Williams drew himself up.

"Speak now; or else for ever hold your peace."

Out of the darkness came a voice. "Just a minute here. I have something to say." Oh God. Margo forced herself not to turn around to look at Philip. Glennie's own father was trying to ruin the wedding after all. Margo should have known it would end this way after that weekend four months earlier when Philip had first met Hari. She should have known.

It was just an informal lunch at Margo's house in Acton, Massachusetts, a quiet suburb thirty miles west of Boston, where she lived with her husband of four years, Mike. She'd been in the kitchen taking the rolls from the oven when she heard Philip's voice, querulous, floating in from the dining table, "What's in this dish?" Glennie answered, "Dad, that's couscous." "Oh, coo-coo? Never heard of it. So we're having coo-coo in honor of...." And he paused. He tried again. "Coo-coo in honor of....." He'd forgotten the name of his daughter's fiancé whom he was meeting for the first time. The silence rolled from the dining room and into the kitchen. Margo stood at the open oven as the silence steadily poured into all the corners of the big house.

"Coo-coo?" Philip was unfazed. "How do you pronounce it, is it 'coo-coo'?" Glennie exploded. "Dad!" It's 'couscous,' not 'coo-coo' which is a Middle Eastern food, and not Indian, and Hari's name is 'Hari.'"

That evening things got worse. They sat in a quiet corner of the lobby of the Meridien Hotel in Boston waiting for Hari's parents, newly-arrived from Bangalore, to join them for a celebratory, get-to-know-each-other dinner. "Ya know, I never wanted to travel to India - too much poverty," said sixty-four- year-old Philip, settling his lanky form into the chair across from Hari's. Philip's hair was gray and dry, like leftover ashes in the fireplace, but his jowls were smooth and flush and he exuded a thick aroma of an expensive aftershave. The studied innocence in his demeanor put Margo on the alert. She smoothed the skirt of her beige suit and braced for the unpleasantness to come.

"Yes," said Hari agreeably. "India is a third world country of 900 million people. You're right. There's a lot of poverty there." Hari was a winsome, slender man of thirty.

"And that democracy stuff - that's a sham." Philip uncrossed his leg and leaned forward with a power stare. Both men wore Brooks Brothers suits and wing tip shoes. Hari stared back.

"Dad! What are you talking about? We aren't here to discuss politics." Glennie, a redheaded beanpole with keen hazel, dressed in a hunter green wool suit, was sprawled on the arm of Hari's chair.

"Oh that's okay, Glennie," Hari said, looking up at her with a smile. "I don't mind discussing politics with your dad."

"Yeah. We men are talking politics." Philip's bared his teeth in a grin. "Now you listen here, Harry."

"Dad, it's 'Hari,' rhymes with 'par,' as in golf."

"Hari?"

"Yes, Dad. Har-ee, as in har-de-har-har-har."

Philip settled back into his chair and clasped his hands behind his head. Margo's stomach contracted. Why couldn't Philip just be pleasant? Why would Philip try to insult his new son-in-law at the first go-round? She looked over at Mike. He was gazing down at his shoes. Philip's new wife, Candy, an athletic, pudding-faced youngster of 43, quietly leafed through the Ski magazine she'd brought with her.

"Okay, Glennie. Now look, Haaah-ree, it's simple. It's clear that Hinduism is the cause of the poverty in India. They don't slaughter the cows; the cows run all over spreading disease, and Hindus don't eat meat so there's not enough protein there, and they starve. India will never rise above third-world status and it's because of Hinduism."

Margo spoke up with the familiar ease that divorced couples retain with each other long after they've separated. "Philip, what on earth are you talking about? You've just made an outrageous statement that doesn't make any sense." She glanced at Mike for help. He gave her a don't-bring-me-into-this look and Candy turned a page of her magazine. "It's okay, Margo" said Hari, "I don't mind discussing India with Philip while we're waiting for my parents." Hari spoke with exaggerated calm, a worldliness that he must have developed working with his more difficult patients at Columbia Presbyterian. He and Glennie would finish their residencies the following June.

Hari checked his watch, then ran his fingers through his shiny straight black hair. "Now, Philip, you were trying to connect Hinduism to the poverty in India?"

"Yeah," said Philip, scowling. "Look at Bhopal. There was a sacred rat got loose in the plant, chewed something...." Margo gasped. "That is the most absurd thing I have ever heard, Philip." Philip turned to her, shrugging, "... that's what a Union Carbide VP told me last week in Duxbury. I'm not kidding!"

Margo stood up. "I can't believe this. If you'll excuse me, all of you, I'm taking a walk." As Margo examined the reception desk before touring the various furniture groupings, including the bell captain's station where she managed to make a friendly comment about the weather, she couldn't place the exact moment when Philip had turned into this pompous, aging stranger. Their marriage, granted, had been in turn romantic, glamorous, tumultuous, then ultimately frightening, but she recalled having married a charismatic charmer who may have been an operator, but he wasn't malicious. She returned to the little gathering in time to hear Philip proclaim in a loud voice, "Well now, Harry, you're being a smart ass."

"Philip. I'd rather be a smart ass than ignorant."

Just then, an elegant Indian couple approach from the elevator bank. Hari continued, "Oh, there's my mom and dad." The woman wore a navy silk sari, the man a gray wool suit. Hari stood. "Philip, I'd like you to meet my mother, Anja and my father, Umang Anantha." Margo embraced Anja. "So glad to see you again, Anja and Umang. Welcome to Boston."

That night at dinner, the conversation inevitably came around to Hinduism again. Glennie tried to explain. "There are many gods, Dad, each a manifestation of various parts of one God." Uman spoke up. "That's correct. (He rolled his r making it sound as if he said "That's codect." He continued. "For example, Shiva is the destroyer of the universe, but in our religion, destruction implies reproduction and regeneration, so Shiva also perpetually restores that which has been destroyed. And Durga is a goddess who rides a tiger, which represents the subjugation of ego and arrogance." He spoke crisply with a British cast to his lilting cadence, and glanced at Philip upon pronouncing the last word.

Margo said, "I've become attached to Ganesha, the elephant-headed god, protector of new beginnings, during the ceremony the Ananthas held during an earlier trip to New York, to bless our kids." Margo had enjoyed that exposure to the strange culture of her new son-in-law, her first introduction to the Hindi pantheon. She remembered the cool, barren sweep of marble in the temple, the intimidating lineup of gods in his or her own small cell, each represented by an exotic statue adorned with necklaces or pieces of cloth redolent of a culture far removed from that of New York. There had been a bare-shouldered priest wrapped in a diaper-like garment, sandaled, who used incense, flowers, and fresh fruits to aid his incantations in a rapid Sanskrit. The strange sounds had inundated Margo's ears in a flood of vowels and consonants, the occasional "Glennie," "Michigan," "January" bobbing up at unexpected intervals in his incantations.

Glennie said, "Anja, isn't there a Lakshmi? I know a Lakshmi on the pulmonology staff."

"Yes, she is also known as Padmavati, and is the consort of Vishnu. She is one who brings prosperity. Her four hands signify her power to grant the four goals of life, one of which is d*harma,* you've heard that word, which means righteousness." Anja's English was beautifully enunciated. She also rolled her "r's" to make them sound like "d's" and she pronounced every "t."

The waiter appeared to clear away the dinner plates.

Philip said, "Aren't we here to talk about the reception?"

Anja turned toward him, folding her hands. "As I understand it, Philip, you have your own ideas about having the wedding reception in Duxbury?" She pronounced it "Dux-bry."

"What d'you mean my own ideas? As far as I know, nothing's been decided, has it? I hope to God I get a chance here. Or has Margo already gone behind my back and made all the decisions?"

"Philip, don't be obtuse," said Margo. "Nothing has been decided except that the kids definitely want to be married at Trinity Episcopal in Concord." The waiter appeared and poured coffee. "Is that decaf?" The waiter nodded. "Please." She turned back to Philip. "What Anja means is the reception, Philip. The kids want to keep the reception in Concord so we don't have to travel forty miles to Duxbury after the ceremony just to get to your house."

Glennie spoke up. "Dad, we love your place, we really do, the landscaping is beautiful and it's next to the seashore and all, but Hari and I want the reception close to the church." She poured cream into her coffee.

Philip picked up a teaspoon. He waggled it between two manicured fingers. "Look, that's all well and good but who's going to pay for this shindig? I had a caterer come in and do a survey. My house is a beautiful place for a reception. He said he could do a tent and serve a snack for thirty people for about $3,000."

"Dad, first of all, we'll have well over a hundred people, not thirty, so your figures aren't right."

"One hundred? Why that number? That's just tacky – and expensive too. I thought we'd do this tastefully, keep it down to just family, have the reception at my place, and your mother and I will go fifty-fifty on the cost. As I said, I think a large wedding would be tacky." Philip exhaled loudly and swiveled his large head around as if to conclude the conversation.

"Dad, Anja's going to bring a lot of people from India. All of Umang's brothers are coming too. Hari's the first born son of a first born son and it's an important day for the family." Hari's parents were sitting up straight, expressionless. Anja's gold wedding necklace, the *mangala sutra,* glittered. (Glennie herself would receive one at the wedding). Glennie continued, "And we want to invite our college and med school friends. That brings up the numbers. And don't you and Candy have some people you'd like to invite?"

"Nah, we don't have any people… just a few in Duxbury… and remember, they're all in their late sixties now, and I don't think they can travel all that far. That's one reason we need to have the reception in Duxbury…." Philip took a sip of his coffee and finished his sentence, "… so my friends will come."

Hari said, "You mean to say your friends won't drive forty miles to Concord?"

"Ya know something, Harry? You're bordering on insulting."

Glennic said quickly. "I can't believe your friends wouldn't come to the wedding, Dad. What about the Simpsons, for example, or Tom, or your old Exeter buddies?" She turned to Candy. "Candy? How many people would you and Philip be having to the wedding? And would they come up to Concord?"

Candy looked up from the packet of Equal in her hands. "Actually we don't have any friends. Nobody would come. So I'd say zero."

The waiter appeared. "Would anyone like more coffee?"

"Glennie," said Philip, reaching over to tap her arm with his spoon. "Where did you get the idea I would agree to all these people at your wedding?" He paused, pursing his lips into a pout. "It's your mother interfering again." He turned to Margo. "If you hadn't butted in, Glennie wouldn't have gotten these ideas that she could invite everybody she'd ever known."

"Don't be ridiculous, Philip."

"I'll tell you who's being ridiculous. You are." The wagging teaspoon moved closer to Margo's face. "And I'll tell you right now, if you don't do this wedding my way, you can count me out. I'm not paying for a penny of it and I'm not coming at all if the reception's not in Duxbury.

"Philip, now you're being a jackass."

Anja and Umang darted looks at each other. Anja's diamond earrings sent sparkles across the table. Umang cleared his throat. He was a professor of biology at Bangalore University. "Now I'm sure we can work this out…"

Philip banged his hand on the table. He turned to his daughter. "It's your decision, Glennie. We're gonna do it my way or I'm out."

"Dad!"

"I mean it. You can take it or leave it."

"Dad. We're having the reception in Concord for the reasons I've given you. We'd hoped you and Candy would understand and see your way to being a part of the wedding but…." She paused and looked over at Hari, her face tight. "If you can't, well, you can't."

"That suits me fine." Philip stood up and said, "Come on, Candy, let's get out of here."

Margo won the fight for the check with Umang. It's only money, she kept telling herself, and it was the least she could do. She could divorce Philip but she couldn't make him a better man.

On the morning of Glennie's wedding day, low September sunlight broke through the blinds. It was a miracle Margo's head wasn't splitting after the two martinis she'd had at the rehearsal dinner. She sneaked into the bathroom. A shower would help. As the warm water poured over her head, the wedding dominated her thoughts as it had for the last six months. Everything was ready. At the stroke of 6:00 p.m. a perfect wedding would begin. She was counting on Philip not showing up. Philip was capable of ruining things - he enjoyed ruining things if it brought attention to himself - and this was one big event to ruin, with 180 guests and $30,000 sunk into the food and music alone. The ceremony would be a blend of Hindu and Christian rituals and vows that Glennie, Margo, Anja and Hari had carefully scripted over the months and had won the approval of the Episcopal priest. Margo scrubbed a heel with a pumice stone as translucent bubbles surfed down on the ribbons of water coursing over her middle-aged stomach. Once flat and inconspicuous, her stomach was now an offensive pouch. It was a perpetual annoyance to her, a holy grail of wishing for which she compensated by spending money at the Estée Lauder counter on small expensive jars of white cream. Toweling off, Margo felt a niggling sense of unease she couldn't identify. It wasn't her stomach and it wasn't the hangover. And it wasn't Philip. Something else was nagging at her, just below the surface. But she couldn't put her finger on it.

She looked in the mirror. Margo was petite, round, with blond, blunt cut hair and large blue eyes. These days Margo only saw the damaging effects of Age the Intruder who mocked her daily in some new way: the graying hairs she covered with the foil treatment; the wrinkles at the corners of her eyes; the slight wattle in her neck. Nothing she could do about the bags under her eyes short of surgery. And of course her stomach. She thought of the time back in high school when she'd hugged her high school Spanish teacher on graduation day and been shocked to feel the flab around the woman's waist. She'd vowed never to have flab around her middle: Never. She fished in the drawer for aspirin to swallow along with her weekly calcium pellet. A few months ago, Glennie, her Daughter-the-Doctor, had run Margo through a machine that printed out a colorful graphic of a skeleton, looking like an image of her future self in a coffin. Glennie had explained in her professional voice, "You're showing a 3% loss in bone density. This is common among post-menopausal women, Mom, and I don't want you to get osteoporosis."

"What's this blue line here?" said Margo pointing at the chart.

"That? That's your calcium. See what I mean?" The line plunged vertically, like a steep decline in the stock market.

The aspirin got stuck in her throat on its way down and its citrusy fumes seared her nasal cavities. Margo thought of her mother who had died two years earlier, and how, back in Michigan long ago, she'd administered aspirin to Margo in a teaspoon with sugar mixed with a few drops of water. She'd poke at the aspirin with a toothpick to break it up in a bit of motherly performance art that Margo loved to watch. "Down the hatch," her mother would say and Margo would swallow the gritty sweet-acrid mixture as if receiving Holy Communion. Margo missed her mother these days and still cried at odd times. Just yesterday she was driving the gift baskets to the hotel for the out-of-town guests and a commercial came on the radio about dogs in heaven. When it registered that the talking dogs were dead, out burbled a sob, right there on Center Street in front of the florist shop.

Margo tiptoed back into the bedroom wrapped in her bath towel. She passed the gray taffeta floor-length skirt and beaded silver sweater set from Saks hanging on the closet door, her wedding outfit being a conscious rejection of fusty mother-of-the bride uniforms of pastel silk or brocade. Mike was still snoring on his side of the bed. Mike was a bassoonist with the Boston Baroque orchestra and he taught at the New England Conservatory. He was on his second marriage too, his own three children having married long ago. He'd given Margo a wide berth during the planning and execution of this affair. Margo went into the closet and Walter, the family cocker spaniel, followed her, hoping for attention. Walter rolled onto his back, spread his mutton chop legs and wagged his tail in ecstasy.

"Hello my little man." She sat down on the little boudoir chair in the closet and hoisted him up for a hug. He wriggled free and ran from her toward the door with his tail signaling left / right, left / right. So adorable. As the wedding day approached, furry little Walter had grown more important to her, as if he were a substitute for the child she had borne who would soon marry and with depressing finality, leave her for good. The other night Margo caught herself cradling Walter in her arms and talking baby talk to him as she watched TV, as if she were lulling a baby to sleep. Good thing Mike hadn't been home.

Margo's mind wandered as she examined the hangers of dresses, sweaters, slacks and blue jeans on her side of the closet. What if Philip actually came to the wedding today? She couldn't imagine him pulling something, but he wasn't the same man she'd married twenty years earlier. Something had gone haywire in Philip since then. When they'd married, Margo'd been nineteen, Philip was thirty-five; she'd been looking for the father she never had; he'd wanted a trophy wife. At the time he'd been irresistible: charming, handsome. And wealthy. She realized she'd sold out on some subconscious level a few years into the marriage. They had married in 1969, around the time the term "sexism" entered the national consciousness via a <u>Time</u> magazine article she'd never forgotten. She'd read the word and discussed the concept of sexism with friends who scoffed. Then came the epiphany and she was forever liberated. If she'd been less liberated, would that have made a difference in her marriage? Could she have hewn to Philip's demands and perhaps, helped him avoid becoming so hopeless?

Before the divorce she'd wanted him dead. A painless death of course, perhaps a fall down the stairs. She imagined putting her foot out as he strode by at the top of the stairs, or better, he'd just trip on something accidentally left there. She imagined him tumbling down, breaking his neck in the fall, dying instantly and solving all their problems. Instead, they'd had a contentious divorce and Glennie had ended up living with her, the two of them against the world, through junior and high school until Glennie'd gone off to college.

Margo's towel slipped as she rummaged for shoes. Sandals or sneakers today? It was warm for September, an Indian summer. She chose sneakers for the support. Mike opened the closet door. "Hey, Ruben," His pet name for her, from "Rubenesque," the term Margo had used unimaginatively to describe herself when she had first talked to Mike on the phone before their blind date. Mike loved her bulk, unlike Philip who nagged her over the years to "do something about that weight."

"Good morning, you gorgeous hunk of womanhood." Mike's hands had found her breasts. He was warm from the bed.

"I want your body. Hmm, you're delicious." Mike's erection poked against her stomach through his pajamas.

"Mike, are you crazy? Glennie and Gillian are asleep just a few feet down the hall." Mike pulled back. "Well, all right, but remember, it's your loss."

"Honey, we've got plenty of time for that kind of thing later. The kids will all be gone by tomorrow at this time."

"I know." He stood there, downcast, frumpy and towseled and suddenly Margo put her hands in his hair, stroking it back off his face. She kissed him and then kissed him again. She said, "Guess what? I love you."

Margo finished dressing. Her depression was creeping in again, and she still wasn't sure what was the cause of it. Dr. Dressler had recommended Prozac for a few months. Margo was resisting such a drastic step, her current belief being that maybe depression was a part of life to be accepted and managed. She had been going to the psychiatrist for several months and still wasn't clear: was she depressed because she was getting old? Was it because her marriage wasn't always perfect? Was it because she felt Glennie no long needed her? She'd had two husbands and now she was old, out of chances, and no longer useful to her independent daughter. How had Glennie been lucky enough, smart enough to find such a wonderful man to fall in love with? It was a miracle.

Nobody like Hari had ever married into the Yarrow family. When Glennie had chosen Hari Anantha, it had been gratifying to Margo to know that Glennie was going to fling in Philip's face all his sneaky little prejudices. "That fucking kike," (applied to Margo's current husband, Mike) or "She's African American!" (whispered, referring to Glennie's best friend in high school.) In great poetic justice Glennie had fallen for a man neither Christian nor particularly white. Philip used to say he'd never liked Indians - couldn't trust 'em. Such poetic justice.

Margo had not warmed to Hari at first; in fact she'd felt an ill-defined hostility when they'd first met in the lobby of the hospital during one of her visits in New York. He was only an acquaintance of Glennie's then, a good friend. Yet when she saw how he looked at Glennie, she knew, before Glennie did, that he was the one who would claim Glennie. The certainty of this knowledge had flooded her veins in a kind of limbic early warning system. And when over the months, Glennie had slowly introduced Margo to the fact that she was falling in love with Hari, Margo's prejudices had surfaced in spite of her liberalism, as if she were marshalling anything to give her a reason to reject Hari. Unrelated images swirled in her head: "Elephant Walk," with Elizabeth Taylor as the plantation owner's wife in taboo love with Richard Burton in blackface. And the Masterpiece Theater rendition of E. M. Forster's "The Jewel in the Crown" about the politicized young Indian rebel. Come to think of it, that guy's name was Hari too. Shiva the god with many arms; erotic statues of southern India where rock-carved deity couples enjoyed timeless coitus; Hare Krishna, Ravi Shankar, the "Kama Sutra;" curried rice and chicken tandoori; Mother Teresa, the stinking holy Ganges; global computer programmers, "Mississippi Marsala." Too confusing a culture; too ethnic. Not what she had counted on for Glennie at all.

She'd discussed her reservations with Glennie frankly. "And think of the prejudice in this country. It will hound you, hurt you. You didn't live during the civil rights movement but I did, and I remember, even though I was a little girl, how much prejudice there is in this country.

And even now. Glennie, I can't stand the idea of someone making a racial slur against you."

"Mom, in the medical profession there are all kinds of mixed couples. We're nothing. These are the people we'll socialize with; today there is nothing to worry about as far as racial slurs go – I just have fallen in love with a universal brown man. This is the man I want to spend the rest of my life with. I want to grow old with Hari."

It turned out that Margo's resistance was not about Hari's skin tone but about letting go of Glennie, of allowing someone else to be the most important person in her life. Once she knew Glennie was in love with the gentle man with the big eyes, Margo gave in. She took a real look at Hari and found him modest, witty, and accomplished. And he adored Glennie. He cooked well, was squeaky clean, could make her laugh, and he was so intelligent that Margo started to tell Glennie he was too good for her. The people Margo had met just last night at the rehearsal dinner (newly-arrived from Bangalore and Bombay and Toronto and Sao Paulo) only confirmed what a catch Hari was. They didn't look like stereotypes but rather like well-dressed versions of her own friends wearing silken saris or elegant *salvar camise* pantsuits and Brooks Brothers suits. They wore good jewelry. They drank scotch and spoke with clipped English accents, told witty stories and published their various scholarly writings in technical journals; they belonged to organizations like the Civil Liberties Union and the Modern Languages Association. If only Philip knew how lucky the Yarrows were that the dignified Brahmins accepted them, and not the other way around.

Margo headed downstairs to the kitchen. Time to make pancakes. The phone rang.

"Hello Margo?"

It was Candy.

"Margo, (she was whispering and talking fast) I just had to phone you. Philip has gone for the mail so I have a minute."

"Yes? What is it?" Margo's head started to ache again.

"I just wanted to give you a heads up. We're coming to the wedding today."

"What?"

"I thought you should know."

"I thought Philip said he wasn't going to come."

"Well, this morning he woke up and said he was 'coming by God.'" She giggled.

"What does this mean - is he going to try to stop the wedding?"

"I don' t know. I hope not, but he's determined to come. He's so... oh oh, I have to hang up now. He's coming up the driveway."

"Can't you stop him?... Candy?" The phone went dead.

Margo put down the receiver. It was all she needed - the Jackass was planning to stop the wedding. She made breakfast and tried to think of a solution.

"Pancakes are ready!" called out Margo and soon the sleepyheads came downstairs stretching and yawning; Mike, Glennie, and the maid of honor, Gillian, a slender blonde with a baby duckling hair cut. The chatting and laughter stopped when Margo broke the news about Philip.

"Oh, shit." Glennie said. "Mom, you and I both know he's insane."

Mike said, peering up from the *New York Times* over his reading glasses, "Do you think we should get Cousin Jugdeesh to rough him up if he shows his face?"

Everybody laughed. (Jugdeesh the imaginary, amusing name Glennie had taken to referring to their future firstborn, now applied to an imaginary cousin.) Gillian said, "I can just see it now Jugdeesh giving Philip the bum's rush out of the church. Yeah, right!"

Glennie stood up from the table and went to gaze out the kitchen window. Margo went over to her and put her arm around her shoulder. "Honey, I don't think he'll try anything."

Gillian put down her fork and pushed back her chair. "Glennie, don't worry - he won't do anything. And I'll take care of him if he comes to the reception."

"What do you mean 'take care of him?'" said Glennie, an eyebrow arching.

"Oh, you know. Talk to him, flirt with him. I know how to handle men."

"I'll bet you do."

"Mee-oww," said Gillian, making a little clawing motion with her hand.

Mike said, "Look, if he does make trouble, we're going to ignore him. That's all we can do. I don't think we can keep him out of the church. And maybe he just wants to see his daughter get married." He was right. Some things were out of her control. Everybody suddenly had things to do and left the kitchen except for Glennie who helped clear the table.

"Oh, Mom, I just wanted to thank you for all you've done; and you've paid out so much money; just to give us a wedding. You've been wonderful! Here, let me do that skillet."

"It's been my pleasure every step of the way, Honey." Margo picked up a dishtowel. "And you'll be the most beautiful bride there ever was."

Glennie made a face. Her hair hung in auburn ropes around her freckled, pale face. She had dark smudges under her eyes.

"Mom, whatever happens today - I mean if Dad shows up - I don't want you to worry about it. Dad can't spoil things no matter what his sick mind thinks up. Because Hari and I love each other too much. We're in this for life and nothing Dad does could wreck today."

"That's how I feel too."

"Do you?"

"Yes, I do"

"You know something? I feel sorry for Dad. It's like he can't help himself. Was he a good dad to me when I was little? It's funny but I can't remember." Glennie handed Margo a skillet to dry.

"Yes, Bunny, he was a good dad and you know he loves you." Margo had an image of Philip rushing out to the backyard after Glennie had fallen from the little apple tree. He'd scooped her up, kissed her knee, and within a few seconds had Glennie laughing, her tears forgotten. Yes, Philip had been a good father. "But something changed him; whether it was his own unhappy childhood or some bad genes kicking in, I don't know. But he changed."

"Mom, he can't hurt any of us. But I just don't want you to worry, okay?"

"'Thanks for worrying about me, Honey. I have a hunch we'll both be fine."

Glennie glanced up at the kitchen clock. "Oh my God what time is it? I have to get to my massage. Mom can you drive me? I'll be right down!" She dashed out of the kitchen, her flip flops going slap slap as she ran, and Margo saw a thin little six-year-old with red hair in a turquoise cotton bikini running away from her down the beach with a seashell in her hand. The house fell silent. She hung up the dishtowel and picked up Walter and carried him to the living room couch. She kissed him on the back of his head and breathed deeply into his black fur.

Glennie had been a darling baby. Margo remembered the ferocious grip of labor – back then natural childbirth was in vogue - and seeing Glennie for the first time, bloody and crying and wrinkled. Soon Glennie was in her arms wrapped like a stuffed grape leaf in tight white cotton, a tiny knitted acorn cap stretched over her skull. Margo lowered her face to Walter's fur and breathed in his doggy smell and thought of Glennie's newborn smell. Glennie had been curious right away, looking out through marine blue eyes with a Yoda expression at once wise and empty. Descartes and the *tabula rasa* idea; Glennie an empty slate, a projection of hopes and dreams. What had this baby been looking at as she had gazed first at Margo and then looked around at the room, then looked back into Margo's eyes, then out at the room again. Glennie had continued to switch her focus back and forth every few moments as if imprinting images onto her brain. Did anything register? Was she writing on her own *tabula rasa*? Or was Glennie just exercising her optical muscles? Margo had been awestruck, and had loved her new baby absolutely, joyously. Margo absently petted Walter. That somber little newborn, so pure and perfect. Her heart swelled. Suddenly Philip's face swam into view out of nowhere and Margo stood up, dumping Walter on the floor. She'd need some backup today.

She called her sister, Ellen, the practical one in the family.

"Ellen, Philip's coming to the wedding."

"No! How could he after what he said the last time?"

"Well, he's coming. What should I do?"

"If it were me, I'd have the police on the scene."

"I can't do that and you know it."

"He just wouldn't dare do anything, would he? He's an idiot but I don't think he'd ruin the wedding."

"I don't know. I'll see you later. Call if you think of anything. Gotta go"

Glennie had appeared from around the corner of the kitchen door, her eyes wide, pointing at her watch.

Margo drove Glennie to the massage therapist then home, then back to pick up Glennie and drop off Gillian for her massage. The hairdresser and make-up woman arrived. Margo answered a phone call from one of the out-of-town guests who had called to chat. She picked up Gillian and paid the delivery man for the pizza the bridesmaids were to share upstairs as they had their hair done. Hari's mother called again - did Margo possibly have a brass or pewter bowl to hold the flower petals for the parental blessing? She found two bowls in the basement and put them by the door just as two bridesmaids arrived to have their hair done. It was getting late. As she tried to get upstairs toward the shower, the doorbell rang again. It was the photographer and her teenaged assistant, his eyes agog.

Sounds of hilarity rang out from behind the door to Margo's and Mike's bedroom suite where the bridal party were dressing. Margo planned to use the guest bath to shower and dress, but she had to enter her own room to get underwear. Murmuring and followed by raucous laughter, the dirty joke kind, stopped when she entered. "Don't bother about me," she said, feeling sheepish, rummaging in her lingerie drawer. The chattering resumed. "Oh, no, how are we going to attach that flower to this buzz cut?" "Here, I've got some crazy glue!" "No, Here! I'll wear the flower in my teeth." "Where's my shoe?" "Ohhh, that shade is trashy, try this lipstick."

Margo showered in the guest bathroom, then dried her hair and poked it into shape, using lots of spray. She did her makeup remembering to go easy on the foundation; today she could overdo it if she didn't watch out. She sidled back into the master suite through the merry throng to grab her Saks outfit before scuttling back into the guest bathroom with its old woman's unguents and colored greases.

Then they were all in the kitchen: the bridesmaids, the photographer, the young assistant who couldn't stop gaping, the hair stylist, the makeup friend, the limo driver and Glennie. Margo said, "Oh, I forgot to offer wine - would anyone like some?"

"I thought you'd never ask. Yes!" Gillian bounded over to the cupboard to get glasses. Margo poured wine all around. "Well, kids, here we go." As Glennie and the bridesmaids rustled around the small area, they transformed themselves into nymphs straight out of an illustrated fairy tale come to life. Glennie stood laughing near the refrigerator. In eleven layers of puffy tulle, a satin bodice and a veil sprinkled with sequins flowing from a pearl-and-rhinestone tiara, she had become a fairy queen, materialized out of the ether to bless their humble cottage.

The more laughter there was; the more the perfume of the satin-gowned young bodies filled the house with an electrifying vitality, the more unexpended energy drained away from Margo. She started to deflate, now marginal to the activity, an unnecessary appendage, a leftover. She'd recently gone into the women's room while shopping at Filenes perhaps a month earlier, and while there, she'd smelled the tang of fresh blood, emanating from the metal receptacle for discarded pads and tampons. The pungent odor had not been unpleasant; rather, it had been fresh and tangy, filling her senses. She could understand how a tiger would kill for blood; how a dog would gnaw at his own wound for the taste of it. She realized she'd forgotten about the peculiar ritual of menstruation that had once been so much an intimate fact of life, before menopause had freed her from its constraints. Her menses had often brought muscle cramping and in her later years, an inconvenient gushing until she'd had a partial hysterectomy. She'd never associated bleeding with fertility back then; there was no gratitude for the monthly cleansing and renewal, preparation for new life and yet.... Was she missing it now?

The bevy of fairies chugged their wine and headed for the door. Margo said without thinking, "Should I ride in the limo with you, Glennie?" and Glennie answered too quickly, stifling the annoyance in her voice, "No, Mom, you ride with Mike." Of course. What was she thinking of? The door closed and then they were gone. Margo stood alone. It was silent in the kitchen. Walter lay on the carpet in the living room, thumping his tail. Walter would never betray her; Walter would never leave her. Margo finished her wine as Mike came downstairs in his dark suit and crisp burgundy tie. They went out together to the garage and drove to the church with little conversation. "Those girls are gorgeous," the limo driver told Margo later at the church when she pressed his tip envelope into his hand, "Just gorgeous!"

The photographer and her assistant posed groups before an ivy-covered wall of the church. Glennie and Hari; Glennie and Hari and Hari's parents; Glennie and Hari and Margo; then the whole bridal party; then all of Hari's family, all of Glennie's family, all the women, all the men, and multiple shots of relatives. Glennie moved in a glass bubble of isolation, her attendants surrounding her in a perfumed unit, first moving across the courtyard to mingle with the lounging ushers, then into the church kitchen en masse, only to reappear moments later, bouquets in hand. Their muffled bursts of hilarity seemed strangely alienating to Margo, as if the young people were mocking her, although how could that be? It was worse. They were ignoring her. Why was Glennie avoiding her? Margo's feet started to feel the pinch of her shoes. "I'm going in to the kitchen for some water, Mike." She managed to stay hidden next to the refrigerator until a few minutes before six o'clock when Mike came looking for her.

People were arriving. Jewel-toned silks mingled with muted New England wool, pumps with sandals. Leather, linen, tweeds and silks flowed into St. Martin's Episcopal Church leaving an aromatic aftermath in their wake. Margo's family, her sister's, her brother and his wife from California arrived and entered the church. And there, getting out of his black Continental, with Candy wearing a pink short-skirted number, was Philip.

"Margo, there he is," hissed her sister Ellen, who had come over to wish her well before entering the church. "What are you going to do?"

"I'm going to tell him that he's not going to ruin Glennie's day." Margo started across the lawn, small jets of pain shooting up from the balls of her feet with every step. Damn those dyed-to-match shoes. She plunged forward. Philip just couldn't be a jerk, not today; she wouldn't allow it. But Philip marched up the walk before she could get to him, his chin jutting, looking comfortable in gray cashmere, white shirt and a red Sulka tie, with Candy trailing behind. They melted into the side entrance of the church before Margo could reach him. Candy had looked at Margo with a helpless shrug before following Philip inside. Mike signaled to a couple of the ushers. Margo started to walk over to him with some piece of useless advice but stopped, unable to think of anything to say.

Then everyone was inside and silence descended outside the carved doors like a weather change at sea when the wind dies and the air hangs heavy and still. Glennie detached herself from her bodyguards and took her place next to Margo, who, it had been decided when Philip abdicated, would give her away. The music started and Hari and his parents entered. The very first part of the ceremony was Hindu, the blessing of the groom by the parents, and it involved flower petals and water. The Hindu priest was a woman in a bottle green sari with a waist-length braid, a professor of English who had flown in from the West Coast for the occasion.

From just outside the large double doors of the chapel, standing next to Glennie, Margo could hear the priest speaking the Sankalpa Mantra, or, "Invocation of blessings from God and all God's creation" in a fast Sanskrit. Her voice was muffled and rhythmic, the cadences punctuated by responses of Anja and Umang. There was at least one instance of polite chuckling from the congregation as well, and Margo recalled, as explained in the order of services, that this prayer spoke about married love as timeless and selfless. Margo shifted her weight from one aching foot to the other. After a pause, the organ and the trumpet struck up the announcement of the bride's entrance, and Glennie's three attendants started their walk into the church, spacing themselves a half aisle-length apart as they had practiced.

With Glennie uncharacteristically silent at her side, Margo waited and remembered all the times Glennie had left her. Glennie the four-year-old off to kindergarten, a shrinking little tyke in blue jumper with white blouse and little white tights and maryjanes on her feet. Glennie going to summer camp when Glennie was nine. Glennie a plump, fifteen-year-old who went off to the island of Saba for the summer to plant trees and help run a children's nursery, and who'd returned in the Fall slim, smoking cigarettes and suspiciously savvy about Rastafarian culture. Glennie driving to college, granting Margo along with the sharp pain of separation, a surprising freedom and a tidy house. Then there was the time Glennie graduated from medical school, sweeping past Margo and the other families in the river of crimson-robed student/doctors with their predictably fulfilling futures laid out ahead of them like a red carpet. Margo had felt flat and empty then too, as if she weren't smart enough to talk to Glennie any more. But still she had not really lost Glennie because Glennie always came home for holidays. But Glennie would have a new home now and a husband who would come first from now on. Things would be different from now on.

The organ switched key, a trumpet sounded and it was time to move out. Crowds on both sides of the aisle craned toward Margo and Glennie with loving grins. The wedding had been a year in the making. It had involved dozens of meetings and a multitude of decisions. Many checks had flowed from Margo's strangled bank account. The cast of thousands swam in her head: the caterer, the florist, the stationer, the

K-Mart clerk (sixteen fake ficus trees and sixteen strings of white lights;) the party store clerk, the fabric clerk (five yards of white netting for the almonds in silver-cup favors,) the Chamber of Commerce secretary, the U.S. Post office clerk who had become a friend with all the mailing of invitations and other related missives, the organist, the musicians, the DJ, the baker, the limo service manager and most recently, the reception hall administrator, a lovely woman whose own Caucasian daughter had married a Chinese doctor, just last year too, a serendipitous coincidence that had thrilled Margo. It was the biggest party Margo would ever throw. It had all come down to this moment. And it was anticlimactic

"Here we go, Honey,"

Margo took Glennie's hand and fixed her eyes in a middle-distance stare. Philip and Candy were on the left side toward the front and near the aisle, Philips face porcine and shiny. She wanted to reach over and slap him as they went by. Glennie's grip tightened and they safely lockstepped past Philip When they reached the front of the church Margo was supposed to hand Glennie over. For a moment Margo hesitated. There was a kind of danger in letting go, as if she needed to keep Glennie from harm by hanging on to her. They were now near the altar, close to Hari, his groomsmen, the attendants and the two priests, and inundated all at once by incense and flowery perfumes, Margo felt woozy and threatened. A long time ago, she recalled, she'd been at the dentist's office and they were going to put Glennie to sleep for a minor extraction. Glennie had been six. Margo had held Glennie's hand during the administration of the anesthesia and one moment Glennie's little hand was alive and the next it had gone limp as she'd dropped off into sleep. It was as if Glennie had died, and it took all Margo's will power to walk back out into the waiting room.

Margo handed over Glennie exactly as they had practiced the night before, her smile held firm. Glennie turned to Margo as she started to back away, and said, "Bye, Mom," in a soft voice.

The Hindu priest struck a match and lit the fire of the *Saptapadi*, the candle nestling in Margo's old brass fruit bowl on a small table in front of the altar. Hari and Glennie walked around the flame and stated their vows with each of seven steps.

Glennie said: "I will not transgress the rights of my spouse in duty or *dharma*, in love or behavior." She took one step.

Hari: "I will not transgress the rights of my spouse in duty or *dharma*, in love or behavior." Hari took one step.

Glennie: "We have traversed one step together. We have become friends."

Hari: "We have traveled two steps together. May you provide me with strength."

Glennie: "We have traveled three steps together. May you bring me good fortune and happiness."

Hari: "We have traveled four steps together. May you bring continued happiness in our lives."

Hari stopped. Glennie's gown was too close to the flame. Hari patted down the layers of fluffy tulle of Glennie's skirt and steered her away from the fire, then they continued circling.

Glennie: "We have traveled five steps together. May we be blessed with a happy family."

Margo's throat constricted. In that one gesture she saw the promise of an entire lifetime of caring and protection in store for Glennie. She didn't think to ask herself whether she wept with happiness for Glennie or a yearning for such devotion she'd never found in either of her own marriages.

Hari: "We have traveled six steps together. May we love each other and fulfill each other in all seasons."

Glennie and Hari together: "We have traveled seven steps together. This seals our relationship and our love in holy matrimony. May we provide sustenance and inspiration to each other." Glennie looked in Hari's eyes as she spoke, proud, decisive and loving.

The Episcopal part of the ceremony came next. Father Williams peered down at the open prayer book in his hands.

"Dearly Beloved, We have come together in the presence of God to witness and bless the joining together of this man and this woman in Holy Matrimony."

Margo took Mike's hand. She'd forgotten about Philip. Would he actually make a scene? The tip of Glennie's veil trembled.

"If any of you can show just cause why they may not lawfully be married, speak now; or else for ever hold your peace….."

And yes, Philip was speaking! Margo squeezed her eyes shut to make him go away. And then a miracle happened. As if Ganesha himself had flown down out of an ancient Indian sky to enact a miracle that could otherwise not be explained, Father Williams kept right on talking, overriding Philip's voice. Yes. Ganesha and his squadron of flying gorgons had deafened Father Williams to the disruptive voice of Philip. Those hands had covered the priest's ears and removed the intrusion. "I require and charge you both, here in the presence of God, that if either of you know any reason why you may not be united in marriage lawfully, and in accordance with God's Word, you do now confess it. Glennie, will you have this man to be your husband; to live together in the covenant of marriage?"

Everybody in the hushed chapel heard Glennie say, "I will."

Margo exhaled. Her heart danced, and Philip faded into insignificance.

Another god, less famous than Ganesha but no less powerful, one named Subrahmanya, came into Margo's imagination somewhere during the last of the Christian prayers. This deity of war and guardian of right and destroyer of evil arrived on his peacock to remind Philip not to let pride and egotism get the better of him, his spear representing the sharpness of the intellect. She saw Subrahmanya slicing Philip in half with the spear and riding away in splendor, leaving Philip's cloven body on the floor.

The wedding ceremony concluded with a mix of Hindu prayers and the staid Christian liturgy, drawing the people in the chapel closer and closer together, weaving a magic web around them all. The candles, the incense, the brass lamps and the flower petals brightened the old place of worship as a ray of sunlight illuminates a clearing in a forest, with Glennie and Hari like pilgrims, displaying their pristine love for all to see. "I now pronounce you husband and wife." When Hari kissed Glennie, Margo smiled. She knew the wedding had been perfect because the love that radiated from the young people confirmed what weddings are all about: an affirmation of honor over dishonor, hope over despair, life over death.

The next morning Margo was up early for the wedding breakfast she was hosting. Washing up in the bathroom, she breathed a small prayer of gratitude, then leaned into the mirror. The woman looked back at her with a new, tranquil expression. It was telling her to wear less makeup from now on; have a simpler haircut; go for more workouts at the health club; get more sleep. Margo knew she was slipping the bonds of her old self-image as a dog plunges into the woods to follow the scent. Age and decrepitude beckoned and she would follow. She had done her best, launching her only child as best she knew how. Now to let go with style. That was the key - letting go.

"Hey, Mom, get your butt over here! Can you come here a minute?"

Margo was replenishing the bread basket at the post-wedding breakfast in her home from which Glennie and Hari would soon leave to catch the 2:30 plane for Hawaii.

"Glennie! Did I raise you to talk like that?" Everybody laughed.

Margo went over to stand between the newlyweds, her arms around their waists. .

"Mom, now when do you and Mike get back from Maine?"

"We'll be back .. let's see ... three weekends from now."

"That's so awesome, you guys going sailing at your age."

"Well we aren't quite over the hill. Why do you ask?"

"We just want to make sure we set up a date for you to come and visit us in New York. We want you to come down and help us pick out furniture."

Margo started to answer but her voice caught. "Of course, if you'd like. Excuse me, kids, but I'd better see about the coffee cake." In the kitchen, Margo brushed back her hair, squared her shoulders, and sighed. Maybe she hadn't lost Glennie, not completely. Not yet.

THE DRIFTERS

"You should do the large bowls by hand." Philip retrieved the Corning ware bowl from the dishwasher and started scrubbing. "We'd save so much on our energy bills if you paid attention to the little things instead of putting big bowls in the dishwasher."

"Honey, you're right." Energy bills, energy bills! As if they were poor.

"We should get going if we're going to make that concert."

"Just give me a minute." She drained her wine glass and headed upstairs to the master bathroom. A Jacuzzi tub sat under a stained glass window. When was the last time she and Philip had used it? Ancient history. She drew a careful line around her lips and filled in with creamy lipstick. The Drifters. While she was eons away from that time in her life, she once loved their music: jangling, drum-and-violin concoctions at once monotonous and sensual. Their music had conjured up images of dark men in striped robes dancing in a moonlit desert in the Sahara, like the picture of Saudi men she'd once seen in a magazine. The sands in her fantasy always resembled the Sleeping Bear dunes in Charlevoix, Michigan, where she'd grown up. She took a last look in the mirror and went downstairs trailing a scent of Coco. Philip stood in the library, coat and gloves in hand.

"I found another poop, this time right on the Chinese rug in the hall for chrissake. You're going to have to do something about this or I'm getting rid of that dog."

"I try to pay attention, Phil, I do, but sometimes I forget to let him out. C'mere, Little Edgar Hoover." She picked up the pug. "Now what is this about a poopy?" She stroked the dog's hairless stomach and cuddled him. "You're such a little cutie. Now get in your crate." She handed in a dog biscuit, secured the crate and put on her coat. Why was Philip so critical all the time? She couldn't do anything right. Maybe he was on edge because of the lymphoma. It was always in remission (she told herself) but last week he had felt a bump on one side of his neck. That meant another treatment. "I am really sorry, Phil."

Philip set the burglar alarm and Brenda hurried through to the garage. She was still upset after their discussion at dinner about the inlaid table. Phil had been a real stinker about it. Brenda had broached the subject while serving the cantaloupe. "Honey, that gorgeous table – you know the one I showed you in the catalogue? I just couldn't resist. I thought and thought about it, and then I just thought it would be perfect in the sunroom. So I ordered it." She sat down and picked up her spoon. Philip set down his spoon.

"Brenda, is that that little corner table that was something like $ 1,200? That one?" Brenda took a deep breath.

"Yes, but let's remember, it's only money and you can't take it with you." Philip shook his head.

"Oh, no, Brenda. We can't afford that. I was okay with the Chihuly bowl you had to have the last time we were in Tanglewood and I don't even particularly like his stuff. But this time…. No, you really can't buy it. Don't you remember? These months I'm still paying for the cruise we're taking with the Codmans to Greece. It's costing a small fortune."

"Oh, I forgot about the cruise." Brenda took a bite of her fruit. "I guess you're right – I shouldn't order anything right now. Maybe in the spring…."

"Mmmmm. We'll see." His expression said no way.

The Mercedes roared out of the driveway into the dark night. Headlights twinkled along the black line of a highway in the distance.

"You remember 'Under the Boardwalk,' don't you?"

Philip brought the car up to a stop sign. K-blink, k-blink went the turn signal. Philip eased onto Rte. 2 and accelerated, his face an emerald mask in the glow of the dashboard light.

"Hell-ow-ow," she said in the singsong voice. "Boardwalk?"

Philip cleared his throat. "Huh? No, not really." Philip's gloved hand searched out a Kleenex from the container suspended behind the passenger seat. He honked then said, "Listen. Can we stay for just an hour or so tonight?"

"Philip, just this once could you not put limits on our evening out?"

"What do you mean?"

"Well, maybe you never listened to the Drifters when you were growing up, but I did, and I loved them way back when."

"Look, I'm taking you to hear them, aren't I? And you know I can't stand rock and roll."

"This isn't rock and roll." Heeeeellp me God! Brenda was sure Philip's ignorance was feigned. Classical music was wonderful, too – they subscribed to the BSO and Boston Baroque for pete's sake – but once in a while she wanted something different. Just this once was all she was asking. They parked and skittered across the frozen parking lot toward the Elk's Club, holding hands for balance. Strains of music leaked from the building. When they opened the doors, a blast of sound exploded in their faces. Brenda laughed out loud and Philip frowned.

"What's the matter with you?" Philip said, shrugging off his coat in the overheated foyer.

"Cyu-pid / Pull back your bow – woe;
And let / Your arrow go – wo;

The place was brightly lit with people sitting at tables for eight as if at a potluck supper. Wheelchairs dotted the aisles and several children were running around. People danced in a roped area at one end of the hall. Brenda and Philip settled down at a table close to the performers Three other couples sat watching the performers, beer bottles and cokes dotting the table. Brenda looked around. Nobody she knew. Not exactly the type of thing their friends would go to. She felt magnanimous, democratic, loving all people of all backgrounds.

Behind the four Drifters sat three musicians on guitar, percussion and sax / trumpet. The stars themselves wore white sports coats and gray slacks with thick gold chains glinting from their open shirts. And pinky rings. Exotic for a town like Concord, Massachusetts. The people with the real money in Concord, the old money, the ones who never wore jewelry and dressed their dowdiest in their boiled wool jackets and Pendleton skirts? None of that crowd was here, of course.

When the song ended, a wave of polite applause rippled through the hall. Brenda clapped hard to compensate for the tepid response. She turned to the man next to her and asked, "Are you Drifters fans too?" The man had a gap-tooth. He held his beer bottle in one hand, his arm showing a large, complicated tattoo. "Yeah, absolutely. This sure takes ya back, don't it?"

"Oh yes indeedy." She thought for a moment and added, "Say, I may be wrong but wasn't "Cupid" done by the Spinners, and not the Drifters?

"Now that I wouldn't know."

Philip lifted an eyebrow and shot her a glance.

Rhythmic thudding started up again, and the lead Drifter crooned into the microphone, "Who remembers this one? Where were you in 1959?"

They started singing "There Goes My Baby."

It was the music of the desert men, a true Drifters hit, heavy and persistent. Brenda's heart thudded. The song belonged to the summer before Brenda's senior year in high school. As the Drifters bobbed through synchronized steps, the years peeled away. She was working at The Menonaqua Beach Club on Little Traverse Bay, a private resort not far from her home. She and Marsha, another waitress, had had a great time sneaking half-glasses of wine and beer on luau nights, making sure to stay late enough at the club so that their parents would be asleep when they drove home. All the waitresses wore short forest green nylon uniforms that buttoned up the front to a V-neck. They set tables, served meals from heavy trays and tried to avoid angering the itinerant cook, Bobby, a frizzy-haired maniac who would take your head off with his violent temper. There was plenty of time to fraternize with the guests and Brenda was conscientious, efficient, and friendly with her people, especially the Clarkes, a family of three cute kids herded around by their sullen, distracted mother and portly father. All the men took special interest in Marsha, whose uniform stretched taut over her full figure, the v-neck never high enough to hide her substantial cleavage. Marsha was a quiet girl and tongue-tied, yet many of the men tried to engage her in conversation, always when their wives were out of earshot. These fathers, whose children Brenda sometimes took to the beach, seemed oblivious to Brenda's own charms – she did have an effervescent personality - and they spoke only to Marsha. Especially Mr. Clarke.

"You must have a lot of boyfriends, Marsha?"

"I don't have any boyfriend, Mr. Clarke. I'm not allowed to date."

"Now that I find hard to believe. What's the story here, a beautiful girl like you without a boyfriend?"

It was Marsha's large breasts that drew the men to her. Brenda still harbored the hope that her own figure would fill out but still…. Sometimes her lack of curves brought her to tears. One day while she was walking down to the beach in her pink and white bikini on her free afternoon, a voice behind her said, "Excuse me, Miss, would you pose for the cover of the Charlevoix "Summerweek? When she turned around, revealing her unsubstantial chest, he stammered. "Listen, I'll have to get back to you to set up a time. Is there a phone number where I could reach you?"

He never called. It's not that Brenda was ugly; she was just plain. And she had no bosom, a stunning physical inadequacy in the era of Jane Russell and Marilyn Monroe. It hurt to discover that no amount of personality compensated for curves. What a naïve girl she'd been.

Amidst the applause, the lead singer announced the sale of CDs and tapes during the break and the Drifters bounded off the platform.

"I'm going to buy a CD." Brenda stood up.

"Not for me to listen to, I trust," said Philip.

"No, don't worry – just for my car."

"Okay, while you're doing that, I'll get us some wine."

Brenda paused. "Hey, how painful is this for you?"

"Let's just put it this way. I'm planning to retaliate with my new Philip Glass CD."

"Ouch." Brenda laughed. "Well, you're being a good sport." And he was, when she thought about it. She looked at him, sitting there in his sport coat and wool slacks.

Philip squinched up his face at her. "Don't buy out the place. Do you need cash?"

"No, I'm fine."

She made her way toward the lobby. The four Drifters stood behind a table loaded with merchandise. She joined the crowd around the table and at the last minute decided on a glossy photo along with the tape.

"What happened to the original Drifters?" she asked the lead singer, Caesar Valentino.

"They're all gone now, all dead, except for B. B. King. I knew Clyde McPhatter; he was still a part of the group when I joined." Cesar Valentino had a warm smile and a heart-shaped face. His black eyes glittered. Brenda noticed his manicured hands and the warm cocoa color of his skin against the snowy cuffs as he signed the photo. He handed it around to the other Drifters. "Here, we need more John Henries for this beautiful woman." When he gave her the photo, his smooth dry hand lightly caressed her own.

"Some of the new guys have been with the Drifters for going on twenty-six years, now," he said, crinkling his eyes.

"That's a long time, isn't it?"

"Well, yeah but we're like brothers, you know what I mean? We like being together." He flashed a smile and Brenda tried to think of something else to say but the moment passed and she left feeling she'd missed something important. Threading her way among the wheelchairs and children, Brenda had a vision of herself alone with Mr. Valentino in one of the Elk's Club's shabby rooms, his gold necklace pressing against her chest. Oh, Brenda, she thought, shocked at herself. She'd never cheat on Philip.

Philip said, "I paid four bucks for this wine. They probably bought the whole fricken bottle for four bucks!"

"Well at least it's benefiting the Fire Department. We can't be too critical," she said.

"Yeah, yeah. All for a good cause." Philip settled back in his chair.

The Drifters had returned. "Let's hear it if you remember this golden oldie from 1959!" The band went into some preliminary thumps and the Drifters started swaying and singing "Up On the Roof." Brenda clapped her hands like a child.

When the Drifters did the next song, "Splish Splash," a Bobby Darren song (!) Brenda felt she had to dance, so she stood up and walked to the dance floor. She caught the eye of another middle-aged woman, arms also held high, and they smiled at each other as they gyrated.

The next song was "The Twist." Brenda sat down again.

"Why are they doing songs the Drifters never recorded?" Brenda asked. Philip gave her a thin smile. She continued, "I have to say that these songs sound all the same. It's funny. I used to think they were unique."

After a few more songs, Philip pointed to his watch. He was ready to leave. Brenda finished her wine – it was pretty awful she had to admit – and moved to pick up her purse when Mr. Valentino started to speak again, his voice intimate and sexy. Was he looking at her as he spoke? "How many of you can go back to 1960 with the Drifters? 'Cause if you can, you made this Number One on the billboard charts and we'd like to dedicate it to each and every one of you."

A single guitar plucked out the signature opening and they began.

"Oh, you can dance…
Every dance with the guy who gives you the eye,
And let him hold you tight."

People in the audience came alive, hooting and clapping, shouting and cheering. They'd all been waiting for "Save the Last Dance for Me." Brenda said, "Just one more, Philip."

In the summer of 1960, when Brenda was a senior in high school, she, her sister Marcie, and their friend Anna Palmer, whose parents had also taken a cottage on Lake Huron over on the other side of the state, drove their dad's Buick Special to the Saturday night dance at East Tawas, Michigan. The dance hall was on a pier top over the lake.

The parking lot was filled with pickup trucks. Brenda remembered the faint sound of music, the softness of the night, and how the waves of Lake Huron made gentle lapping sounds against the shore huddling in the dark beyond. The girls in their halter-top sundresses and Capezio flats made a flurry of checking their hair and lipstick in the mirror before leaving the car. Ascending a narrow pine staircase to get to the hall, they passed under the reproachful stare of a moose head mounted at the landing, its antlers casting spidery shadows on the walls. Upstairs the hall was dark. It smelled of cigarette smoke and floor polish. The girls clustered and started whispering and laughing to show they were having a good time. Brenda darted glances into the void on the other side where shadowy silhouettes of boys moved. It wasn't too long before a boy appeared in front of Marcie; then another asked Anna to dance. The two girls stayed on the floor with their partners for a second dance, and then another.

Brenda kept watch through the next few dances. Surely someone would ask her to dance. Someone had to. Time passed. She fought her sense of humiliation and the invisible arrows identifying her as a wallflower. The music was good, of course, and she kept smiling. Marcie glanced now and then in her direction from behind the backs of her partners; once she even came and stood with Brenda for a few moments. Brenda's hopes withered and she could no longer quell her inner voice: You're too tall, too plain, flat-chested, geeky, ugly.

When she couldn't pretend any longer, she started to leave. She'd wait for the others in the parking lot. It was okay, she told herself. At least they were having fun. But it felt awful, too, to have this empty place in her stomach, as if all her happiness had been sucked away leaving behind a sickening vacuum. A new record began. The latest Drifters hit.

> *"Oh I know, (Oh I know) that the music is fine,*
> *Like sparkling wine;*
> *Go and have your fun."*

"Wanna dance?"

The boy standing before her had dark hair. He was okay looking. Not ugly or a loser at all. She could hardly believe it. He was wearing blue jeans and lumberjack boots, and his t-shirt smelled freshly washed.

"Sure." His hand was calloused and hard and he was like the boys who took shop and automotive science, boys she didn't know in high school. They moved around, pumping, hesitant, and Brenda, gripped by indecision and a fear of breaking the spell, could find no words. He broke the silence. "You here on vacation?"

"Yes, our parents have a cottage for a couple of weeks. It's fun here, isn't it?"

"Yeah, it's fun." They danced past Marcie who flashed her a huge smile. Brenda said, "Do you live around here?"

"Yeah, I work over at Cohoon's granary. I drive their truck most of the time, but I also help in the yard."

"Did you grow up around here?"

"Yeah, I'm just a hick from East Tawas."

"No." She spoke with passion. "Why would you say that?"

"Well, you know, you probably think I'm a hick."

"I don't think you're a hick at all."

"Well, that's good."

He pulled her closer. She reveled in the soft cotton of his t-shirt and in the contours of his arm and shoulder. His smell was soap, cigarettes and Mennen aftershave. When the music ended, Brenda prepared to be left alone. She looked around, casual, indifferent so he'd know it was okay for him to walk away. She could still go to the car and wait it out.

But he didn't leave. When the music started again, he took up where he'd left off, taking her hand into his callused paw and wrapping his arm around her.

Each time the music stopped, she waited for the boy to leave, but he just gripped her tight around the waist again. They stopped trying to talk and when the DJ played "Unchained Melody," she found herself clinging to him, her cheek against his neck. The music was transporting; it invoked a mystical experience that brought her close to ecstasy. The lyrics suddenly made sense to her; she "hungered for his touch." She knew she wasn't in love, but her heart ached with something like love. And joy. When the music ended the boy asked if she'd like to get some fresh air. They hurried down the stairs past the moose head and crossed the parking lot to the beach. The breeze from the lake was warm. A golden strip of moonlight flung itself across the water from a million miles away. She felt outside herself. This was not happening to her – it was too important, something that happened to other girls, but not to her. She watched, spellbound, as he steered her to a dark corner by some rocks. He kissed her, shocking her by putting his tongue in her mouth. After awhile he had her on the ground. He slid his hand under her skirt and found her pubic hair beneath the elastic band of her Lollipop cotton underpants. She'd never known a boy would want to put his hand on her private parts and she felt a sense of wonder.

And then he ruined it. The boy had gone too far; all of a sudden he was forcing himself into her and things were real, frightening. Brenda fought him. After a brief struggle, he stood up. "Why?" he said as she pushed him away. She ran to the parking lot. She hid in the car and huddled, sheltered and rebuked at the same time. The silence was oppressive until after many minutes the faint sound of music reached her ears, reminding her that other kids did have fun at dances. She unlocked the car, knowing the boy was gone, began to hate herself. She was the one who'd ruined things, not him. Why was she such a scaredy cat? The words of her mother clanged in her head. "Good girls keep their legs together," "You're a good girl." "Save yourself for your husband." The words had imprisoned her just when she had begun to learn about love. She hated her own prudery and cowardice.

Driving home through the woodsy back roads, Marcie and Anna dissected their various dance partners with much hilarity. "Come on, now, Brenda, we saw you with that boy. Did you like him?"

She only said, "He was okay," but as she drove the Buick along the dark asphalt, a ghostly run through the pine forests in which every black tree loomed Disney-like, she mentally reviewed every gesture, every word, every nuance of her evening. Listening to Anna and her sister, her head swirled. It astonished her how they were so objective, so unimpressed with the dance, while she'd been so deeply affected. A maelstrom of joy, guilt and regret raged in her head.

Brenda was suddenly pulled back to the present as she realized that the concert was coming to a close.

> *"But don't forget who's taking you home,*
> *And in whose arms you're gonna be."*
> *And Darling, /save the last dance for me.*

Brenda's tablemates, the people near them, and in fact, the entire roomful of people were smiling and swaying to the music as if they were all joined by a sacred cause. She fought back the lump in her throat, the sadness welling up in waves. What was going on? Why sadness? Was she feeling sorry for herself, for her lost youth? Philip pointed to his watch again but without impatience. Just one of their signals they had developed over the years. She started to object, to voice her frustration with him for his prim and controlling ways, and something stopped her.

"But don't forget who's taking you home, …"

Philip was the man who was taking her home. She had someone. And she remembered Philip was fighting lymphoma. The oncologist had told them it would flair and then fade with treatment, then flair again. An unpredictable and deadly invader of their lives, something which Brenda had yet to acknowledge as something that could kill Philip. And it came to her how Philip endured his illness with stoicism, never complaining while she, buyer of expensive furniture and perfume, drifted in and out of her selfish worlds, often burdening herself with self-pity.

He said, "Honey, are you sure it's okay to leave after this song?"

Suddenly and with the intensity of a slap, Brenda came out of her dream, the cocoon in which she had lived for so many years. Philip was there in front of her, and he needed her to care about him. She reached across her wine glass and grabbed his hand. She put it up to her face.

She'd forgotten how to feel much of anything, so swathed had she become in the routines of her comfortable life. At seventeen she'd endured roller coasters of emotions, but had learned to hide from emotions that could bring pain. Yet standing in front of her, her husband (who stood astonished), was a dear and caring man. This man was someone who lived with her, who cared about her, and who was someone to care about. He continued to stare, his eyebrows pinched together, head lowered, mouth open, his bewilderment becoming absolutely comical to her. She laughed long and hard then wiped her tears on his wrist (and Rolex) before finding a Kleenex in her purse. "I'm sorry, Honey. I don't know what has come over me. I'm just so glad you're here with me right now."

> *"Oh darling, (do-do-do) / save the last dance for me;*
> *Oh save (cha-cha-cha) / the last dance for me."*

A moment of grace hovered in the air and then all hell broke loose. Everyone cheered. Where was that exit? Brenda reached for her coat and purse on the back of the chair and grabbed her husband's arm. She whispered in his ear as they headed for the door. "Honey. When we get home, we're going to get NAKED and jump into the jaccuzzi. And I'm going to wash every part of you with slippery, slithey, sexy soap." Charles smiled and picked up the pace.

The Drifters (Encyclopedia Americana)

American rhythm and blues vocal group that produced a series of chart-topping hits from the early 1950s to the mid-1960s. The Drifters were actually two groups--one built around lead singer Clyde McPhatter, the other an entirely different group that took the name. The early group reached number one on the rhythm-and-blues charts with "Money Honey" (1953) and scored several other hits, including "White Christmas" (1954). Three lead singers later, in 1959, Treadwell replaced the entire group with another ensemble, led by Ben E. King. Still recording for Atlantic, now under the guidance of writer-producers Jerry Leiber and Mike Stoller, The Drifters cracked the pop Top Ten in 1959 with "There Goes My Baby" (remembered for its innovative use of strings and Latin rhythms) and took "Save the Last Dance for Me" (1960) to number one.

INNOCENCE

"You!" All the kids were looking at him, turning around in their seats to get a good look, third grade sanctimonious eyes. "Yes, I'm talking to you!" Mrs. Sears stood at the front of the class, her nylon green and white polka dot dress stretched taut over her big breasts and buttocks. Her blue eyes shot anger at him.

"You go right back and pick up that piece of string you were kicking."

He looked at her, uncomprehending. "Okay."

He turned back into the hall and walked down toward the gym, scanning the clean linoleum floor for a piece of string. He was in trouble again but this time he didn't know why. After a few minutes he found a dusty segment of an old shoe lace. He picked it up and brought it back. They were on arithmetic. He walked up to the front of the class where she stood, chalk in hand, and extended the shoe lace.

"No, that's not it. Now you stop playing games with me young man and go get that string, do you hear me?"

"Where was it?"

"Don't you sass me, young man!"

"But I didn't kick no string, No ma'am." He knew he was going to get it.

"That string you were kicking in front of the gym door. You go pick it up and bring it back! And then you'll stay after school for all the time you wasted in getting back here."

He was now sitting in the vestibule, the school empty, oblivious to the smell of floor wax and the pungency of his own socks. He'd be late getting home. He had struggled getting into his green wool snowsuit. His mom made him wear it any time the thermometer dipped below 40°. He sat, pulled on his rubber boots, and fastened the metal clasps. On went his khaki cap with the earflaps over his hair. On went the yukky mittens Aunt Cathy had knitted him for Christmas. The yarn went from red to orange to yellow to green to blue to purple and back to red. Matt said they were sissy mittens. He hated them and he hated Matt. He picked up his lunch pail and pushed open the heavy outside door. Clang! The noise broke into the silent air as the door shut and locked itself.

Outside was a dazzling surprise – the front walk, the telephone lines, the shrubs – everything within sight was coated with snow, a sugary fairyland beginning to turn beige in the setting sun; the same color as them meringues his mom sometimes made. It was the time of day when afternoon turns into night, a kind of slack tide, when everything stops moving and the world stops breathing. Lights glowed dully from the few streetlights in front of the school and from the windows of the silent houses along the street. But nothing stirred, not even a car. A dog barked somewhere far across the playground, shattering the silence that hung in the air. The snow was falling in large flakes. The boy put out his tongue. A flake landed on it and turned to water. He caught another flake in his mouth, and then another.

He had been crying back in the classroom and his nose was still running. He hadn't known the right answer. He thought about the problem standing there and felt bad all over again. Why do you carry the number to the next column? He still didn't get it, even though Mrs. Sears tried to make him learn by yelling at him. His dad would have a cow! He decided his parents would never know about today if he could help it.

He lingered. The cold stung inside his nostrils. He wiped his nose on the back of his mitten, then inspected the clear ribbon of thin mucous he had made. It sparkled in the sun and magnified the fibers of his mitten. He was hungry. He found a half a peanut butter sandwich under the crumpled waxed paper in his lunch pail. He ate most of it in one bite. A streak of peanut butter was smeared on one cheek. He put out his tongue and cow-like, scooped around as far as his tongue would reach until he had cleaned his face. Noticing that snow was fast covering his snowsuit and melting on his thick glasses, he stepped off the stoop to head home.

Picking his way in the knee-deep drifts where he thought the sidewalk was he soon grew too hot. He took off his mittens and stuffed them into a snowsuit pocket. He unzipped his snowsuit a couple of inches and tugged on the neck of his blue-striped tee shirt. The cold air rushed in to caress his sweaty neck. When he reached the corner of Carpenter and Eastman he did a quick check for cars then took a running jump off the curb and landed flat on his feet making two big hollows. One of his mittens flew out of his pocket, unnoticed. He took another leap, feet together, then another. He was an arctic rabbit bounding across the snow-covered tundra, just like the big buck rabbit in the book they read during Science. He remembered that in the Arctic Circle the animals turn white in the winter. Now a bear was after him and the boy started making great two-footed leaps, faster and faster. When he stopped, panting, he sat down on the far curb, thinking I love this snow, I love messing it up.

The temperature dropped as the sun set. A car approached the corner where he was sitting. It slowed, windshield wipers whooshing steadily, then turned right, tires crunching, trailing a blurry cloud of cherry-red. The color hung in the gray gloom for a moment, then disappeared. The world was quiet again. The boy sat looking at the spiraling flakes of snow until his feet got cold. He would drive his own car when he grew up, like Lonny next door. Lonny was in high school. Lonnie drove a used black RX7. When he grew up he was going to get a candy-apple red Grand Am with duals.

The boy stood up and walked on. A snowplow came toward him, its muffled wheel chains going "clack" "clack" clack." The boy watched the large unbroken wave of snow that rode high before the truck. That's so cool! Oh man! I'm glad I ain't standin' in the path of that plow! I ain't dumb. It could really smear me, crush me, grind up all my guts and blood and squash me flat. He remembered the frog Billy Jensen stepped on last summer on the sidewalk in front of his house. Frog guts mushed out on the dry cement. Why did Billy have to do that? The boy didn't get it. He loved all animals, even bugs. He'd never kill one, especially not a frog, even if it peed in his hand. The plow was passing him now and the snow it was pushing cascaded majestically in huge mounds, higher than the boy. Then the truck was gone leaving the smell of diesel in the air.

The snow came down more rapidly now. The boy wanted to try a snowball although he knew the snow wasn't going to pack. The best snow for packing was after a storm when the sun warmed up the air. Then you could make good snowballs. And snowmen. He tried to make a snowman last week. He had asked his dad to help him but his dad never came outside. He said later that he forgot. The boy had used dead leaves for the eyes but they didn't look right. And then he used his dad's hat. He was just going to borrow it for a little while and then put it back in the closet but they caught him. Oh man, when his dad went to get his hat and couldn't find it, and then when the boy tried to tell him why he took it, his dad just reached out and grabbed him. Then his parents were shouting. His mother had come running but she didn't stop his father from hitting him. She stood there watching with big eyes, afraid. "Fuck you!" he had screamed, giving his father the opportunity he'd been looking for to punch him in the face. That hurt. He knew his dad didn't like him. He didn't like his dad either. He hated his dad. It wasn't his real dad anyway. His real dad was in California. He knew his real dad loved him and was going to come home one of these days. Even if California was just something he made up to tell the other kids.

The boy put down his lunch pail and scooped up some snow and the snow became a small core that melted in his wet red hands. Yup. This snow wasn't no good for a snowball. He bent down and gathered an armful that he threw against a tree, the fluff pleasantly cool against his bare wrists. It brushed by the tree and disintegrated. The next armful blew back into his upraised face making his cheeks tingle, then hurt. His eyes widened behind his smudged glasses and he wished he were home with his mom in the kitchen baking cookies. Or just sitting at the kitchen table watching her make dinner.

He reached into his pocket to put on his mittens, wanting to get home as fast as he could. Oh-oh. Only one mitten. Where the heck's the other? His dad was going to kill him. He did a search of the ground around him, then he put on one mitten and picked up his lunch pail. He shoved his free hand into his pocket, wiggling his wet fingers. He started back towards the school and the corner where he had watched the car turn. He searched the ground as he walked, looking for his footprints. It was completely dark now but he could see by the warm yellow light that spilled from the curtained houses that there was no mitten. The wind was blowing straight into his face. He was cold. He wanted to go home but he wasn't going to take any more beatings. No sir! No more. He had to find that mitten. He trudged resolutely. He wished his mom would tell him where his real dad went so he could write him a letter to come and get him.

*   *   *

The boy's mother looked out of the window, then at the kitchen clock. Four-thirty. Time for her husband to come home. She hoped she had done everything she was supposed to do. Let's see. Laundry done, socks and underwear folded and put away. Chicken stew on the stove, ready to go. She'd shopped for beer, picking up a bottle of Chablis for herself. He probably wouldn't object. Money was tight but hey! If he can drink beer, why couldn't she drink wine? She'd made it home just before the storm started in earnest with time left to do the cooking. She turned on the TV. One of her soaps was on. She knew the story. Would the girl find the courage to leave her family? To take a chance on her own? The story was just getting exciting.

"Dad, for the last time. I have to go take care of Tom."

Rosalie's voice rose to a shrill hysteria as she stomped toward the door, dragging her backpack. Her father grabbed her arm.

"You're not going anywhere.

"I'm going and you can't stop me."

Rosalie's father threw her on the sofa, her book bag knocking over the lamp as she fell.

The camera moved in on the man's contorted face, then Fadeout.

At the commercial, the boy's mother turned off the television just as the phone rang.

"Oh Hi, Mama…. No, Buddy's not home yet……. We're doing okay. I really don't need to burden you with my problems. …….. Okay, okay. Maybe we'll visit soon. Yeah, we'll come on over. I really need to make this work, though….. Yes. Mama."

It was almost five o'clock. Her son hadn't come in yet. She looked at the clock again. Why wasn't he home from school? They lived only two blocks away from Madison Elementary and she'd made sure he wore his snowsuit today in spite of his objections so she knew he'd be protected against the cold. He'd probably had to stay after school. His dyslexia made every day such a challenge and they couldn't afford the special help she knew he needed. She sighed and wished she could go back to work. Okay, okay, he doesn't want me working. It's going to be okay - not to worry – that little tiger will be home from school in a little while. She sank back into the kitchen chair. She remembered his sweet smile this morning as she'd kissed him goodbye. "Now you stay out of trouble, you hear?" She had smiled as she spoke and he said, "Aw, Mom. I will." He was such a good kid. She wondered at her luck to have him in spite of his father that no-good bastard who had walked out on her soon after she became pregnant. Her little tyke deserved better. She had had hopes for success with her new husband, but things weren't ...... She heard the car in the driveway and the little hollow in her heart opened up to let in the sadness. She tried to fight her disappointment by making sure her two men were happy. She wanted this marriage to work. If I try hard enough, I can make a go of it.

Her husband came in, stomping the snow off his shoes and bringing with him a cloud of cigarette smoke and moisture. "I'm home," he called from the vestibule with more stomping. "Did you get the beer? I'm ready for a cold one." He took off his overcoat. "That fucking Janiken gave me a load of shit again over safety glasses." His voice became girlish. 'Now if you don't wear your safety glasses at all times, I'll have to turn you in and it'll give the company a bad mark.' Who gives a shit about the company?"

She got up from her chair and went to the refrigerator. "Hi Hon. Oh that's too bad. Did you take off your glasses in the plant for some reason?"

He looked at her and started to say something.

She backed away, remembering that he always had good reasons for what he did. "Of course, why did I say that? Of course you had a good reason. Janiken's a jerk."

She opened the beer and handed it to her husband. He was a dark-haired man, lean, an ample stubble on his narrow jaw, a handsome face if not for thin lips that always seemed pursed in discontent. He took a swig of his beer then held out the bottle in front of his face.

"What's this? Buckbear Beer? What the fuck kind of beer is this? Don't tell me they didn't have Bud."

"Well, yes, they did, Hon, but I thought you might like something better, kind of a treat, so I bought this. It's ar-tee-sinal – I think that's how you say it. The man at the store said it was good."

She sat down and coughed. She'd made another mistake.

"For Christ's sake. Can't I even have the beer I like?"

"Sorry sorry sorry. I was trying to give you a treat."

He took another swig. "Next time spare me the treats. Tomorrow get me something I can drink...." He settled into an easy chair in the living room. "What's for dinner? Where's the kid?"

"He's not home yet and I'm getting worried."

"He'll be along. You know him. He's probably in a snowball fight. Or just dawdling like he always does. I've told him a hundred times to come home on time and here he's late again. Tryin' to pull my chain. I know him. Well, when he gets home we'll see about how much TV he gets tonight." He took another drink.

The woman walked toward the closet and took out her coat and boots. "I'm worried. I'm going out to look for him."

The man stood up. "You'll do no such thing. I'm getting hungry and I don't want my dinner delayed just because your kid can't get home on time. You spoil him, you know. And if you go out to find him, he'll just think he can get away with delays all the time."

"But Hon…."

"No buts about it. Let's eat. I'm going to change my clothes and then I'll be ready."

The woman stood in the living room, coat in hand. She stood still, then moved toward the door. She stopped and sat down clutching her coat. She buried her face in the threadbare wool. After a long moment, she stood up and fetching her hat and boots from the closet in the vestibule, headed for the door.

* * *

The boy found the corner where the snowplow had come through and he knew he had to cross the street. There was some light traffic, so he waited until every car had gone by, then looked to the left and to the right as he had been taught ("Stop, Look, and Listen, Before you cross the street. Use your eyes, Use your ears, and Then use your feet.") Okay. Go. It was tough to wade through the deep drifts and he stumbled when he reached the opposite curb. He was tired and so he sat down for awhile, wondering if he'd ever find that stupid mitten. It was comfortable to sit on the curb with all the snow swirling around him and he liked watching the cars that cautiously rolled by, plowing through the fluffy stuff. The mound of snow next to him looked inviting, like a big pillow, and so he decided to lie against it for a bit, his snowsuit hood keeping his head warm. He took care not to lie too much on his side because if he did, he might break the frames of his glasses. He heard another car come by but he didn't bother to look at it. It was nice to just watch the snow close up, his nose almost touching the icy stuff. He thought he could pick out a few flakes that looked just like those in the book that his mother had read to him. They were so pretty. There was no hurry in getting up just yet. It seemed warmer to be on the ground than trying to fight the wind. He stopped worrying about the mitten and sang a chorus of "Frosty the Snowman" to himself. Spider Man came drifting into his mind. What would Spider Man do in this situation. Maybe Spider Man was even in his town. He could just see Spidey flying from rooftop to rooftop through his neighborhood. But the picture didn't quite work. The houses were too close to the ground. Spidey climbed skyscrapers. No, that was a stupid idea.

When his mother found him he was half covered by drifts but he was alive. Half awake but alive. She thought about how he'd always been a warm little body, never cold even when she herself needed a coat. She bent down to him.

"Hi Mom, I was just taking a rest." He sat up. "Mrs. Sears made me stay because she said I kicked a piece of string but I didn't. I really didn't." The boy pushed his glasses up onto his nose, then wiped his nose with his other hand as he spoke.

"Buddy, of course you didn't kick no string. I'm sure you didn't." His mother helped him stand, then brushed snow from his snowsuit with her gloved hand. "But Buddy, since you didn't come home I had to come out. Your dad's gonna be pissed, and worst of all, I almost didn't see you. You were half covered by snow. Did you know that? You were almost hiding from me." The boy kept talking.

"And I lost my mitten. And I had to go back and look for it. I'm sorry, though. I don't know what happened to it."

"Well, we will just do without your mitten. For now, we're going to get home as fast as we can and get some hot soup into you."

"Can I have chicken noodle the way you make it with milk?"

*   *   *

"Where the fuck you been?"

"Now let's not get all in a twitter. Buddy was told to stay after school but it wasn't his fault, and then he went back for his mitten and got sorta lost. It's lucky I found him when I did." She didn't look at her husband as she removed her hat, coat and boots then turned to help her son with his snowsuit.

"I don't give a damn about no mitten. You get over here, Buddy. You are gonna get a whippin' for this after dinner. Right now all I know is I'm hungry."

The woman stopped unzipping her son's snowsuit. She slowly turned to stare at her husband. The ball bearings that had been running all loose in her insides for as long as she'd known him, started to set off the usual nodes of anxiety as in a pinball machine. It was an unbearable moment, to expect once again the same loss and humiliation she always had when he acted like this. But the ball bearings never got very far. A new feeling stopped them, a feeling that was stronger than her fear. Her new feeling made sense; it knitted together her insides into a kind of armor that made her solid and strong. She knew at once she was through with trying. She would talk to him, to tell him that she no longer loved him; that he was a man without compassion, without empathy, a man who would rather put her down than take responsibility for her feelings.

She knew for certain that all that was left to do (and it would be hard but not impossible), was to say the words that she'd had enough, that she was taking Buddy with her that very night, and he could go to hell. Even if she had to take a beating, she was ready for it.

"Keep your snowsuit on, Buddy. And go get your best toys and books. We're going to Grandma's."

THE 7-ELEVEN® PARKING LOT

Moira rang the doorbell. She was ready for her first teaching adventure having just received her MA from Michigan State University. She'd been thrilled to be hired by the hoary old private school, Briar Roughly, in mid-New Hampshire. That fall, she drove East, unloaded most of her stuff from her Corolla, and hurried off to attend the faculty get-together the Saturday before classes began the following Monday. When Moira entered the headmaster's colonial home, she took in the unmistakable signs of New England-old-money: shabby-elegant living room, two Irish setters sprawled on the enormous chintz sofa, a lovely oil painting over the fireplace – Turner? Out on the large glassed-in porch the faculty gathered in little groups, wine glasses in hand, balancing plates of small sandwiches.

The headmaster, Dalton Westerly, led her to the porch and poured her a glass of wine. The guests barely looked up from their conversations, indifferent as grazing cows. Dalton approached a tall woman who stood talking with an older, gray-haired man.

"Bobbie, Jack. Excuse us. This is Moira Gaughan, the new Spanish teacher." Watching Bobbie, he said to Moira, "Bobbie Pettibone is the heart and soul of our Spanish Department." Bobbie let out a yip. "You are an unconscionable flatterer, Dalton."

Bobby was young-middle-aged, curvy, with luxurious brunette hair cut long. Her mouth was a slash of dark red lipstick, her eyes hooded and sparkly. She spoke with an assured, upper class drawl particular to a segment of Northeast society. Moira had hoped Bobbie would be her mentor, her ally, in this first job right out of school, but as Bobbie slowly gave her a shrewd look, Moira could feel envy. Or was it just bad manners?

"Welcome to Briar Roughly. Did you just arrive?"

"Yes, up from Providence."

"Gaughan, Gaughan…. Are you related to the Gaughans of Marblehead?"

"No, my family is from the Midwest."

"Oh. That name is so familiar….. Where'd you go to school?"

"Well, both undergraduate and masters at Michigan State and then…"

Bobbie interrupted, attracting the attention of the people around her. "Michigan State. I seem to remember something. Don't they have a live cow with a window in its side, so you can watch milk being processed, *in situ* as it were?

Bystanders were gathering around, forming a tight little circle of onlookers, as if craning in at a traffic accident.

"You're right, I'm afraid. No longer, though. That was during my mother's time there."

Bobbie's smile disappeared. Moira hadn't meant to imply that Bobbie was her mother's age.

"So, Dear, where'd you go to prep school?"

"I didn't go to prep school. Plain old public school for me. Midland, Michigan? Dow Chemical Company is based there."

"Of course, I know it, doesn't everybody? I suppose I'd really date myself if I said, 'napalm.'"

Someone tittered. Moira shifted her feet, looking for an exit.

There was silence. A gawky man with hooked nose asked, "So your field is Spanish – What's your take on the Generation of '98? I take it you've read Unamuno."

"I have, but it's been awhile. My specialty was Cervantes."

Another man asked, "How do you find us, compared with the Mid-West?" The people in the circle moved closer, bird-like. (All except the gray-haired man, Jack, who made a point of looking through the back window as if he just had to wait to return to his private conversation with Bobby. Jack, taught part-time French for a dollar-a-year salary, was distantly related to the Saltonstalls.)

"I think Midwesterners are friendlier, somehow, than Easterners. There is a certain reserve in the East, you know, with so many people per square mile." As she talked, Moira became aware that an older, very good-looking man over by a bookshelf was watching her.

Bobbie continued. "What you're really trying to say is that Easterners are unfriendly?" Bobbie's eyes were widened, imputing rudeness on Moira's part. Someone in the circle smiled. This was getting good.

"Oh, no, I didn't mean that. People are essentially the same wherever you go. But Midwesterners are more open. There, that's the word I should have used. 'Open.'"

"Oh," said Bobbie. "That's an interesting way to put it, Dear." Bobby turned toward the gray-hair man. "Okay, Jack, where were we?" The crowd melted away. Moira moved to the buffet table, picked up a sandwich and a plastic glass of white wine, stunned by the way with which Bobbie had treated her. How soon could she get away from these people? She was thinking up an excuse when the man by the bookcase approached and stuck his hand out. "Hi. Roger Pettibone. Bobby's husband." He waved his other hand in Bobbie's direction.

"Oh. Yes." Moira shook hands with him. "Hello."

"I'm the Chaplain. Live right here on campus, same as you, but we have our own house. Don't mind these people, including my wife. They don't accept newcomers easily. They'll like you soon enough….." Moira

131

just smiled. What had she gotten herself into? Roger continued talking. "I guess they've got you living as floor master over at Woolsey?"

"Yes, I'm afraid that babysitting with the Woolsey boarding girls was part of the teaching job offer." The man was at least six-feet four, and Moira, at five-nine and used to meeting men at eye-level, enjoyed standing next to him. She felt protected. In fact, after the cool reception from her new colleagues, she wanted to bask in his apparent interest in her.

"Yes – third floor. I have an apartment up there."

"All set for classes?"

"Hope so – I still have a little work to do." Moira took a sip of wine and looked at this man. Graying sideburns, strong jaw, athletic build. "Do you teach as well as conduct the weekly services?"

"A couple of classes: Comparative Religion and Ethics. I also handle the Drama Club."

"Oh, then we'll be working together. Dalton informed me yesterday I was to assist the Drama coach. I guess that's you." She smiled.

"I know. I asked for you."

"You did? How do you know I can even read a script?" Roger smiled easily and touched her elbow. He leaned close and lowered his voice. "I saw you in the office when you interviewed last spring. Thought we could use some young blood. I hope that's okay."

Moira paused for a moment. Hi breath was sweet. Then she said, "Yes, it's fine. It'll be fun. But I don't know anything about drama. Is this another one of those duties that come with the privilege of working at a private school?"

"That's for sure. They just throw you to the wolves. At least you're not coaching track – or are you? I had to handle Saturday study hall when I first came here. Gads, the kids couldn't wait to get away to smoke their weed and mess up something. Drama Club is fun." Moira twisted her paper napkin into a hard spiral and put her wine glass and china plate down on a little table, next to a silver-framed picture of Dalton and his family in ski gear, a jagged line of Alps in the background.

"As I said, I'm really not a good actor or director. I guess I could paint scenery."

"You don't have to know anything about drama. That's what makes it fun."

Bobby was watching them. Moira began to move toward the door.

"Well, it's nice to meet you, Roger. See you soon. You'll have to excuse me, I'm still unpacking." Moira sought out Dalton to thank him, and left the house. She drove her Toyota to the large girl's dorm on the other end of the campus. She was tasked with making sure the girls on her floor kept the strict hours imposed by the school, kept their rooms relatively neat, did not smoke in the dorm, and did not get too homesick.

She unpacked the last of her boxes, hanging several fleece jackets in a colorful row in her tiny closet. She wondered what she had gotten herself into. She'd been lucky to get the job and felt a certain pride in teaching at the prestigious prep school. Briar Roughly had been founded by two bachelor Methodist minister brothers in the late 19th century, becoming co-ed in 1979. At first, Briar Roughly was one of the top-tier schools in the country but over time, the School's reputation sank to its current status as an Arts-and-Athletics institution for rich kids.

That night after she had eaten her grilled cheese sandwich and was just settling in to prepare a lesson plan for her first Monday, the phone rang.

"Hi. This is Roger."

Moira had to think for a moment.

"Roger Pettibone. Chaplain."

"Oh, Roger. Hi."

"Sorry to barge in on you, but I forgot to mention the faculty play today when we talked."

"Oh?"

"Yes, I am hoping you'll consider joining it. Lots of fun. And we make money for the Scholarship fund."

"You know, right now I'm trying to get my lesson plan done. Roger I can't think about a faculty play. I'm really not an actor. But I appreciate your calling. May I think about it and tell you later?"

"Or course, of course. I just wanted to prepare you for the idea. We have plenty of time."

"Okay, that's good... Say...." She didn't want to hang up. "What's it like here when winter closes in? I have visions of "The Shining" and being cut off from civilization by the snow up here with Jack Nicholson running around with a knife."

"We do get a little stir crazy. They say that back in ought-seven, one teacher tore off all his clothes and ran, stark naked, down the hill and into the Obegannicut River. Trouble was it was frozen. They caught him sliding around on the ice yelling, (and here Roger raised his voice in mock outrage,) "'None' takes a singular verb. How many times do I have to say it? 'None' takes a singular verb!'"

Moira laughed. If that's the worst, I think I can weather it. No pun intended. I'm used to rough winters, coming from Michigan."

"I'll let you get back to your unpacking. See you a week from Tuesday at the Sperling Auditorium. We start at 7:00 p.m."

"Okay. Thanks."

Moira played with her pencil. It was nice of Roger to think of her for the faculty play. Could be fun. The phone rang again. It was her ex-boyfriend, Chris.

"Why are you calling?" Moira didn't bother to hide her annoyance.

"Because I wanted to wish you luck with the Eastern Establishment."

"We have nothing to say to each other."

"Don't hang up, Moira. I just need to tell you I'm sorry about what happened. It's all over between Cindy and me and I was sitting here – I'm doing field work now – all alone, with nothing but coyotes and snakes out here. I'm about a hundred miles south of Albuquerque - and I thought about you."

"Well, that's certainly flattering. Go back to your coyotes, Chris. I'm busy now." She hung up. She would not forgive him for finding him in bed with someone she'd considered a friend.

She picked up her lesson planning book, then she put it down again. She'd dated Chris during her senior year and their breakup still hurt. She remembered the drive to an off campus party. He stopped for an injured baby squirrel on the side of the road. Using a spare towel from his trunk, he'd picked up the creature and put it in her lap then driven fast to the emergency animal clinic. They'd hustled into see the vet and then in the glaring white of the sterile room, the squirrel had died in her hands. She sighed then picked up the phone and dialed her mother's number in Michigan. A machine voice came on: "Hello – I'm hoping you'll leave your number so we can talk. Have a wonderful day." Good old Mom. Always cheerful. Probably at her quilting club or playing bridge. Moira looked around her apartment at the particleboard bookcase, the daybed, the kitchenette and tiny bath. Her shoulders slumped. It would be a long winter.

On the first day of school, the air was warm and dry with just a hint of freshness in the breeze that harbingers the end of summer in New England. Moira looked out at her students, a class of Remedials. Second-year Spanish students were ability-grouped at Briar Roughly into Fast Track, Normal, and Remedial, the latter consisting of the poor souls who had squeaked through Spanish I last year with low C's and D's. They had to pass two years of a foreign language to graduate and these kids weren't in her class because they loved Spanish. Language learning, as Moira was fond of telling her students, is not an intellectual exercise, but a motor skill, like riding a bicycle, that you learn with guts and repetition.

She said, *"Muy buenos días, y ?qué buen día está hoy día, no?"* The students remained stock-still. *Contéstenme ustedes. Muy buenos días...."* She switched gears. "Remember, we're hitting at the hard-wired habits – you gotta just jump in."

One of the boys who'd been eyeing her breasts, shifted in his seat and said, "Are you going to always talk in Spanish because if you are, I'm not going to make it through this year."

Dean Ramsay had been explicit. Second year Spanish would be taught entirely in Spanish. She said, *"En español lo más possible."* Then she switched to English. "No, not always Spanish. But you will learn it better the more you hear and speak it. *Van a aprender con el esfuerzo con que ustedes escuchen y hablen.* Anybody catch the subjunctive in that sentence ?"

She spent the morning drilling introductions, numbers, and days of the week. After class one of the girls came up to her and said she loved Moira's sweater set. By the end of the month, some of the students could dredge up a few phrases. She praised them. She gave out simple exercises for homework. Thank God she also had two normal beginning classes and an AP class of smarties to motivate her.

A week after classes started, Dalton called. "I hope you're comfortably ensconced."

"Oh, perfectly. Still learning a few names, but the girls and I are doing fine."

"Don't let those girls get to you – they have a way of crushing you if they sense any weakness."

"Oh, so far so good. They're actually kind of sweet. I have a young one, who's pretty homesick. Can't ship her back to Santiago, though, can we?" They both chuckled. "What can I do for you, Dalton?"

He cleared his throat.

"I'm calling to let you know you'll be receiving three more students tomorrow. Apparently they all insist they can't do the work in Bobbie's normal Spanish II. I'm calling you at this hour because I wanted to prepare you. One of the new students you'll be getting, a freshman, is a Brewer. You know, of the "Brewer Brewers.""

"You mean as in Senator Brewer? Is it his daughter? She's on my floor here at Woolsey. Baby fat, freckled, homesick?"

"Yes, that's the one. Think you can handle having her in Spanish?"

"Why not? Is there something about her I need to know?"

"No, it's just that her father's so famous, we just wanted to give you a heads up."

"I'll do the best I can." She returned to her lesson plans thinking *he figures I didn't know how to handle celebrity kids*. There was a knock on the door. It was Joey Brewer herself. She was crying, showing a mouthful of braces studded with lavender rubber bands.

"I think you better come quick, Miss Gaughan. They've put Penny Macy down the laundry chute."

Moira raced after Joey to find indeed, a small girl tied inside a bundle of sheets being lowered into the laundry chute by a couple of two hard-looking scholarship girls from Chicago.

"Get that girl back up here, and make it quick!"

They hauled the victim back up, then Moira said, "Look. I'm going to overlook this behavior this time. You're new, it's a different environment for you, and you deserve a break. BUT. Next time you're involved in anything like this, you will go on suspension. Understood?" The girls nodded. *How would those scholarship kids, African American* from the ghettos of Chicago, ever fit in? She vowed to give them extra attention, the good kind of attention, she said to herself. She turned away toward the two culprits. "Hey, by the way, drop in my room tonight if you have time. I'd love to talk about Chicago. My sister lives there. It's my favorite town." The girls smiled. As Moira headed back to her room, one said, "I bet her sister don't live where we come from."

Joey Brewer came to Moira's room almost every night for some reason, fearful about her Spanish homework. Or her braces hurt. Or she couldn't reach her mother. Moira did her best to cheer up the homesick girl. On Parents' Day, the Senator and Mrs. Brewer came to class. The Senator had just been on the cover of *Time* magazine as a possible presidential candidate. At the end of the session, Mrs. Brewer approached. "Miss Gaughan, I don't know what you're doing, but keep on doing it. Joey has never been happier." Senator Brewer pumped her hand. "Great job, great job. And she never told me how pretty you are."

Drama season began in early October. Moira kicked through the leaves en route to the theater, shivering in her fleece jacket. Must get out the down coat. It was getting dark earlier and earlier these days. She entered Sperling Auditorium to find Roger down on the stage talking with a group of teenagers. He looked up. "Oh, here's Miss Gaughan. Go to her if you have trouble finding props or costumes. I'll bet she's got a lot of good ideas." He looked over at Moira and winked. "Okay with that, Miss Gaughan?"

"Sure, Mr. Pettibone. That's what I'm here for."

Roger said, "I thought you'd say that." He turned to the students. "Okay, let's get organized. Did everybody get a copy of the play? Who's going to read for the part of Lana? We'll start there." A sullen blond girl spoke up.

"Mr. Pettibone, should I try for Lana or would I be better as Betty?"

"Who do you feel suits you best, Debra?"

"I can't decide whether I am more bitchy or nicey-nice."

"What do the rest of you guys think? Is she bitchy or nice?"

Everybody shouted, "Bitchy."

'There's your answer." More laughter.

Moira watched the tryouts sitting next to Roger and when the students had left, said, "Debra's got real talent. I also thought the boy in the checked shirt was amazing – what subtlety for such a young guy."

"Yeah, we have a few stars." He stood up. "Let's get together later this week to do the casting. How's next Wednesday after chapel in my office?" Roger locked eyes with her for a little too long and the warning ping rang in the back of her head. Just friends. He was just being friendly.

"That should work."

Roger picked up leftover scripts. "Oh, by the way, we're going to need a big tub of Stein's Cold Cream Makeup Remover and a few other items. Would you mind ordering them? There's no hurry. I'll send you the website and give you the tax-free code and payment information."

"No problem."

The door to the auditorium opened and Bobbie breezed in, coat flying. "Roger, we'd better get on the road if we're going to get there in time for cocktails." She came down the center aisle, wafting Chanel. "Hello, Moira. Are you going to the Colter's too?"

"No, actually not."

"Oh, sorry. I thought you were invited. Well, come on, Roger. Chop chop." Moira trailed the couple out.

"Can we give you a lift, Moira?" asked Roger, locking the door to auditorium.

Moira quickly answered, "No thanks. I'll enjoy the walk home." The Pettibones sped away in their Lexus as an icy wind caught her by surprise. She pulled her collar tight and set off for Woolsey as the first snowfall of the season began in earnest.

Winter term was as isolating as Moira had suspected. The students settled down and the sessions of Spanish class became a familiar drill for both Moira and the students. She'd gotten the Remedials to greet each other and to give their birthdays in Spanish by November. But there was nowhere to go in the frigid, dark New Hampshire world outside the campus and Moira felt trapped. The entertaining among the adults increased exponentially, with cocktail parties every week. Moira had been invited to join some of the other floormasters for Friday night drinks – there were men and women with apartments like hers in each of the other seven dorms on the campus – but she was never included in the parties of the clique of long-established faculty, most of whom had some pedigree that certainly did not reflect a Midwestern public school background. At the pre-Thanksgiving party given by the headmaster and his wife, Moira ran into Bobbie and Roger again, along with some of her younger friends. Moira was on her second glass of wine when she realized the noise in the rooms was overpowering. She headed for Dalton's library, stole in and closed the door against the noise. Ahhh, peace. She began perusing Dalton's collection of books. She saw he liked Updike along with the usual cluster of nineteenth century English masters. Maybe he'd lend her the Hardy book she'd always meant to read – *Tess of the D'urbervilles*. A voice spoke from a corner of the room and she jumped.

"Have you thought over my suggestion that you join the faculty play this year?" She whirled. It was Roger.

"Oh Hi, Roger." How had he had the same idea? "What are you doing here?"

I had the same idea. You know, these parties are always the same, and when the decibels get too high, I like to hide in here. Just like you. So, as I said, faculty play this year?"

"I had a feeling we would be having this conversation sooner or later. I have a terrible secret. I can't act my way out of a paper bag."

"You don't have to know how to act."

"What's the play?"

"'Little Red Riding Hood.'" Moira raised her eyebrows. "The scholarship money we'll bring in justifies every moment of making yourself look ridiculous in the eyes of the students."

"What would be my part?" Roger walked toward her as they talked.

"I'd like you to be one of the woodland bunnies. I'll play the lead, of course."

"You mean the wolf."

"No, I'm Red Riding Hood." Moira burst out laughing.

"Oooh, a cross-dresser in our midst. The kids will love it!"

Moira paused. "Okay. I'll do it."

Roger put his arm around her waist and squeezed. "I knew you'd play with me."

"Ooo-la-la," Moira said. She pushed down the little warning bell in her head. Mustn't flirt with this guy. He's married. She said, "Well, I'm going back for more shrimp. Have you had any? Fabulous." Roger smiled, a knowing smile, a smile that unnerved her while flattering her at the same time. Playing with fire, she thought. Don't.

Rehearsals were unalloyed silliness. Moira discovered that appearing in the play endeared her to her students. She also realized on opening night when she saw the project was soon to end that Roger had presented her with the opportunity to develop a satisfying camaraderie with other faculty members in the cast, and she was grateful. She wore a form-fitting Playboy bunny outfit, along with two other young women, all three vamping Roger's Little Red Riding Hood who played every line for laughs in his long curly wig and leering manner. Her two sister bunnies were the Headmaster's secretary and a part-time French teacher. Later, Allen, her friend the Physics teacher, told her that Bobbie had gone around telling people that she thought it was a disgrace that Moira and the other women would take such sexist roles.

After the cast party, Moira drove Roger home, full of exhilaration. She stopped the car and left the motor running. The warmth generated by the heating system in her car blasted defiantly against the frozen night, making her feel cozy and intimate.

"You were a riot with that ridiculous wig. I thought it was going to come off in the second act when Grandma threw you the cookie, but you caught it just in time. You know, the wig was crooked for the rest of the scene."

"The kids loved it. That's what counts." Roger paused. "You were beautiful tonight, you know that? And I'm not just saying that because you were wearing tights and a fluffy tail. You've got an inner beauty that makes you radiant."

Roger leaned over and kissed her on the lips, a light, exploratory kiss. Moira drew back in surprise then without thinking, kissed him back. His kiss had turned on a switch, one she'd believed was closed and out of commission. She sank into his embrace, feeling appreciated for the first time since she'd arrived in New Hampshire. When one of Roger's hands began to unbutton her coat, she pulled away. "Don't." She stared out of her side of the car.

"I had no idea how lonely I was."

Roger took her hand.

"I've wanted to kiss you for months."

"Roger don't say that. What about Bobbie?"

"When I married Bobbie, I was in love with her. She was my life. But over the years she lost her love for God, and for me. Twenty years and we've lost respect for each other, and we've devolved into a holding pattern these days. When she flirts with others – Oh, I see her - she needs to be reassured she's still a knockout – it hurts, but I keep thinking that one day she'll come back to me. I'm afraid she thinks I'm stodgy because I don't keep up with her drinking."

Moira paused, then said, "I hope she finds what she's looking for and that she comes back, Roger. I have tons of fun with you and you've been a good friend." A flash of desire ran through her body as she remembered the kiss. She shivered. The kiss was all the more satisfying that it came from Roger, the husband of Bobbie with her ongoing little slights against Moira as the school year progressed. Revenge was a dish best served cold. Who said that? No. No. Moira took a deep breath. "Roger you're married, and besides, we live in a fishbowl. Think what a scandal we'd create, and for what? A few moments of pleasure that wouldn't last."

"But think of the pleasure. And it's more than pleasure for me. I'm lonely too."

"Don't say anything more, Roger. Please don't." They sat in the car, the motor running, and gazed out at the driveway, now white with snow. Thick snowflakes sparkled in the headlights in the black night. When a light went out in the upstairs window of Roger's house, Moira woke out of her reverie.

She roused herself. "So. We are going to remain good friends?"

Roger waited a long time to reply. "You're one classy lady, you know that?"

During rehearsals for the Spring play, *Our Town*, Moira and Roger pretended they were not attracted to each other, a tactic that only intensified their lust. Then one night after the kids had left the building, she told Roger, "I'm going to look for a shawl for Jessica in the prop room." Roger followed her in and pinned her against a pile of burlap in the corner, where he proceeded to kiss her neck, her forehead, the other side of her neck, and finally her lips, in slow increments of passion. Gone were all objections – they wanted each other and their need was so intense that they only managed to undo their clothing from the lower parts of their bodies and fall, feet tangled, into a mad joining of their bodies. Afterwards, they knew that there would be many more times that they would, "make the beast with two backs," as Roger put it.

Thereafter, it thrilled Moira when Roger took terrifying chances with a stolen kiss or concealed caress during rehearsals; Moira lived on the edge of excitement, constantly afraid they'd be seen by one of the students. The fat little prompter, Leo Tepper, had an unnerving habit of appearing by her side wherever Moira went, once almost catching her with Roger's hand on her back. Moira skipped the cast party after the last performance, avoiding obvious opportunities for the gossip mill, and realized after a couple of months that she was becoming a tiny bit worn out by the subterfuge. Did she love Roger? No. But did she love their trysts? Yes. During a March faculty meeting, Bobbie proposed that the School assign academic observers for new and second year teachers. Bobbie kept looking at Moira as she spoke in favor of oversight.

In March, Chris called again from New Mexico. This time he begged Moira to stay on the phone, and they had a long talk. Moira had to admit to herself she had missed him. "You know, Chris, I am surrounded by older pseudo-intellectual people. Oh some of them are really smart and well-read, and those are the people I've become friends with. But some of them – help me, Jesus. And the worst ones are the wives who spend half their time gossiping about other faculty people. And God knows who's sleeping with whom. It's incestuous here, I'm telling you."

"Wow — that sounds bad. Can you get away sometimes?"

"Yes, I do, and as I said, there are some nice people here so I shouldn't complain."

Chris said, "I'm coming up to Boston. To work next year. I got a teaching fellowship at MIT."

"Why are you not going to stay in the field?" she asked.

"I have enough data to go for my PhD. So how far is Briar Roughly from Boston?"

"Why do you want to know?" Moira stifled a laugh at her question.

"Come on, Moira. Don't give me a hard time."

"Chris, I can't lie — it's good to hear your voice again." Her voice became serious. "But you hurt me and I am not sure I can trust you."

"Give me a chance, Moira. Let's just leave it that we'll have dinner when I get back, okay? I need to talk to you and I can't do it over the phone."

"Give me a call when you get to town." They hung up. What could it hurt to see him? Her old feelings for Chris had come rushing back when she had heard his voice. She really was desperate for company her own age. But of course, she was still involved with Roger. This could get sticky. At least the semester would end soon. It would be good for both of them when summer vacation arrived. She really needed a break from Roger.

In late April, the snow was still on the ground but sunshine started sneaking into Moira's room before her alarm went off. The School threw a centennial party to celebrate its long history. The party took place one Sunday evening in the cavernous field house that held the more than two hundred faculty members, Trustees, spouses, significant others and School administrators. It was a feast: open bar, shrimp cocktail, oysters, aged cheddar and brie, a pasta station with Bolognese, marinara and carbonara sauces, a carving station with beef and turkey, and one table laden with petit fours, crème brûlée and tiramisu. Moira arrived late to avoid the forced gaiety of the long cocktail hour. She negotiated her way through the crowds, looking for the bar and finally found an area where they were dolling out the drinks. "What'll you have, Moira," asked a Science teacher and junior varsity soccer coach who stood in line ahead of her. "White wine, please, Jerry." She noted that some people were sitting in the bleacher, eating, plates balanced on knees, wine cups tucked by their feet.

Moira looked for Roger. She moved on to the carving station, took a plate of food, and with her wine in hand, plate and silverware in the other, climbed up a few tiers of the nearest bleacher and settled down to eat. She saw the animated, well-dressed groups below as if she were watching TV with the sound turned off. You didn't need to hear what they were saying if you knew the people. There was Allen Fisher over by the pasta table shamelessly vamping one of the male servers; Dalton commanded the area by the dessert table, holding court. Bobbie wearing a lime-colored linen summer dress with three men at her side, laughing, her head thrown back. Moira finished her dinner and left her purse and jacket at her place on the bleachers to go to the dessert table. En route she chatted with Dalton and then had a few words with Allen who swam through the crowd toward her, a silly smile on his face. "Did you catch that dreamboat at the linguini station?"

"Hey, I'm telling Roy on you."

"Just don't let Roy get to him before me, Sweetheart."

The party had reached its loudest, most raucous stage.

She got back to her bleacher seat just as Roger appeared. "There you are! I was looking for you," he said. She gave him a brilliant smile. They sat down together. Roger cut himself a hefty bite of roast beef and took a swig of wine and Moira caught a whiff of his aftershave, or was it cologne? She noted the junipery minty freshness as if he came straight from the evergreen forests that surrounded the School. She had already started taking afternoon walks in the shady trails. She said, "Did you see Allen? He's invited me to join him in Provence this summer. Allen and his partner, Roy, are renting a villa."

Roger stopped smiling. "Moira, we haven't talked about this, but how are we going to get through the summer without seeing each other? And by the way, why would you go to France?"

"Why wouldn't I?"

"Of course, of course. You have to have your plans. But Moira, we have to be able to see each other some time this summer. You in France, and Bobbie and me at Bobbie's parents' place on Lake Winnipesaukee – how is that going to work?"

"What's the matter? You sound bitter just now, as if something's wrong."

"Well, I'll miss you." Roger put down his sandwich, chewing.

"And something else.," he continued. "Nothing that hasn't happened to me before." Ping went Moira's warning system. What did he mean? What was he going to say? "But if you want to know, there's a rumor going around, my dear wife has brought to my attention, that says you and I are having an affair."

Moira sat upright. "Who would believe it? You're the Chaplain and theoretically, you're a good boy."

"Yeah, you'd think that they'd know I was a good boy. But there's talk. Don't get upset, but Cathy Gardner saw us leaving the auditorium a couple of weeks ago and drew her own conclusions. I told Bobbie she was wrong, but she doesn't believe me."

Roger took another bite. When his face turned red, Moira thought he was angry. She turned away while she tried to think of something to say.

Roger pawed at her arm and Moira looked at him, annoyed. Then she did a double take. Roger eyes were popping and he didn't seem to be breathing. She panicked. She needed someone to help. Who could help? She stood up on her bleacher seat and scanned the crowd. No one she knew. Her eyes moved across the scene which predictably had gone into slow motion: people taking sips of drinks, laughing soundlessly, a movie full of strangers playing out in exquisite detail across a far away field.

Roger began clawing at his throat, dumping his plate of food, drink and napkin on the floor at his side. Moira came out of her trance. She'd taken first aid as a life guard in high school. The Heimlich Maneuver. She climbed around behind Roger and straddled him with her knees. She put her arms around his waist and tried to remember. Center your fist over his belly button. Where was his belly button? The voice of her instructor came back to her. "The belly button in men is usually at the belt buckle." Her hands found Roger's buckle. She braced herself and remembered again the instructor's words. "Don't hesitate, don't take a practice shot. Give it all you've got the first time. Commit."

She made a fist of her right hand and placed her left hand over her right hand and took a deep breath, then drove her fist into his solar plexus. It didn't work. Roger still wasn't breathing. Again. With all her strength, she drove her fist deep. Out flew a piece of meat, arcing up over the head of the woman sitting in front. Roger gasped, inhaled, then breathed out. He was going to be okay. He fell back into her lap until his weight toppled them both over sideways where they wound up partially wedged between the bleacher seats and planks.

A plump member of the Mathematics Department who had been sitting behind them lifted Roger back to his place as Moira climbed back to her seat.

"Roger, shall I get a doctor?" the plump woman asked.

"Dorothea, I'm fine. No, thanks anyway. Just a piece of meat stuck in my windpipe."

Roger settled himself, staring straight ahead. Moira said quietly, "You okay?"

"Yeah, thanks. That was awful. I'm so embarrassed." His face was gray.

"You just choked. Could happen to anyone…. Here, take a drink of wine. It's all I have." She laughed. Roger took a small sip and his color began to return to normal.

Several people who had witnessed the event offered help.

"I'm fine, fine," said Roger, waving them all away.

When they were alone, he said, 'Now I owe you my life."

"Let's not get dramatic about this."

"No, I do owe you my life. I'll never forget you." He looked at her with complete trust, and Moira's warning bell rang again, loud. She would make sure to get away this summer. She'd take Allen up on his offer of a week in France, then spend time in Michigan of course.

"Roger, I won't forget you, either." She decided she would not ask him what he meant by "this has happened to me before." She knew.

Roger said softly, "I want so much to make love to you right now. I know I can't touch you, but just imagine if I were touching you, where I'd be touching you, and what I'd be saying."

Bobbie came rushing up. "You're all right! Jerry Pritchard came and got me. What on earth did you eat?"

The following Thursday, one of those days when it's going to rain all day, when the only thing to do is to stay inside with a cup of cocoa and a good book, Moira sat in the armchair she had stolen from the prop room. The phone rang. All the kids had left the dorms for the summer and Moira had finished her paperwork. She just had to drop off her grades at the main office along with the comments she'd completed the week before. She'd be through for the school year.

"Hello?" It was Roger.

"I need to see you. Meet me at the 7-Eleven®."

"Roger, its raining buckets."

"I need to talk to you and I can't do this over the phone."

"Okay." She sighed. She had to drop off the grades anyway at the main office. She could swing over to the 7-Eleven® en route. "I'll be there in twenty minutes."

As she drove, her heart was thumping. What was up with him? She was looking forward to the break from Roger – it had been going on too long. The windshield wipers moved in harsh swipes across the smeared glass, giving everything outside a blurry, patchy look. She was cold; why hadn't she worn something warmer under her slicker? She pulled up to the store and Roger bounded out to meet her. She got out of the car.

"Roger, what's so important that we have to meet like this?"

He pulled her out of sight of the road, and kissed her.

"Oh, I desperately needed to see you, Moira."

"I'm glad to see you too, Roger." Roger wore jeans under his parka, and flip flops. He hadn't shaved.

"You look awful. What's wrong?"

"Please listen to me. I'm leaving Bobbie. She's not happy but I've made up my mind. I'm going to start over. I'm leaving the ministry and going to Alaska where they need people like me who care about the environment, who can teach, who want to make a difference." A cold fear stole over Moira as he talked. The rain poured down on Roger's head, parting his hair into thin greasy clumps. His eyelids were red. As he talked, the rain ran in rivulets down his face.

"I'd like you to go with me. Will you marry me?"

Moira saw the gray in his whiskered jaw and the creases that lined his face; she imagined him wearing bedroom slippers. He was old. She searched for the words that would assuage her guilt for trifling with him as a small horror invaded, the realization that Roger would think of making their relationship permanent.

"Oh Roger. I can't. I'm so sorry." His face fell.

The rain beat down on them both, an accusing patter of heavy drops that did not hide his tears.

Somehow she made it back to her room where she sat for a long while in her easy chair. How had she been so selfish as to think she could play with this older man? He was halfway through his life. She was just beginning hers. Surely he understood….

Many years later, that moment in the 7-Eleven® parking lot coalesced into something almost solid, like silly putty, a lump that dwelled in her attic of memories, occasionally popping out when one of the old gossips of the faculty pried open the door. Dorothea (of the choking incident) waited for Moira one afternoon after an all-school faculty meeting. Moira had joined the senior ranks of the teacher-snobs by then and Bobbie had also stayed on at Briar Roughly until recently she was asked to leave the school, rumor had it for her advanced alcoholism. Dorothea, a casual friend (now twenty pounds heavier than she had been at the centennial party), pulled Moira aside as she left Randolph Hall. "Moira, do you remember that poor Roger Pettibone, the Chaplain?" They stood by the door as other streamed by, heading to their evening cocktails.

Moira shifted her shoulder bag, keeping her expression neutral. "Yes, of course I remember him. I believe he went to Alaska?"

"It was in the *Globe*. He drowned."

Moira gasped. Dorothea's face settled with satisfaction.

"He'd been documenting the effects of climate warming on the polar bears and apparently vanished in the Arctic Circle. They think he drowned."

"I'm sorry to hear that, Dot. He was a nice man."

Dorothea continued talking, watching for Moira's reaction. "His widow, one of the researchers, will publish his work."

His widow, Moira thought. His widow. So Roger had married again. Something opened up and took wing, leaving Moira relaxed and happy. She put out her hand and touched Dorothea's arm.

"Thanks for the news, Dot. I'm sorry he's gone but glad his work …" She looked at her watch. "Oh, excuse me, Dot, Chris is waiting for me. Big date!" And she winked.

It's a Living

Lorraine entered the conference room. A few men appraised her as she walked by – thirty-eight, attractive, well-groomed, nice figure, a bit hardened in the face. Career Woman, not an easy mark. Habituated to ignoring men in a meeting like this, she sat and poured herself a glass of ice water from the metal pitcher. Her thoughts were about the conversation she'd had in her hotel room with her husband back home. He worked for an NGO that brought food to hungry children in Africa and spent much of his time lobbying corrupt leaders. "You go kick butt, Honey. The kids are fine…. And if you just can't handle the corporate politics, well, you can always look for another job." Sure. As if she could find another job that paid as well. Another job that would come with so many perks and benefits. Like the stock options her former manager, Richard, had doled out at the end of the fiscal year. And the travel. She could spend a week with her husband in St. Johns, first class, on the travel miles she earned in a few months and still have miles leftover. She and her husband were growing used to the money she brought in, but she sometimes wondered. Was it the money or did she like being away from cooking and cleaning? And while her husband talked of the good he did every day in his job, she had to admit to herself that she was not really doing good for anybody except perhaps other workers who benefited from her salary-bias corrections during salary planning times.

"And how's the HR Manager today?" A red-haired man in an orange and black Daffy Duck tie sat down next to her. Oh great, she thought, just who I don't need to see. He'd been the first to brown nose his way into the new VP's inner circle. "Hello, Jamie," Lorraine replied tepidly. He was a real piece of work. Yesterday he'd taken credit for Shirley's work on the Putnam project, butting in to answer the questions people were asking Shirley about the progress as if he, and not Shirley, were the senior member of the team. It had been difficult to watch and listen in silence as Shirley had let Jamie take over the meeting. But what was worse was Jamie's veiled hints at bonus money when the time came for her recommendations to the senior managers for the new Performance Management system.

They'd run into each other at the bar the previous night. "How about one more nightcap?" Jamie had said. "Hi Jamie. Thanks but I'm about ready to get to bed." She was tired from the air travel that had been required for this meeting. He said, "Hey, Lorraine. Before you go, what's your thinking about the Performance Management system we're going to get?"

"I'm pretty impressed with Collie Corporation. It's user-friendly and I liked its bias-checking formulas. I've already hinted to them I'll probably pick Collie."

Jamie clamped his lips as if in pain. "Oh, I'm sure it's a good program and all that. But listen." His bourbon breath mingled with his cologne. "I'm gonna tell you – Dan wants Villareal. I heard him talk on the phone after last week's status meeting. I think between you and me he's buds with the Villareal's CEO but you didn't hear it from me." Villareal was way more expensive than Collie. What was going on? Lorraine said, climbing off the bar stool, "I looked at it but really, Jamie, it's not as good a program."

Jamie shrugged and put on an innocent face. "There may be some kind of bonus if you find you can live with Villareal. Just sayin'."

Oh, so there was pressure here. Lorraine left the bar in disgust but en route to her room and to her own amazement, she wondered what kind of bonus was he talking about? She hated herself for even thinking about it. That night she mentioned the conversation with her husband. "I'm surprised you'd even think about this, Lorraine. That's not you at all."

"Maybe not, but do you remember when I refused to hire Clem's friend back when I was Project Manager in Tewksbury? That friend was nice enough but she had no credentials. Clem pressured me over a few weeks, I kept refusing on principle, and about three months later, he transferred me to the lower pay category, different site. Remember that? It almost killed me. When I went to HR to complain, that bastard backed Clem." The demotion still hurt although she'd moved way beyond by landing the job in HR that eventually led to her current job. Could she live with Villareal? Maybe....

Lorraine took a sip of ice water. She asked herself, "Why am I here?" I should have been an English teacher, her major in college. But she had gone where the money was. She told herself that she did make a contribution. HR personnel were never highly valued by the inmates, yet everyone accepted that the company needed the pre-screening of new hires, the salary bias-adjustments, the arbiter of quarrels, and her favorite, the keeper of ethics and rules. Periodically she sent websites to senior managers with required viewing on ethical decision making. No gifts over $50, for example. Yeah.

At exactly 8:30 the new VP, Dan Bernard, strode in, followed by the pretty assistant he'd brought with him. The assistant instantly assumed a serious expression and sat down, back straight, long legs folded in sharp angles under her chair. Lorraine studied her outfit. Short skirt, jacket, fashionable high-heeled shoes. Her legs were thin and slightly bowed, but over all a good-looking woman. And great hair. The assistant had pulled back her brunette mane into an upswept, Dorothy-in-Kansas pony tail that didn't match the cool expression in her eyes. Lorraine had seen the assistant earlier in Dan's office when she had gone in to pick up the Fed Ex package she would use later for her own presentation. The assistant had been in conversation in the far corner office, sitting forward in the same attentive pose. Lorraine said to herself with a certain unkind but satisfactory venom that she hoped the woman was making a lot of money since for all anyone knew, the assistant might be sleeping with the new VP. Evil thought. And then came this thought: And even if she weren't sleeping with him, how could she toady to his every whim? Lorraine had become more and more cynical of the tricky political environment at the more senior levels of management.

The new VP waited for the audience to come to attention. He folded his short arms over a pear-shaped stomach, his small hands folded like those of a Russian nesting doll. She'd already had a run-in with him. During his first month he'd cancelled the sexual harassment training that had been mandatory and had failed to agree when Lorraine pointed out why the training saved the company millions in lawsuits. He'd even insulted her obliquely by stating, "There's no need for training in our department. It's a waste of time and money."

When the lights dimmed and the slide show leaped to the big screen, the VP began to talk and pace in front of the projector, casting a huge shadow as he walked to and fro. The tassels on his loafers bounced as he walked. He began by tracing his rise to power. He claimed that his predecessors "had neat jewelry and shit" and that he wanted to "be like them when he grew up." A few guffaws came from the audience at that one. Lorraine took notes, feeling compelled to record his boorish statements so that she and Shirley, the senior finance manager, could laugh about him later on. Shirley didn't like this new VP either and felt the business was going to suffer under his Little Napoleon-style rule. Lorraine lost interest in the VP's boasting and her thoughts drifted. She'd heard these clichés before.

"... We're selling some magic here, like I said. We can get this company going again, and would not have the profit without you people so thank you very much, okay?"

Lorraine winked across the table at Shirley. The senior managers' use of poor grammar and slang had amazed Lorraine when she was new to corporate culture. But after fourteen years with the IT company, Lorraine understood grammar mattered little to people whose only focus was on the bottom line. Sighing, she took up her pen again, capturing the forecast numbers against the current year's budget.

The numbers were important; the new VP spent time explaining them, rapidly firing out comparisons and points of interest. Lorraine had been busy processing all the changes in personnel in the recent reorganization. Corporate money was like play money to Lorraine, the amounts were so enormous. Not that she was careless with the company's money. She had been mostly honest in her transactions, engaging and negotiating business partners with integrity and she always provided meticulous travel accounting. Yet over the years she had learned that everybody charged expensive meals and big rental cars. Today for example she would pull out her corporate credit card and charge to the company the exorbitant Xeroxing fees the hotel imposed if the Fed Ex of materials didn't make it to the meeting on time. Group dinners at conferences such as this went into the thousands.

"We're not mainframe guys.... and gals, okay?" said the new VP, remembering the three women in the room. He had hired males - his cronies - who had come up through the ranks with him, his assistant being the lone female. Lorraine's former boss, Richard, had been a casualty of the reorg, a fact that Lorraine resented. Richard had been the best boss she had ever had for the simple fact that he had shown courtesy and consideration to his staff. He had acted out of genuine kindness coupled with an ability to make his vast group of underlings, all the way down the management levels, feel as if they counted. This quality was so unusual that she had bonded to Richard and considered him a mentor. When Richard lost the power play last summer, Lorraine lost some of her faith in the company.

Then the VP said that he had had to "take out" some of the players. He meant Richard. Lorraine could hardly hide her disgust when he looked her way. The VP's voice was low and monotonous, spoken at rapid-fire pace. Lorraine thought the fast delivery was an important element of his rise to power. She had read somewhere that people who talk fast gain more respect than slow talkers.

"Before I took over, we never made a profit, okay?" said the VP, peering at his audience. "While I was in Europe, bad deals were happening. In the time I took over, we grew from a minus two percent to a profitable eight percent, okay? I created a horizontal value chain and it was a winner with the executive committee. People hate change, but finally I was able to put it together…"

The darkened conference room was a cocoon – warm and soothing with the constant whoosh of the gentle air conditioning (they were in Miami after all) and the VP's voice was lulling, soporific. Lorraine's thoughts drifted again. It was common knowledge that this guy had nudged his way into favor by discrediting Richard with the senior VP (there were many VPs) – details not known. Lorraine knew that there had been questionable ethics involved in the takeover of Richard's job.

The VP continued to talk on and on and his words blurred together. He started to look porcine. Definitely piggy. VPig. He was well-dressed with pink jowels and short, cloven-hooved forelegs. Porky Pig. Lorraine, her mind whirling, raised her hand with difficulty because her arm was so heavy. "Excuse me, Mr. Pig, but why did you just say you built up the business when everybody knows Richard Meyer did it?" Why was she talking? She knew she was throwing away her job but she couldn't control her mouth.

Heads swiveled. Mr. Pig said, "Excuse me? What did you say?"

Lorraine said slowly, clearly, "Why did you just say you built up the business when everybody knows Richard Meyer did it?" Silence in the room, the stillness of a wax museum. Lorraine was watching herself perform and noted she was wearing the same high heels as the pretty assistant.

"You know, you are almost right. Richard did build the business up. I have to say you caught me by surprise by bringing it up. But yes, I had help. Richard was a fine manager. It was just that there are things that happened that meant that Richard had to leave the company. Reasons I'm not at liberty to disclose, okay?"

Lorraine put together her papers and put them into her briefcase. She rose from her seat and walked around the table. She picked up the end of Mr. Pig's tie, looking him in the eye. She flipped the tie in his face. Gasps all around. She was walking on air, feeling proud. She left the conference room in her special shoes, flying low through the front doors of the hotel and into the parking lot like Wonder Woman, leaving behind all the little people in the room. Her car rose up into the air over the treetops and buildings that grew small and distant. She flew toward the sun.

Her elbow slipped and she woke up. The meeting was breaking up and the lights were on. Jamie of the Daffy Duck tie stood up and said "Well, Young Lady, good thing you didn't fall over, ha- ha. Oh I saw you snoozing.…. I know – it was pretty boring." He gathered up his papers. "Catch ya' this afternoon." He started to leave then turned. "Oh, hey. Dan sent me a resume he'd like you to look over for the Project Manager position we're interviewing for. Fred doesn't have much experience, but he's a friend of Dan's and Dan said he could vouch for Fred's strong work ethic. He'd be a great member of the team. Do you think you can fit him in?" Lorraine had already chosen the candidate she would recommend – a young woman with exactly the kind of credentials that would fit the job. With a sick sense, she knew she'd have to hire the VP's candidate over the qualified woman. There was too much political capital at stake to object. "Sure. Send it over."

Lorraine gathered up her notebook and pen. It's a living, she said to herself. That's what Bugs Bunny always said. It's a living. When Bugs ended up capitulating to get the carrot, he'd say that. It's a living, with a shrug of his thin shoulders.

As Lorraine made her way to the cafeteria, she couldn't stop thinking. She'd never dreamed she would rise so high in this company and yet she wondered. Are there layers of corruption, some worse than others? Where was she on the corruption ladder? Low? Medium? Or did her work have nothing to do with ethics? Was it all just business? Just a living?

She stopped.

"Hey, Jamie." She spotted him by the elevator en route to the cafeteria.

"Yeah, what's up?"

"About that friend of Dan's. I've thought it over. No dice. First of all, the candidate I have in mind is super qualified. Second, she's female. And Native American. I get to kill one bird with two stones. And the main thing is she's best for the job."

Jamie entered the elevator and as the doors closed called out, "It's your funeral."

Lorraine went looking for the VP in the Bay Room Restaurant. He sat in a corner with his pretty assistant. Bugs Bunny once defeated the Crusher in a wrestling match. He didn't always give up with just, "It's a living." She squared her shoulders and walked over.

"Hi Dan. Hi Maggie. Dan, sorry to bother you but Jamie mentioned you had a candidate for that Project Management job? I'm sure your candidate is worthy, but I've already decided on a very qualified candidate."

"Oh, and who is that?" Dan frowned.

"You'll like this. She's super qualified technically and she's Native American. Female, non-white. Great for our statistics with Corporate next month, since we've been in the doghouse over minority hiring."

"Well, I... I guess you make a good point." He was still frowning.

"And another thing, Dan. I have already decided on going with the Collie system and not the Villareal. Just a reminder that Villeal is hugely more expensive and Collie handles bias the best I've ever seen."

"We'll have to talk about these decisions later – and would you excuse me? We're eating right now..." He turned to his assistant. "Maggie, make a note to set up some time with Lorraine next week."

Lorraine said, "I know I am being rude to interrupt you and I apologize. I just thought maybe someone might be pressuring you to go with Villareal and I wanted to be there for you with all the backup you'd need if anybody pushes you." She smiled and backed away. "Enjoy that sandwich – it looks delicious."

As she walked out of the restaurant and toward the elevator, Lorraine's knees were weak, yet she felt good. This was a living she could live with. Even if she lost her job.

She pushed "UP."

MOTHERLY LOVE

The speedometer hit 87 as I shot past the Buick plant in Flint. Driving through the snow-crusted fields, the glare hurt my eyes. I always drove too fast when I came to Michigan; it was as if I went fast, I could get the visit all over with quickly. I loved my mother but I had a busy life back East. My plan was to go straight to the nursing home, spend a few hours, take Mom out to dinner, stay at the Super 8, drive back to Detroit Metro early the next day and be in Boston by 3:00 in the afternoon.

I turned off US 75 toward Midland, en route to Mr. Pleasant. Having grown up in this sleepy little company town I had gone straight to New York after college with $200 dollars in my pocket and a return bus ticket my mother had handed me just before I had boarded. "Now you come right back home if you don't get a job right away, Dear," she'd said. "Yes, Mom, I will," I'd said, comfortable with the lie. Over the years, visits home had dwindled until now, thirty years later, I returned only twice a year.

The pine-studded countryside en route to Mr. Pleasant displayed the hard-times Michigan was experiencing – an occasional convenience store, taxidermist's signs, impoverished little shacks and trailers along the highway. But nearing Mt. Pleasant, the Soaring Eagle Casino rose up like a mythical city. I remembered back when I was growing up that the Chippewas dwelled in the lowest rung of Michigan society, the Indian kids oblivious to my own world of country club dances, National Merit Tests, Oberlin College. I silently congratulated them for their new-found wealth. Strangely, a map appeared recently of all indigenous tribes in America. Nowhere are the Chippewas to be found on that map.

I swung into the parking lot by the side entrance of the Pleasant Woods Home and entered through the side door. It triggered a loud siren when anyone wearing an alarm bracelet left the building. In past visits I had gotten used to the random alarms wailing through the halls. Bleep Bleep Bleep Bleep and a couple of the aides would look at each other then one would take off running.

We had been forced to place both my parents in the home at the same time, a difficult time for my siblings and me. At first I believed the residents to be people whose lives were all used up; people who inhabited barely living bodies. But that was not so. This place was a self-sufficient little microcosm with its share of rebels, cliquey types, connivers, thieves, and sweet and trusting souls. In fact, most of the residents read books, wrote letters, went on excursions and related to the staff as functioning adults. I had to laugh, however, when I learned from one of the nurses that a couple of old women had asked my mother to join their exclusive social group. I'm sure my mother was pleased but she would hardly make much of a contribution, being in the latter stages of Alzheimer's.

I passed the staff smoking lounge and the line-up of laundry carts and entered the corridor that led to the residents' wings. It was 12:30, just past lunchtime. At the end of the corridor ahead of me a figure slumped in a wheelchair, far away and tiny, as if seen from the wrong end of a telescope. I hoped to pass without incident, but as I approached the old woman lifted her head. "Help me! "Help me!" I recoiled and stepped widely to avoid being touched by her outstretched claw. I felt ashamed. Later, I would learn how to treat the demented with kindness.

Ahead of me, people moved across my hallway field of vision as if actors on stage: from the right, a nurse pulled a medications cart; from the left came an aide pushing the wheelchair of an old man. By the nurse's station, two women inched forward in wheelchairs, serenely blocking traffic until an old man walked over and pushed the chairs out of his path, frowning as he unblocked the snarl.

My mother's room was empty, so I headed for the dining room. I wondered if my mother would know me, a question that occurred every time I made the trip. Maybe if she still knew me, I would feel comforted. I peeked in and saw her at a table with three other women, each silently eating. Although they always said at the care conferences that Irene conversed with her table mates, I had never seen evidence of this. All three women were alone in their own worlds. I waited outside the dining hall until she finished, and when she came through the double doors, I stood up, and said "Mom?" In a split second, she broke into a wide smile and said, "Well, Honey! What brings you here? I'm so delighted." My heart relaxed.

"Well, Hi, Honey!" my mother said again, after we hugged. She looked calm and healthy. One thing that Alzheimer's had done for my mother was to erase all the old anxieties and insecurities. Her manners and charm remained and the nurses and caretakers at the home liked her because she was gracious and uncomplaining. In fact, graceful behavior was something my mother had taught herself after surviving a poor and unhappy childhood. She had invented herself so completely in her pre-Alzheimer's days that the Difficult Woman Mother I knew in my adolescence, a woman prone to depression and fits of anger, was gone. Gone was Loving Mother of my childhood. And now, with Alzheimer's, the Gracious Woman Mother had emerged.

I kissed her and we returned to her room. She was dressed in the same dress she had worn the last time I had been in town - four moths earlier - and it was looking as if she had been wearing it every day. They always told me at the care conferences that it was hard to get my mother to change clothes. We did the photo album ritual. The Alzheimer's literature advised using photo albums to help jog the patient's memory. I would settle in the armchair next to the single bed and work through all the pages. I would tell her who the people were. The photos spanned my mother's life from early childhood through her sixty-second wedding anniversary. Her husband and my father, Roy, had died a year earlier but she never remembered that fact. She would often refer to "Daddy" in the present tense during our conversations. At first everyone had corrected her when she forgot he had died, but she kept looking up horrified, saying "What do you mean, he's dead? Daddy? Daddy's dead?" so we learned quickly not to remind her. I became very good at dodging the truth. I followed a personal code of never lying to her, and soon saw how easy it was to divert her attention with a question or a comment. Even first-born son, Phil, was gone from her mind, although she thought his photos looked familiar. She laughed at her own silliness when I told her who he was.

In later visits she would refer to her own childhood family in the present tense, as if she still lived in Montana with her father, the town sheriff, in the early 1900's. She'd say, "Dad probably bought me that," as she leafed through the album. It was clear that my mother lived in a zen-state these days, a perfect nowness with the world. For her there was no future and not much past, and she had found the tranquility that had eluded her in her mature years.

I insisted she change her dress to go out to dinner. She'd always cared about her appearance, and yet with the vanity of certain handsome people, she never gave herself enough time to get ready, counting on the forgiveness of others who had to wait for her. I remembered how the family prepared for church when I was young. We would sit conversing at the breakfast table until someone noticed the time. Everyone flew into a panic. We girls put the breakfast dishes into the sink and rummaged in the closet for hats. Our mother began to fly through the house, becoming angry, looking for a lost glove or standing in the bathroom before the big mirror, finishing her makeup and barking orders through the door. "Ohhh, where IS that choir robe? Roy, would you please go to the laundry room and bring me my choir robe?" She'd fuss with her hair and mutter, "Where is that man?" He'd have been in the car by then, engine running. "You girls get into the car. I'll be out in a minute." My father would drop my mother at the church before parking, and she'd rush to catch up with the choir through the back door. Our family then filed into a pew maybe during the processional hymn but sometimes well into the First Reading. After church she was always calm and serene.

My mother returned from the bathroom and said "Okay, Honey. I'm ready." Her breath was foul, so I put her back in the bathroom using words she'd use with me so long ago. "Here's your toothbrush. We need to get those pearly whites clean before we can go out to dinner." The nurses had told me she resisted oral hygiene and I'm sure they probably had given up. She also had a problem with staying clean after urinating, which I didn't know at first. But that afternoon when we drove to pick up the $600 custom-made orthopedic shoes we'd ordered for her, I learned in a hurry. My mother had sat down in the store, ready to try on the shoes, and in the act of sitting, she released an appalling, ammonial odor. The salesman knelt in front of her as I quietly told her to keep her knees together. The kindly salesman took minutes fitting her feet into the kid glove leather oxfords. He talked and joked in his mid-west flat twang, showing the unrelenting friendliness of Michiganders. I sat stiffly, afraid to move myself as if I, too, might release an odor. My mother blissfully and cheerfully helped him with his measurements. He finally finished the fussing and we were allowed to leave. When we returned to the nursing home, I went straight to the nurse's station and asked to speak to the head nurse. Could they bathe my mother? Right now?

Although the aides were busy getting the residents ready for lunch, Linda, the head nurse, heard something in my tone. Soon a male and female aide, along with Linda, went with me into my mother's room. I stood in the doorway, telling my mother I'd return later. I said nothing about her needing a bath. Like lions on a gazelle, the aides attacked, stripping away my mother's clothing. She tried to fight them. When she accepted the futility of resistance, she looked at me across the room with bewilderment, and then with sadness as she recognized my act of betrayal. I said, "Mom, I'll be back in a couple of hours to take you out to dinner." But she did not accept the bribe. She just looked at me with the naked look of the powerless victim, and I saw for the first time the underbelly of the placid life of the nursing home, the complete powerlessness of the patients.

My mind flew back to my early years in our old house. "Sally, go get the ruler." My mother pulled out a chair from the dining room table. I backed away, my fear heightened by the look in her eye. I was sweating. "No, Mom, I just didn't hear you. I would have come home if I could have heard you." I started to cry.

"You know that when I call you, you are to come home. I distinctly heard you playing with the other kids. I had to call and call. Now go get the ruler."

I went into the den and opened the top drawer of my father's desk. There it was, the beige wooden ruler with little strip of metal on one edge. I picked it up, trying not to think about what was coming, and hurried back to my mother, my fear growing with each second, desperately trying to think of a way out.

"Mom, I didn't hear you." I wiped my nose and tears with my hand.

"Now bend over my knee."

And she spanked me. It was a humiliation I could hardly bear. It hurt, but I cried more out of shame. Afterwards there were no hugs, no discussion about right and wrong. I just returned the ruler to the top drawer and went up to my room until dinner, when nothing more was said about the incident.

In my adulthood I had long forgiven my mother for not being perfect. She'd done the best she could and I admired her for her charity work as well as for her wonderful sense of humor. I have friends back in Boston who are still trying to understand their sadistic or narcissistic mothers —I have heard appalling tales over the years. I appreciated that I had been a much-loved child. Yet this memory of being spanked, only one of many times, came down around me like a ghoul whispering "payback, payback." I didn't like myself for it.

The attendants continued to force my mother to undress. I turned away, and as I left, distress and guilt mingled with a pleasurable vindication.

That night, I took her to the nicest restaurant in Mt. Pleasant. She had forgotten my treachery (had even forgotten I was in town and greeted me as a long-lost daughter when I showed up again) and was in good spirits, as always delighted to be with me.

"Mom, what would you like to order" I asked. My mother picked up the menu. She put her index finger upon her upper lip as she scrutinized the menu.

"Well, let's see. I wonder what's good tonight?" she said. "I always love a good steak."

"Well, you can certainly have one, Mom," I said. "They have a couple of them that look nice. There's a filet mignon and I see they have a New York strip sirloin."

"I always say you can't go wrong with a good steak. Good meat. Daddy and I like our meat. You know that, don't you, Honey?"

"Yes, I do, Mom. It's amazing you have lived so long with all the meat and bad stuff you have eaten over the years. Today they are saying that all that cholesterol isn't good for you. Must be heredity. You used to have bacon and eggs practically every day for breakfast too for the last sixty years. Amazing!"

I laughed and she joined in. I was truly astonished at the physical health of my mother. No salads in my childhood but always plenty of beef. I recalled how my mother could take a cheap cut of roast beef, put it into a pan after sizzling it brown on both sides, throw in some onions and vegetables, clamp a lid on it, and shove it into the oven for a few hours. It came out savory, pungent, deliciously moist and tender, and the vegetables managed to keep their shape.

The waitress approached. She had large dark eyes and a dimple in one cheek. "Hi. How are you tonight? Can I get youse something from the bar?"

My mother turned a radiant face to the waitress, smiling with anticipation.

I said, "My mother would like a Manhattan on the rocks. For me, an extra dry martini, straight up, Beefeater gin, and an olive, please."

The waitress moved off to fill the drink orders and I turned back to the menu.

"Mom, they also have salmon. You like that."

"Yes, I do. What are you going to have, Dear?"

"Well, I think I'll have the salmon. And I'm going to start off with a Caesar salad."

"Oh, dear, now what am I going to order?" my mother said, studying the menu again.

"Well, Mom, you always like steak. And, if you're not in the mood, they have Coho salmon. And they have chicken too."

"Why don't you tell me what you are getting?

"I'm going to have the salmon, Mom."

"Oh," Mom glanced down at the menu. "Let's see what looks good. Honey? What are you going to order?"

I looked at my mother. "Mom, I think I'll have the salmon."

The waitress brought our drinks. "Are youse ready to order now?" People in Michigan were so friendly.

"She'll have a filet mignon, medium rare."

Later after she almost finished her banana cream pie and coffee, I drove her to the nursing home and hugged her as we said good bye. As I drove to the Super 8, I knew that by the time I had reached the parking lot, my mother would have forgotten all about my visit.

That night I had a powerful dream. My mother was a young woman standing in the sunshine on the lawn of our old house on Sayre Street. She was holding a garden hose and laughing as she directed the rope of water at somebody unseen in the dream. Was it me? Her dark hair hung long and wavy in the dream, her lean body clothed in slinky harem pants and a polka-dot halter top. Her facial bones defined her beautiful face. She was relaxed, happy, at peace.

PLAYGROUND PEACH

Last week Cynthia cheated on Eliot.

Eliot had gone to Prague on business and yes, Cynthia had missed him. He was a very good catch, this Eliot Goldsand. She knew he'd had a series of lovers before her – they had shared some of their histories on their first date - but somehow she felt that she could keep him amused, primarily because she was so unlike him. She could make him laugh. And he was such a gentleman. She was charmed by his little attentions, his witty, acerbic opinions on practically everything. Eliot was an orderly person, a saint really - predictable, stable - good for her. Under his influence she was now taking vitamins and had begun regular workouts at their club, getting up at 5:30 a.m. just like Eliot. Early to bed; no television. Eliot scheduled meaningful fun things weeks in advance, like hiking the White Mountains or attending a Boston Baroque concert. They often dined out at chi-chi restaurants on fancy meals like lamb *moustaffa* with salads of goat cheese and candied pecans. Her life had gotten so busy once she started dating Eliot, she'd even given up whitewater canoeing so she could go sailing with him on weekends although truth be told, she'd only done the canoeing in the first place to meet men, so everything equaled out. She had also quit her pottery classes to have more free time for Eliot on Saturdays because they sailed in the summer and in the winter they zoomed North in his Lexus for ski weekends at Bretton Woods or Sunday River. Strangely, when Eliot called from Prague to say he had to stay another two weeks in Europe, she discovered she didn't mind at all. She had now time to paint her toes…. work on reducing her thighs…. watch reality programs on television.

One night after work she went to Sears to buy paint for the choir room. Cynthia was now attending church, Eliot's church, and she'd joined the choir. One Sunday after the service, Cynthia stood in the choir room next to Ruth Willowby as they removed their white cottas and long black robes. Ruth was a soprano and first in the social pecking order of choir members but not all that great a singer. Cynthia had heard a distinctive shriek coming from her on the high E during last Sunday's anthem. But it was an all-volunteer choir after all so what's a person to do?

"How are you doing on the refurbishment project, Cynthia?" Ruth asked. Cynthia had volunteered to take it on (before she'd met Eliot when she had lots of free time; now it was something of a drag). At only five feet four, Ruth had a way of crowding into a person's space.

"The first thing I'll do is get the paint. Carl helped me with the measurements."

"Cynthia, don't you think we should try for something warm for the walls, maybe a pink without being pink? I'm thinking pinky beige." Ruth reached for a coat hanger. Until now, Cynthia hadn't realized just how much she disliked Ruth. Cynthia had already decided that taupe was the best color for the room and now here was Ruth horning in. Cynthia paused, her hand on the bottom snap of her black robe, weighing the political fallout of crossing Ruth.

"You're absolutely right, Ruth," "Pinky beige would be great." Cynthia ripped open the snaps of the robe in one brisk motion then stepped out of the robe and reached for her own hanger. "I'll be scouting paint prices tomorrow night. Any suggestions on where I should go?"

"Oh, Cynthia. I meant to tell you." Ruth's voice went low with suppressed excitement. "There's a paint sale at Sears."

Cynthia ate a Big Mac in the car on the way to the mall. Choosing paint was a new experience for someone who dealt with budgets and long-range planning all day. She knew nothing about paint. She found a parking place and walked into the big Sears store. Passing through Men's Wear, she saw tables loaded with cheap ties that Eliot would never touch in a million years. She headed past the bathrobes and down the main hallway looking for Paint. There were many people in Sears, families shopping together, people who acted as if they were on an outing of some sort, husbands pushing strollers, couples holding hands, kids running around as their parents solemnly regarded a stove. Passing Optical and Tools she found Paint near the Pick Up Center in the back. Paint was a large department. There on display were brushes, stirring sticks, masking tape, turpentine and paint thinners. Gallon cans, half pint cans, spray paint cans lined up on multiple tiers of shelving. How could there be so many types of paint? Lacquers, enamels, stains, indoor and outdoor and flat, semi-gloss, and gloss. And that was before you got to the colors.

Cynthia started sorting and jotting down prices. She moved to the color wall where hundreds of fans of color samples hung from little slots. She pulled out a fan: Deer Lodge, Water Fowl, Kitty Hawke, Rushmore, Stone, Bill of Rights. She moved to the right, looking for pinky/beige: Turkish Delight, Peach Fuzz, Tiger Lily, San Antonio Beige. One slot lower she found two possibilities, Wet Sand and Playground Peach. How did they come up with these names? Resisting the urge to gather up a whole armload of fans and just go home, she studied the colors one by one, carefully replacing unsuitable strips in their slots. Eventually she found a good color family: Peachtree Plaza, Scented Candles, King Salmon, Tinsel Town, Popsicle Stick, Playground Peach.

"Excuse me." The salesman was kneeling in the aisle, putting a woolly roller cover back on the shelf. "I wonder if you could help me for a minute."

"Sure. What do you need?" The man stood and turned toward her as he rose. Many men were shorter than Cynthia's height of five feet nine, and she wasn't used to tall men. This man kept rising, passing her on the way up like a god emerging from the sea foam. She caught her breath.

"Well," she said. The man was certainly tall. She suddenly wanted, absurdly, to be protected by this man. He had a not unattractive Prince Valiant haircut and a strong jaw festooned with just enough stubble to be in style.

"I was wondering about the difference between the Sears brand and Dutch Boy. They've both got the right colors but Dutch Boy is more expensive."

She was alone with him in the shiny linoleum aisle, surrounded by high walls of shelving that closed them off into a kind of sanctuary, making their exchange seem intimate and personal.

The man shifted back on his heels. "See, the two brands are essentially the same quality because they're made by the same manufacturer. I know because I used to be a painter before I started working at Sears."

The man's hair is too long. He probably smokes, she was thinking, Blue collar, hates yuppies, drives a truck, votes Republican. Catholic, working class. Out of habit, she checked for a wedding ring on his left hand. None.

He said, "I shouldn't tell you this, though, because I get a better commission if you buy Dutch Boy." He smiled showing even large teeth.

"We wouldn't want you to miss out on your commission, now would we?" she said, giving him her most dazzling smile. His beauty was stunning.

"Oh, that's okay. I do pretty good anyway. And I hate to see people pay more than they need to." he said. "You'd be surprised at the markup they put on this paint. Now you take the Sears Best - that stuff is as good as anything in the store, including Glidden."

She studied him. Her interest was detached, intellectual. Physical beauty in others intrigued her. His shoulders. Broad and muscular. Probably football in high school. Probably hadn't gone to college or why would he be selling paint in Sears? Good teeth. Had a little paunch. Too many beers, too many potato chips, too much television. For a moment, Cynthia felt a rush of contempt. This football player had received his beautiful body by some genetic accident, not through merit of character or achievement. And now, barely out of his twenties, he was squandering it on beer and potato chips!

". . . and so if I were you, I'd go for the Sears Best. It's really just as good and it's on sale right now."

She came back to earth. This man was not only gorgeous, but incredibly, he was nice. He was helping her, giving her real information. Against her better judgment, she trusted him. She liked to be absolutely sure of things in the years since her divorce. When life offered reassurance in small truths, she was pleased.

"I guess I'll buy the Sears Best if you're sure it's going to provide the same coverage and durability," she said primly, wondering if she sounded like some kind of weird librarian or lab tech always stuck in a dark room working with other dweebs.

"Hey, you won't go wrong, believe me" he said.

No, you lovely man, she thought. I do believe you. She took a step forward, drawn to him, as if pulled by a puppet master. Checking herself, she said briskly, "I really appreciate your giving me the real story on this. My budget is tight."

The salesman smiled. "I can relate to that."

He seemed unusually warm for being handsome. Her experience was that good-looking men were never as evolved as the less attractive ones. Kind of a natural law: the better looking, the worse personality. She had known a lot of men in her forty-two years, handsome, plain and downright ugly. She had been married to a handsome man once, many years ago. At first, living with Glover had been like being on an amusing merry-go-round. But the merry-go-round stopped and the music soured. Ultimately she had escaped and reclaimed her life. She'd sworn never to get involved again. Then she started to date but this time she sought only the nerdy types, men who would not steamroller her. Like Eliot, she thought.

What was going on? This guy was just a salesman. And too good looking to be interested in someone like her (she unconsciously recited her defects: angular face, athletic shoulder, brainy). She was happy with Eliot (his defects: chubby face, narrow shoulders, brainy). She had a chance, maybe, to settle down with Eliot. She was involving herself in the community, she was being a good citizen. She was a hospital fund drive volunteer; she was waving to her neighbors. She went to a Tupperware party just last month (she didn't tell Eliot, who would have made a sarcastic remark.)

She turned back to the samples as the handsome salesman spoke to another customer. She tried to imagine each color on the choir room walls, then decided to take some samples and let the choir committee (Ruth) make the final decision.

The salesman was now at the cash register, "I'd hate to make a mistake, even if I'm getting a good bargain here" she said to him, keeping her voice light. "I'm going to take these samples back to the church gang."

She instantly regretted saying "church gang." She was unnerved by this man's good looks and wanted to make a good impression. She felt like a goody-goody in mentioning a church committee for God's sake. Like a teenager she started to babble, to explain.

"You're not going to believe this, but this paint is for a church choir room. I'm on the committee. I don't know why, but it strikes me as pretty silly to be here in Sears buying paint. I'm the last person who should do this," she laughed, feeling happy and amused at herself in the role. She said, "They're very picky, so I don't want to get it wrong."

The paint salesman took in her self-deprecating laughter. Then he laughed too. They were conspirators in a little game, the cool guys vs. the church people.

He said, smiling, "Okay. That's fine. We'll be here when you're ready. What exactly kind of room do you have to paint?" he asked, "I mean, does it have insulation in the ceiling or anything?"

"No, it's actually a basement room, with plaster walls. We're going to do the ceiling too."

"The ceilings are a bitch," he said. "I busted my neck on my last job with that effing ceiling."

"Yes, I know what you mean," she said. "Effing?" she thought. Eliot never said "effing" – he'd *never* say "effing." It had a risque sound, foreign, a word her friends never used. Maybe she'd try it on Eliot some day, just to see if she could pull it off. She said, "Okay. Thanks a lot for your help. I think I've got what I need now. See you later." She started away, then called back, "By the way, how long does the sale last?"

"For you? As long as you need it, Doll."

"Doll?" Her stomach lurched. Ohmygod ohmygod. She cut through Vacuum Cleaners searching for the exit. Passing the Bissells, she thought maybe she'd had a hot flash. She changed her plans; she needed time to think. He'd called her "Doll." She felt a surge of energy and swerved toward the mall in the direction of Lord and Taylor's. She went straight to their shoe department and bought a pair of pumps for more money than she'd ever paid for shoes, then drove home thinking about the paint salesman's big hands with the clean, neatly trimmed nails. She thought about him all the next day. But by the weekend, she had cooled down. Eliot called Saturday night.

"Oh, hi." She said. "I was just raiding the refrigerator for celery and peanut butter."

"What kind of a meal is that?" he asked.

"I'll have you know celery goes really well with J & B on the rocks."

When he said goodbye, he added, "Be good." Her heart lurched. What did he mean by that? No, he couldn't possibly know about her trips to Sears. She wondered what he was doing during his evenings in Prague.

Cynthia was back in Sears with her paint strips the following Monday after work. She looked for her paint guy as a weary middle-aged salesman approached. He was wearing a brown polyester jacket, gray pants and a tie an unnatural shade of aquamarine printed with large tropical flowers. "Can I help ya find somethin'?" he said in a whine. He took in her breasts as he spoke.

"I was helped last week by someone else. He was tall, mid-thirties? Oh, there he is over there. I'll wait for him, thank you." Cynthia had spotted her guy down the aisle, talking to a middle-aged couple.

"Suit yourself."

She wandered around the aisles of paint cans, loitering near the cash register for awhile before Himself finally appeared. He came up quietly, looming larger and handsomer than she remembered.

"Hello," he said.

"Hi. Remember me? I was looking at paint for the church choir room? How are you doing?" He didn't answer. She continued, "I've got the sample picked out.

The salesman looked at her and slowly smiled the sweetest smile she had ever seen.

Then it happened, something shifted inside. Cynthia wanted this man. She wanted his hands on her body. Her desire rose up through an excited, almost sick feeling in her diaphragm. She was the terminus of an invisible river flowing between them - a feeling so radical for Cynthia that her brain became disconnected. She observed, as if perched on a ledge over the store that the man moved around with an economy of effort, gracefully, no wasted motion, like a football player making every second count before he makes the pass. He looked at her obliquely, studying her the way she had studied him a week earlier.

"So you decide on a color?"

"What?"

"Oh." Cynthia rushed with her answer, as if a contestant in a quiz show. "Yes, I'll take the Playground Peach, Number 384. Sears Best. Six cans should do it."

Get a grip! she thought, furious with herself. She felt like the self-conscious teenager she used to be a hundred years ago: too tall, too plain, a girl who never attracted the football players in high school. And here was a football player standing in front of her, acting friendly.

Oh, no. Hold it! she told herself. He's a salesman, remember? He's not a football player. You're projecting. You have some unresolved issues to imagine this man a football player. Grow up. He's just a paint sales guy. The other part of her was saying, The hell he is! Hang on to this, woman! This man, this god, this football player, at long last, is interested in you! Take it and run!

He mixed the paints, consulting a card for the formula. They made small talk as the cans shimmied in the claws of the mixing machine in the back room. As they chatted, her inner voices argued. Look! How can you be interested in someone who has to work with a machine like that all day? A machine that makes a racket like an air hammer. The other voice countered. Oh, no, you're wrong. This man is helpful and kind to people. And he's clean. Look at the neat cut of his pleat in those khakis. He's got wonderful shoulders and he's so nice.

She produced her Visa. He rang up the sale on the cash register. Would she like him to carry the cans of paint to her car? That would be so great. She went outside to the parking lot and drove to the customer service entrance. She released the trunk latch and walked around to the back of the car where he stood next to the box of cans on the sidewalk. He hoisted the box into the open trunk. She watched the muscles move under the smooth skin of his arms. Those beautiful hands again. He carefully closed the trunk.

They stood there, silent. Cynthia fingered the sterling pin on the collar of her new navy coat. Now what? She could think of nothing clever to say. She walked toward the driver's side of the car and got in. She slammed the door and immediately rolled down the window. She said, "Good bye and thanks!"

She pulled away and he called out, "When am I going to see you again?"

"I don't know," she answered in a sing song voice, dissociating. She drove away fast.

When Eliot called that night she was in her kitchen planning their Christmas open house. Eliot said his project was going well. He'd had time to get to a concert - Schubert's "Trout" Quintet. After Eliot hung up, Cynthia sat there, motionless, her "Silver Palate" cookbook open to 'Hors d'ouvre.' She looked at what she had written down: "Gruyere asparagus tarts," "Strasbourg paté," "Tangiers couscous salad," "Good brie." She thought about the paint guy's narrow hips, big hands, broad shoulders and his Prince Valiant haircut.

The next morning she called Sears and asked for Paint.

*　　*　　*

Greg was in the stock room when Cynthia called. He wanted to impress Fardino so he could get a promotion and make more money. It wasn't hard to do a good job since he used to be a house painter. A moron could do well if he just worked hard and sucked up to the big bosses.

He walked onto the floor toward his boss. "Mr. Fardino, what do you think of the new arrangement over here?" he asked. Greg had taken the initiative and re-arranged a corner display to show some overstocked Glidden's latex indoor-outdoor to more advantage.

"I noticed." said Mr. Fardino. "Sorry, but you gotta put it back. We gotta keep the Glidden all together. I thought you knew that. I don't want ya doin' nothin' like that again without checkin' with me." Mr. Fardino was forty-nine and looked sixty. He had a beak nose, black bushy eyebrows and a gaunt, hunted look. He had been with Sears for thirty years and was just promoted to manager of the paint department last year.

"Oh," said Greg. "Sorry about that. I was just trying to get more mileage out of that Glidden. That's where the bucks are."

"I know, I know." He sighed. "But Mr. Thomas didn't tell us to move no paint

Greg was ringing up a sale when Cynthia's phone call came. "Paint Department," Greg sang out, hitting the TOTAL key on the register pad.

"Hi. Is this the man who helped me buy paint last night? I was in last night buying paint for the church choir."

"Yeah, I'm the one." Greg said, smiling to himself. Bingo! She called! "Would you hold on for just a minute please?"

Greg put down the phone, took cash from his customer, bagged the Zip-Strip paint remover, expertly scooped out the change from the drawer, and handed the bag to the customer. He picked up the phone again. At least Fardino was on his break and wouldn't eavesdrop.

"Well, hello," he said.

"Hi. I am calling to thank you for your help the other night. The choir committee liked the paint. They even liked the color, hooray, especially the tenors, and I just wanted to say thank you. I would not have known what kind of paint to buy. You saved us some money with your advice about the Sears Best."

"Glad I could help," he said.

"Well, it was a rousing success."

Greg was silent.

"Um, I was wondering something." Here it came. The windup. Annnnnnnd the pitch.

"Yes?"

"I wondered if you wanted to have a drink after work."

"That could be arranged. What night?"

"Well, I was thinking about tonight."

"Yeah, that would be all right." Greg said.

"Great. Let's do that. Do you know someplace we could meet?"

"There's a place near here, down the Westminster Turnpike, called the Eldorado. It's next to the Wal Mart. Do you know where I mean?"

"Yes, I think so. Is it near the book store?"

"You got it."

"Well, that's great. What time would you be able to meet?"

"I get out of work at ten. How about ten fifteen?"

"Oh, that's a bit late, isn't it? That's just about my bedtime." She laughed and when Greg didn't respond, continued, "Oh well, what the heck. I guess I can stay up that late."

"Okay." She thinks 10:00 is late? he thought. How old is this broad? "By the way," he said, "What's your name?"

"Oh. It's Cynthia. What's yours?"

"Greg."

"Okay, Greg. Well, hey, maybe we can discuss painting techniques tonight," she said, flirting.

"Yeah," he said. There was an awkward silence. Then he said, "Hey listen… Sorry, but I gotta go now. I have some customers and I'm alone on the floor." He spotted Fardino coming from the direction of the employee's smoking lounge.

"Greg, that's fine. Have a good afternoon and I'll see you tonight."

Greg hung up the phone. So she called him. He had not expected it after she drove away with the paint. Cynthia. Something of a dingbat maybe, he wasn't sure, but not bad on the eyes. He liked the idea of running his hands along those aerobic-hard legs. He had noticed her, the Little Miss Executive suit she was wearing, the expensive perfume. And she had a classy haircut. Not that punk cut his ex-wife Missy wore. He was intrigued - sick and tired of silly broads who spent your money and then started looking for someone new before they finished fucking you. Greg walked over to Mr. Fardino and said, "Mr. Fardino. I'll be in the stockroom if you need me."

Fardino stared. Greg had never volunteered to work in the stockroom. He thought it was a trick. Greg walked away whistling.

*   *   *

"You have beautiful eyes," Cynthia said. They were on their first drink in the darkened room.

He shifted around in his chair to address her, checking to see if she was serious..

"It's funny you say that. I have a glass eye." he said.

She was speechless. He continued.

"It was the result of a hockey accident. In high school. I got a puck in the eye. They couldn't save it."

Later in the conversation, Greg said, "I'm only temporary at Sears. I'm going to save up to buy a restaurant. I'll do the cooking. Italian cooking. I know a bunch of good recipes." Cynthia said, "Oh what a great goal. So you can cook?" "Yeah, I'm pretty good." That smile again. Cynthia felt drawn into a dark cave of emotions, helpless, unwilling to leave. So much exotic stuff swirling around her; glass eye, restaurant, kids, hockey.

They talked for two hours, drinking steadily. She drank martinis, he stayed with beer. She paid the bill. When they went out to the parking lot they were both drunk. He walked her to her car. He put his hands on her arms and she swayed toward him, face uplifted, ready for her kiss. He bent down. She said, "Why don't we find someplace?" He said, "Hey, all in good time, Doll. You gotta work tomorrow; I gotta work tomorrow. Let's wait until Saturday." They looked at each other for a minute and then lunged together. She melted into his body, reveling in the protective cocoon of his arms. The kiss lasted until she started to breathe heavily.

He would come over to her condo the next Saturday and cook his Italian chicken dish for her. He dictated the ingredients to her; she tucked the shopping list into her purse and drove out of the parking lot, hitting the curb with a loud thunk as she turned East.

The car kept making a funny loud noise as she accelerated. It must be a tire, her alcohol-soaked brain concluded. Cynthia's cell phone rang. It was Eliot from Prague.

"Hey! How are you?" he asked.

"Hey, yourself. I'm fine." Cynthia frantically searched for a place to pull over.

"What's up? You sound like you're in your car."

Cynthia's brain shut down momentarily while she maneuvered the car to a stop on the busy road. What to tell him?

"Yeah, well, yes, I'm driving home."

"At this hour? It must be midnight there. I just got up to take a run before my meeting today. Oh before I forget, I am going to have to swing by Thailand before I come home. Or I should say, I have the privilege of going to Thailand while I'm abroad."

"Thailand? Why?" Cynthia caught her breath.

"Oh, the customer wants me to meet someone. I'm kind of excited. I've never been. It will only delay me a couple of days." And then he returned to the real subject as she knew he would. "Now what's this about you driving home at this hour?"

"Well yes, I was shopping."

"The stores close at ten."

"Well, guess what?" Think, Cynthia. Think. Long pause. "I was reading in my car and I fell asleep. I don't know why but that's what happened."

"Reading in your car? What are you talking about? That's crazy. Why would you do that?"

"Well, it's such a good book, I couldn't put it down."

"What book is that?" Think. Think. Okay, she had it.

"Oh it's the new Grisham – I forget the name. It's a keeper though. I'll save it for you when you get home." Cynthia's head was swimming. Those martinis were killers.

"Well, Sweetie. Listen. It doesn't sound good for you to be out on a work night, this late. I'd hustle on home if I were you. Read the book later, okay?"

"Of course, Honey. How is Prague?"

"Oh usual stuff – meetings, big dinners, lots of that crazy dessert called *Palatschinken*- a gorgeous crepe stuffed with strawberries and what they call *schlag* – whipped cream. Mounds of it. Or you can get the crepes with jam or chocolate sauce. All this after a dinner of goose-fat bread, potatoes and gravy and beef. I will be going on a diet big time when I get home."

Cynthia almost gagged. Gotta get that image of goose-fat out of her head. Hold it together. Get off the phone. "Well, that sounds great. I'd better get going now. But you have a great time. Call me from Thailand. I miss you." This last word she drew out, hoping it sounded sincere, making it "yeewwwww." By the time she had called AAA, gotten the spare tire mounted, and had driven home, it was 3:00 a.m.

*   *   *

Cynthia's head ached. That second martini always did it. When would she learn? Even the two aspirins she'd taken hadn't worked. She hobbled out of bed (her left knee was acting up again) and went into the bathroom, looking in the mirror. The woman who looked back had small but definite wrinkles around the eyes. And her hair was gray at the temples again. When was her next hair appointment? She'd have to get one in before the weekend. She picked out the blouse she'd wear with her navy suit and laid it on the bed. So Greg was a hockey player, not a football player. But he was an athlete! Last night she had given in to the fantasy. She had no regrets. She thought about the kiss as she showered. She added a dollop of salon conditioner to her blonde-streaked hair and turned her body under the drizzle of warm water absent-mindedly. He seemed so independent and manly; okay a little childish with that swagger but really, a nice guy. What would it be like to wear a glass eye? She wondered if it hurt. How strange. His eyes spoke to her. Silent depths, she thought. Poetic words came to her: eyes like velvet pools of unconsciousness. She ran a razor over her shins. He had Sparky's eyes. Her last dog, Sparky, a cocker spaniel. He always looked a bit wistful.

So what if one of Greg's eyes was glass? She thought the terrible loss of an eye must have given him psychological depth. Having had so many privileges in her life, she was attracted to those whom she imagined had suffered. She knew that during their coming date he'd open up to her about his tragic life since the accident. She couldn't wait to sympathize.

Cynthia got out of the shower, toweled herself dry and put on a matching bra and panties to celebrate and began putting on her makeup. Greg was truly a hunk. His shoulders were phenomenal. Broad, dense, Michelangelo's David shoulders. She carefully smoothed the liquid rouge – mustn't do too much. Greg was too young for her. She sighed. They were all getting younger - the policemen, the mothers in the supermarket, they all looked like teenagers.

She finished with a careful application of light coral lipstick and grabbed her earrings. Suddenly she felt wonderful. Ain't lust grand! She opened the closet with its jumble of hats, tennis gear, puzzles and games on the top shelf, catching a baseball cape that flew out as she grappled for her coat. The closet she had yet to clean while Eliot was out of town. Yanking out her coat from the thicket, she drove to work and put in a full morning getting rid of two performance reviews and three meetings. At 4:45 she called the salon to change her appointment and worked until 8:00. She left alone, the last one to leave the building.

*   *   *

She greeted him in a silk pantsuit. He wore jeans and a cotton shirt.

After dinner they went into the living room. The drinks were starting to wear off. Cynthia offered Greg a glass of scotch, asking if he took ice. He asked if she had some beer. They sat in her living room in front of the marble fireplace. Cynthia had by now learned that Greg had no conversational skills. He was a man of action. He started moving restlessly around her living room furniture, like a panther, pacing.

Going from one side to another, examining her little tchotchkes, picking them up, appraising them. He paced around as they chatted, and once he turned on the television set, turned to a sports channel, watched for a few minutes, then walked on. She was dumbfounded. She started to believe they would not make love after all. Of course, he had to make the first move. In truth she had started to turn off, now that her own drink was wearing off.

Greg prowled gracefully, dominating the room, relaxed and in control of himself. Was he evaluating the expensively furnished living room as he prowled?

"Do you have any more beer?" he asked.

"Oh, I don't think so. I'm so sorry. I do have scotch and some wine. Would you like some Chardonnay?" He had drunk the only two bottles of Moosehead she had.

"No, I'll survive. So what did you pay for this condo?"

Greg picked up the Mexican sterling letter opener as he passed by the end table, then put it down. He was interested in her money.

"The cheapest sold was in the low $300's; the most expensive was $450," she answered. "I have a great broker who got me a good deal on it." She felt embarrassed at the question and that she had answered him. It was none of his business. Why was she such a patsy?

"Let me have some of that scotch," Greg said. He walked to the kitchen and drank two shots in a row right out of her shot glass. She couldn't help be fascinated with his self-confidence. She was also thrown off her guard by his casual indifference. She wondered if he was being rude or just didn't have good communication skills.

A sudden thought came into her head. Ohmygod. Maybe he was thinking of robbing her. Casing the joint. He'd take what he wanted and she'd be powerless against him. Greg circled back to sterling letter opener. She just hoped he'd leave the Don Quijote carving alone, the one she'd carried back from Spain on her lap. He could have all the silver but not the carving. Maybe he didn't see it sitting on the floor next to the stereo. When he continued to wander around, it occurred to Cynthia that he was playing a game, toying with her. Maybe she was supposed to be doing something. He seemed to be playing hard to get. Or did he want her to make all the moves? She had no idea what to do. At last, Greg clicked off the television set. Cynthia asked, "What are we doing? Do you want to go? It doesn't look as if you want to be here."

Greg turned and approached her. She was sitting on the couch. Without a word he pulled her to her feet and kissed her. So things were going to be all right after all. They weaved together in a sloppy, embrace. Cynthia's fear of rejection melted. She returned his kiss, allowing all her feelings to travel into her arms as she hugged his big body. Suddenly Greg swept her up in his laborer's arms, high, and carried her into the bedroom.

They undressed. She pulled off his boxer shorts and got into bed. He stood still for a moment, facing her, with his back to the moonlight that filtered between the slender slats of the mini-blinds while it spilled past him onto the beige carpet in soft even patterns. At last she knew she was going to be screwed by the football player. Hallelujiah!

He pulled her up in a sitting position and stood over her. The moonlight flowed around him, filling with shadows the curves of his shoulders and thighs. He lifted her up, and she straddled him, her legs around his waist. Gently, carefully, he entered her, moving her up and down, grinding her against him, a piston moving within. She was back at Central High, but instead of making out with a clarinet player in the band she was a cheerleader with her boyfriend the star quarterback; she was the prom queen on the float; she had the cutest boyfriend in the school.

After it was over, they disengaged, holding on to each other gently. They fell into bed and Cynthia curled up under Greg's arm, wanting to feel small. Greg went to sleep instantly. Cynthia remained wakeful for a long time, wondering at herself, at her situation, at her life. She could never tell Eliot. That was one thing that was certain. Eliot could never know. She marveled at how coldly she made the decision without a whiff of shame.

In the morning she awoke first and quietly showered and dressed. By the time Greg stirred, she had read the paper and made coffee. They'd already started to become bored with each other. When he left, no false promises were made by either of them. It was a courteous parting. Cynthia felt relieved when the door closed and she was alone in her condo. Over the next weeks she did pause occasionally to wonder at what she had become. She'd almost put Greg out of her mind once Eliot returned and they took up where they had left off. She needed Eliot to ground her. That was the one certainty in her life.

*   *   *

She was in bed a few weeks later, fast asleep, Eliot at her side, when Greg phoned. It was 1:30 a.m. although she had told him they couldn't continue the phone sex. She said, teeth gritted, "You have the wrong number," and hung up.

Three days later Cynthia arrived at her appointment with Doctor Torney. After she had dressed, she sat facing her doctor across her desk.

"So, Ms. Warren, you have felt this way for over a month now?" The doctor was recently out of residency and young, but she had an intelligent look and a calm, reassuring manner. Dr. Torney's hands were plump and white with tapering fingers. She also had curly auburn hair atop an alabaster, slightly plump face. Botticelli's "Spring." Dr. Torney to a T. Had anybody ever told her that?

Cynthia answered, "Yes, Dr. Torney. I have this burning sensation when I go to the bathroom. When I pee. It's really bad. What's going on? I'm so used to being healthy, I don't know how to deal with this! It's probably just a yeast infection but I thought I better let the expert take over." She laughed.

Dr. Torney didn't smile. She looked steadily at Cynthia. "Ms. Warren, we're going to run some tests. I would like to get some blood work done. I don't want to worry you, but I am going to ask you a question. It has to do with your relationships, with your sexual relationships. Do you have a steady relationship now?"

Cynthia answered, "Yes, I do sleep with a man on a regular basis. We have been together now for about eight months."

"Have you both been tested for the HIV virus?"

"Yes, I was tested the last time I gave blood, which was before I started a serious relationship with Eliot. We agreed to do that before we started sleeping together. I've had no unprotected sex except with Eliot. And he...."

Cynthia stopped. Her eyes caught something white behind the doctor's desk, something she couldn't stop staring at but had no way of interpreting since her brain blocked comprehension. The doctor's words bounced around in her head: "unprotected sex," "unprotected sex." She looked down at her hands. She looked back up at Dr. Torney. Dr. Torney said, with a touch of gentleness, "It may simply be an STD, like chlamydia. We can clear that up with antibiotics."

Cynthia remembered that Greg hadn't used a condom. How stupid of her. What had she been thinking? So much bullshit about sleeping with the football captain. No! It couldn't be Greg who passed along the disease. Could it?

"Are you and your partner in an open relationship? In other words, could your partner possibly have picked this up?"

Cynthia said, 'No, not at all."

Then she remembered Eliot's quick trip to Bangkok. He had said he visited the Buddhist temples but it was a city known for the open availability of prostitutes. Did he…? Had she….?

"Excuse me, Dr. Torney. May I use your bathroom?" Cynthia closed the door behind her and looked into the mirror. She put her hands up to her cheeks and rubbed at her skin. Then she rubbed her eyes and examined the little witch hair (as she called it) on her chin. Then she looked deeply inside her mouth. She left the Dr.'s office, jumped in her car and drove fast, almost running down a man trying to cross the street.

Ruth and the choirmaster were talking one day after church. They always joined the others for the after-service coffee soiree in the Hall. Ruth leaned in and whispered, "Do you have any idea why Cynthia quit?"

The choirmaster answered, "She said something a time crunch. But no, I have no idea. Come to think of it, nobody's seen her at church at all. Too bad. She had a good voice."

Ruth said, picking up a cookie. "At least she got the paint right for the choir room before she left. I like that peachy color, don't you? I told her that peach was just what we needed."

ALL'S FAIR

Wally came to live with the Buchanan family six months before his twenty-seventh birthday, February 15, 1953, two months before he fell for Alicia Buchanan. Being a young man of little experience in the world, he'd been unaware of his feelings until one night when lying in bed, he looked up to see the watery stain on the ceiling in his rented room turn into an outline of Alicia's face with her pale yellow hair. Suddenly he was thinking about the little hollow between Alicia's clavicle and shoulder bone that was visible when she bent to pour him coffee or when she reached over to slap his hand when he was teasing her. In his imagination Alicia was laughing, and then she unbuttoned her blouse. Boy this was getting good.

Briiiiiing! Alicia swirled away into the icy air. It was time for another work day at Dow Chemical Company. Wally padded to the bathroom, the freezing linoleum burning his feet. He shaved with practiced swipes, swishing the razor fast through the hot water in the bowl with flicks of his wrist. He remembered that today was his birthday. He thought about his parents and Bruce back in California. His mom made the best cakes, with her special frosting. She always cooked him his favorite meal when it was his birthday: roast beef, mashed potatoes and peas. He finished with his shower, then dressed, knotting his tie and grabbing his suit coat. He opened the door that led to the Buchanan's kitchen. In three steps he was warm. Steam from the percolator had iced the kitchen windows opaque.

"Morning, Wally. It's seven degrees below out there so dress warm." Mrs. Buchanan set down a blue bowl of oatmeal at his place. She took the milk bottle from the counter and poured the thick yellow cream from the sloping neck into a small pitcher, then some of the milk into another smaller pitcher which she set on the table. "The milk was darn near froze this morning. I felt sorry for the milk man, I can tell ya."

"Morning Mrs. Buchanan. Brrrrrr. Does it always get this cold in Michigan?" The family beagle sat at his feet looking up at him. "Hey Jackie. How do you like the cold?" The dog's tail thumped.

Mrs. Buchanan laughed. "Oh, Honey, this is nothing. Wait 'til the thermometer sticks there for three weeks in a row - you'll know what cold feels like. You better borrow Lyle's boots out in the vestibule - you'll need 'em." Wally went to the vestibule and came back carrying the black rubber galoshes, metal clasps clanking. He looked at them suspiciously. (Mr. Buchanan had already left for work. He was an hourly man, worked in Security.)

"Morning everybody," said Alicia as she pounded down the stairs and swirled around the banister into the kitchen, her Lana Turner haircut shiny and neat. Wally always thought of her as a skinny little dervish, but this morning the buttons on her blouse reminded him of his dream and he felt himself get the familiar tingle in his pants. Damn. He bent down to put the boots on over his shoes.

"Say, Mom, I had a thought. Would it be okay if Wally has dinner with us tonight? It's too cold for him to eat downtown."

Mrs. Buchanan gave Alicia a look and said, "Well, I'm planning to fix some chicken and dumplings. I guess I can buy more chicken today."

"Oh, great – how about it Wally?"

"Oh, I don't want you to go to any trouble." He straightened up to look at Mrs. Buchanan. Alicia said, "It's no trouble at all." She winked at him behind Mrs. Buchanan's back. He blushed.

In 1953, Midland, Michigan was booming. Wally had worked only one year for Shell Oil in Martinez, California, when Dow offered to double his salary if he'd come east to the Metallurgy Department. After explaining to his mother it wasn't going to be forever (although she knew better) he accepted. Wally'd had to look on a map to see where Midland was. A little town in the middle of nowhere in a nowhere state. Since there was a shortage of housing and virtually no apartments in the small town, he'd signed up with the Buchanans. The terms were simple: Wally'd get the den next to the living room with the day bed, access to the downstairs bathroom, and breakfast. He'd get his own lunch in the plant and eat dinner at one of the restaurants on Main Street before he came home

After Wally finished his oatmeal, he bundled up in his new gray herringbone wool overcoat and added fedora, ear muffs, scarf, and mittens. Mrs. Buchanan said, "You'll need an extra sweater." He clumped back to his room, put one on and returned, sweating.

"Bye," said Alicia, waggling her fingers at him behind her coffee cup. "See you tonight." Damn! He was blushing again.

The cold air hit him hard. It was an aggressive cold that sucked up all the oxygen; it hurt to take a breath. He walked down the path Mr. Buchanan kept neatly shoveled, his galoshes squeaking in the thin layer of sparkling Fels Naptha flakes that covered the hard ice. He'd learned how to put each foot straight down, never to walk normally in this kind of weather. When he'd fallen the first time, it seemed as if the ice-covered ground had risen up to knock his head hard. He'd lain to see if he was really hurt or just insulted. Then he scrambled up and made it to the bus stop in a slithering sliding motion barely in time for the 8:15. As the bus pulled up to the main plant, he wondered again why he'd accepted the offer to live in this godforsaken town.

Alicia had time to kill before leaving for work. She put her coffee cup in the sink, planning to write a letter to her grandmother. She was a clerk at Boyd's downtown and didn't have to be there until 8:30. Mrs. Buchanan was scrubbing the oatmeal pan. "Don't you get any ideas about him- you're way too old for him."

Mom, I'm gonna get that guy to take me out."

"Alicia, does he know how old you are?"

"No, and I'm not about to tell him."

"Well you just watch your P's and Q's, young lady, or you're going to get yourself hurt."

That evening Wally stood in line with the dozens of other men shuffling toward the punch clock. Over the musk of overcoats, earmuffs, mufflers, and blocked felt hats wafted a pungent musk of cigarettes, mothballs, and Brylcreem. Wally thought of his brother staying warm out on the coast. Bruce smoked Luckies. He drank too. He was the wild one. Bruce would always give him a joke gift for his birthday, like pinups of Marilyn Monroe or Jane Russell. Oh well, Wally would make it through the day without a fuss about a birthday. His parents had already sent him a check and a card. He was truly grown up now and past the birthday fuss.

When he walked into the kitchen after leaving his coat and galoshes in the den, his mouth watered at the aroma of chicken stewing with carrots, celery, onions and peas.

"May I do anything to help, Mrs. Buchanan?"

"No, Wally, you've had a hard day. Alicia will set the table when she gets here. This is woman's work. Why don't you go in and read the paper until we're ready?"

When Alicia arrived, she looked around. "Where's Wally?" Her mother motioned to the living room. Alicia dumped her coat and boots in the vestibule and carried a shopping bag into the living room. Wally was sitting under the floor lamp with the *Midland Daily News* opened wide before him in imitation of Alicia's father, feeling foolish but afraid to defy Mrs. Buchanan. Alicia sneaked up.

"Ta-da!" She pulled a pink wool Jonathan Logan dress out of her shopping bag. "Twenty-one bucks. A steal. Whadda ya think?"

Wally put down his paper and said, "Nice, Alicia. Did you get it at Boyd's?"

"Yes. Wanna see me in it later on?"

"That'd be great." He had an image of her trying on the dress upstairs before her mirror, barefoot, the cleavage of her small breasts showing above the white nylon edging of her underslip as she prepared to step into the dress. He imagined her neck above her white back; the tunnel of bones along her spine as she bent to step through the unzippered opening.

"Oh, and I got you something for your birthday."

"How'd you know it was my birthday?"

She pulled out a thin box. Wally opened it up. A maroon silk tie nestled in apricot tissue paper.

"Alicia, you shouldn't have done this."

"You told me a few weeks ago, don't you remember, silly? I hope you like it." She lowered her voice. "Don't tell Ma - she'd think I was being forward or something."

Mrs. Buchanan called from the kitchen, "Alicia, come and pour the milk. We're almost ready to sit down." Wally took the tie to his room and returned to the kitchen. Mrs. Buchanan opened the door to the basement and hollered, "Lyle, come on. Dinner's on." When Mr. Buchanan appeared from the basement, his hair flecked with sawdust, he said, "The doghouse is almost done. Then Jackie can sleep outside - we'll just put some straw in there."

"Where is Jackie?" said Mrs. Buchanan. "Oh, there he is." She put her hands on her hips. "You know you're not supposed to be there." The beagle came slinking out from under the kitchen table, his tail wagging. Alicia swooped down, hitched up her skirt and sat on the floor for a tussle with Jackie. Mrs. Buchanan said, "For God's sake, Alicia, get up this minute! We need to have the table set and there you are, wrestling like a boy on the floor."

They ate in the kitchen, the dining table in the living room, always with its thick folding protective covers, white lace tablecloth, reserved for company and Sunday dinners. "Mrs. Boyd is such a fuss-budget," said Alicia as she heaped chicken and dumplings on her plate. "She had me cleaning the jewelry cases, then the display window. I had to crawl past the manikins just to get at the glass and I felt like an idiot. I never got to sit down once the whole damn day."

"Well, you're paid to do whatever she says, so I wouldn't complain. You make a decent salary, and even got a quarter an hour raise last month, "said Mrs. Buchanan, wiping her lips with her napkin.

"Do you know she shaves her arms? They're always so smooth, like a baby's bottom, above those thick-nailed, manicured hands."

"Well, that's great table talk!" said Mrs. Buchanan.

"This is delicious," said Wally. "Sure beats the Chat 'N Chew."

"Their liver and onions aren't bad, but Mom's cooking's best," said Alicia. She took a drink of milk leaving a smear of Tangee lipstick on the rim of the tumbler. "Do you like liver, Wally?" She grinned at him.

"Uh, no, not really."

"Oh, it's good for you with all that iron. Mom makes it with bacon and onions. Dee-lish!"

"No, I've never cared for liver in any form but they do a decent burger at the Chat 'N Chew. Say, any Mexican restaurants around here? I kind of miss those California tacos."

"Mr. Buchanan spoke up. 'No Spicks around here unless you count the migrant workers who come up to pick the apples and harvest the beets over in Bay City."

"Dad! Spick is not a nice word!"

"Well, that's what they are!"

"Dad, you should call them Mexicans, not Spicks. That's really rude."

Mr. Buchanan scowled and his voice took on an edge. "Listen here, young lady, I'll call 'em what I like in my own house and as long as you're under my roof, you'll hold your tongue. You understand?"

Alicia's face reddened and she said, "Excuse us, Lyle. Our family is a bit crude."

"You're too big for your britches, that's what's wrong with you," said Mr. Buchanan. "Miss Hoity-Toity thinks she's better than us because she's had a little education. You don't have to work with the Spicks like I do. You'll keep your opinions to yourself do you hear me?"

"I can't take this." Alicia stood up and stalked upstairs to her room.

"Don't come back 'til you remember where you are."

"She's usually not so high-strung," said Mrs. Buchanan, embarrassed. "She'll get over it."

Wally struggled for something to say. "I'm sure, Mrs. Buchanan." Big mistake, taking this job. The phone rang. Mrs. Buchanan went into the living room to answer it. She came back into the kitchen. "It's for you, Wally."

It was Bruce. "Hey, Man, how're you doing?".

"Hi, Brew Buddy! You remembered!"

"Happy Birthday, you old creep. What are you now, about twenty-five?"

"You know I'm twenty-seven - and catching up to you. Just because you're two years older doesn't make you the king of the hill."

"The question is my man, how are you doing – where are you – in Michigan? said Bruce.

"I'm okay - but it's a pisser, that's for sure."

"Well, you come back to California sunshine when you're had your fill. Mom and Dad say hi - they're at Grandma's in Seattle but said to say hi."

"What's happening with the band"?

"We got a lot of gigs - not making any money but it's a hell of a party. They invited us to the Monterrey Jazz Festival again, so that's not too bad."

"Well, keep your lip and don't do anything I wouldn't do."

"That won't be hard. But I try to have fun in spite of your bad influence on me, Little Brother. Well, listen, I gotta go - we're heading in to San Fran for some fun tonight. You be good. And come back to paradise soon as you make a pile of money."

"Will do, Brewster - Stay cool."

Wally turned off the floor lamp, ducked his head back into the kitchen to say he was heading for his room. "Thanks, Mrs. Buchanan – dinner was delicious." Avoiding the kitchen, he groped his way through the dark living room to his den past the piano, wondering why you notice musty smells more in the dark than during the day. He lay down on the daybed and replayed the conversation he'd had with Bruce. He missed him, the independent one of the family, with his good looks and musical flair, who chose playing jazz trumpet over the corporate life. Wally burrowed into his pillow, feeling safe in his dark room, away from the clangor of the Buchanan family dramas. He was homesick. With the pillow over his head, he remembered a game they used to play when they were kids, a thought prompted by the smell of the Buchanan's living room. They'd take turns climbing into the upstairs window box and get buried in the clothes and rags while the other sat on the lid. Each tested the other how long he could stay buried in the dark with layers of clothing over his face, as oxygen seeped away. A game of dare. They called it "airplane." He'd have to go home for Christmas - he'd just have to find the money. Alicia was the only bright light of his days and she was unfortunately not his type, being a little older and too skinny. But there was something about her that kept him interested, an honesty and worldliness that intrigued him.

Mrs. Buchanan took a plate of food upstairs to Alicia's room. Alicia was perched cross-legged on her twin bed in a pink chenille bathrobe putting her hair into pincurls.

"I'm getting out, Ma, I swear it. He can't treat me like a child." Her eyes glistened. "What's wrong with me? Why can't I find somebody to love so I can start my life? If only Roger hadn't died on some godforsaken island in the Pacific, I'd have my own house and maybe a baby by now. You know Ma I miss him so much sometimes."

She wiped at her eyes with her sleeve, and picked up a handful of bobby pins and jammed them into her mouth. Mrs. Buchanan sat down on the bed. "There, there. Roger gave his life for our country. It was a shame that we lost him so soon after you married; you were both so young. But you have your life ahead of you. You just have to move ahead. You're doing okay at Boyd's, Honey, and things will turn out all right."

Alicia took a strand of hair and curled the lock around a finger, her elbow an inverse "V" over her head. With her other hand she took a bobby pin from her mouth and prying it open with her teeth, slid its prongs over and under the curl, then placed another across it to secure the curl. She remained silent.

Her mother spoke. "Steve called again. I think he's sweet on you. If you gave him any encouragement he could take you away and make you a fine husband."

"Oh, Mother! Steve's just a good friend, not a boyfriend. I've known Steve since kindergarten! He's just somebody to go to the movies with. And that's not the point. Dad's so...." She stopped, remembering her mother had married him. She wanted to say Dad's so crude and why did her mother marry him. Alicia selected two more bobby pins and made another pincurl.

"Oh, I'll get over it." She turned to her mother, taking the plate of food from her hands. "Thanks, Mom." She took a bite and chewed thoughtfully. "You know, Wally is cute. I wish he weren't so damn young - he's so much fun and I like him a lot."

"Wally? Well, now looky here. You've said that before and I don't like the way you're thinking. Wally's a bit liberal for my taste - I think he's a Democrat from something he once said about Truman. But that's not the point. He's certainly a nice young man, but you're too old for him. If you like him just make sure you don't spill the beans about your age. That would spook him."

"Mom, is that cheating?"

"All's fair in love and war, I always say. Does he have any idea of how old you are?"

"Not that I know. I never talked about it with him, if that's what you mean."

"Well just don't ever let on, and meantime, just have a nice time with him. Of course I don't want any funny stuff going on under this roof, you understand."

"Mother-r-r-r."

Later that night Wally got up, ravenous and sneaked into the kitchen for a cracker. Alicia'd left a tube of her Tangee lipstick on the kitchen table. Wally pulled off the cover and brought it to his nostrils. It smelled like Kool-Aid. Alicia's smell. He replaced the tube on the counter, took a handful of crackers, then went back into his bed thinking about Alicia and how her coral lips opened wide when she laughed. Jackie followed him into the den and jumped up on the bed. Wally didn't push him off. Jackie had started sleeping on his bed a few weeks back and Wally liked the company.

On the walk to the bus stop the next morning the cold stimulated Wally's nasal passages. He struggled through the folds of his overcoat to get at the handkerchief from his pants pocket and dropped his mitten. After a quick swipe at his nose, he found an outside pocket for the handkerchief: it was too cold to go through all that again. He hitched up his scarf over his face, and pushed his glasses over the wool before stopping for the mitten to pull onto his hardened fingers.

That night they all watched *Make Room for Daddy* in the living room. Wally watched Alicia when he thought nobody was looking; her face was so alive. He imagined making love to her and watching her as they gave each other pleasure. That night his fantasy was that he made Alicia lie down on the kitchen table. He was pushing apart her bare thighs. Of course Wally was a virgin but he had a good imagination. He'd had two girlfriends in his life back in California, both of whom had tired of waiting for him to ask them to marry him. They'd gone off and married other boys just months after they'd broken off with Wally.

On Wednesday, Wally could hardly see on his way to the bus stop. The wind blew snow into his face. He tried to gauge how far it was to the corner. Just five more houses. He could see two figures braced against the wind not too far ahead. Good. The bus hadn't come yet. A clot of melting snow lodged inside his sock. He thought they'll find my body here one day in the Spring when it thaws, frozen like a chunk of ice, forgotten, never even missed. The bus pulled up and he got on.

He was working in one of the metallurgy labs later that morning - he rotated between his lab and his office - when Earl Cunningham, a local guy with a degree in chemistry from Case, came in. "What do you know about Dow's process of electrolytic reduction of magnesium from the seawater?"

"Don't they pump it from Galveston Bay, down in Texas? I don't know if they still take it from Midland…"

"Yeah, but do you know when it started up?"

"All I know is that Dow invented the process. Got the National Science award in '41 I believe, but I don't know anything more."

Wally worked in extraction, based on electrolysis and thermal reduction, usually spending most of his time in the lab surrounded by tanks and fantastic structures made of fine glass tubing that Wally bent and shaped using an acetylene torch. He sometimes had to make the instruments he needed for his electrolytic experiments. Wally's team was trying to develop a commercial dry cell battery. At the lab Wally wrote up the techniques he had been using on his latest experiment - that should wow them - and worked on the presentation he was scheduled to make later in the week. He had dreams of getting a patent in his name.

"Ya know, Wally, there are no bars in this hick town - do you believe it?"

"That's a crying shame," Wally said, as if he knew a Schlitz from a Pabst. He wasn't much of a drinker.

"Yup, Midland's a dry town. If you want a drink you gotta go to Alpena or Bay City."

At least a bar was a place you could go after work. Midland had one movie theater, one Country Club for the swells, and a couple of restaurants. Main Street was three blocks of diagonal parking lines. That was it. The Tittabawassee River on one side, Eastman Road on the other and tree-lined streets of small houses, except for the golf course section, all the way out to U.S. 10. Beyond the Tittabawassee to the west, nothing; beyond the plant to the south, nothing. Only flat farm countryside dotted with little red barns and an occasional hick town like Auburn or Freeland or Oil City.

Wally had taken the Super Chief across country from San Francisco to Chicago and then a bus for the last six hours of the trip. When he'd first stepped into Midland, his heart had sunk. First there was the smell– a sulphuric, rotten egg smell that emanated from the elaborate brine water processing plants. Then there was the bleak, unbroken horizon with no mountains, no hills, just fields of corn or sugar beats or potatoes as far as the eye could see. The Dow plant had impressed him. The Tinker Toy network of thousands of thin red, yellow and blue tubes streaming at right angles from stark boxy buildings carried the chemicals Dow got from the brine wells around an eight mile square area. Here was one of the premier chemical plants in the world and they wanted him to work for them. For a lot of money. It was staggering to know Dow valued him so much. He itched to get his hands on their equipment so he could prove he was worth every penny. But why did the town have to be so small and raw? He had been certain he'd never have any fun or make any friends.

One Saturday in March, Wally returned from his usual weekend breakfast of pancakes and eggs down at the Chat 'n Chew. He was about to sit in the den and read the papers when Alicia intercepted him and said, "Let's make snow angels." Alicia was dressed in her jeans and wool jacket and hat and mittens.

"I am way too old to do that kind of thing," he said with a smile. "You gotta be kidding."

But she had insisted and there they were out in the front yard like a couple of kids. He knew better - at twenty-seven he was a grown man - but she soon had him laughing like a fool and getting snow inside his collar. She had been right. It was fun lying on his back working his arms and his legs back and forth, letting the sun warm his face. It felt good to do some exercise, too. He'd become a lab rat and could stand to lose a couple of pounds. After they'd had a brief snowball fight and sucked on icicles they'd discovered hanging from the side porch awning, they had gone inside to the kitchen, all red-cheeked and wet and gotten out of their snow-covered coats and boots. Mrs. Buchanan made cocoa for them as if they really were kids. Real Hershey's cocoa made from powder. Mrs. Buchanan mixed the cocoa with sugar and milk and stirred with a big spoon a bubbling mixture on the stove. She put a bowl of whipped cream and a thick blue crockery plate of chocolate chip cookies on the table and then went down to the basement to do a load of laundry.

"So you thought you were too old to play in the snow." Alicia said as she stirred her cocoa. Her cheeks were wet from the cold and her bangs hung in wet strands. She took a drink and put down the cup, leaving a smudge of cocoa on her upper lip, revealing a furze of fine blond hairs on her lip. Her bottom teeth were charmingly crooked.

"Yeah, well I guess I found out I was wrong, didn't I?" Wally wondered if he should tell her about the smudge on her lip but decided there was no way he could ever mention such a personal thing to her. And besides he loved the way it made her look even more childlike and small, even if she was older than he.

"Hey, when's your birthday?" he asked.

"In March Why?"

"Well, I'll get you a present."

"Oh, you don't have to do that."

"Yes, I do I want to. What do you want?"

"Gee - I don't know."

"Do you like records?"

"Yes, I love records. I have a few albums. I like Johnny Ray."

"Yeah, he's pretty cool. I'll get you a Johnny Ray record."

"Oh, that'd be cool. But you don't need to."

Wally took another sip of cocoa and tried not to look directly at Alicia's breasts beneath her pink sweater. She had tucked the sweater in the waistband of her skirt, making it stretch tight across her chest, so it was hard not to look. She was small-boned and not really built. But Wally knew he'd love to get to first base with her but it was tricky living in the same house and all. Maybe she'd go for a ride with him. He'd have to find some kind of social life here.

"So you've got a PhD. Was it hard to get it?"

"Not really, except for the dissertation. And the orals. But I was pretty well prepared for it."

"You're such a smarty."

"You're not dumb. Why'd you stop going to college, Alicia?"

"Ran out of money - simple as that. With the War, and then Ron's death. I just couldn't swing it." She licked her spoon and put it on the saucer. "I plan to go back some day so I can be a kindergarten teacher. I love little kids." She fluffed her bangs.

"Yeah, you'd be good with them too. Except when you get 'em outside in the snow and force them do snow angels and get snow down their necks and they catch cold."

"Now you cut that out!" Alicia said, mock angry, and stuck out her tongue at him. Wally liked the way her hair waved just right. Must be naturally curly, he thought.

Later that day Wally was alone in the house. Alicia and her mother had gone shopping and Lyle was at work on the Saturday shift. Wally'd gone upstairs to look for a ruler in the Buchanan's bedroom office. Returning, he noticed the door to Alicia's room was open. He casually glanced in then walked into her room. The usual girl things - a pair of nylon stockings flung over the boudoir chair in the corner, a plastic tray filled with hairpins and ribbons and nail polish on her little vanity table. A pink Philco on one side of the bed, a bookcase in the corner. He scanned the books. *Black Beauty, How Green Was My Valley, Peyton Place, Babbit.* Along the bottom shelf were some yearbooks. He knelt down and took out her high school yearbook. 1939. When he saw her picture in the graduating class he knew. She was thirty-two years old, five years older than he.

That information was a shock. Kind of put her out of the running once and for all. He felt sorry for her in a way. The only man who ever came around to see her was Steve. Wally wanted to know just how good a friend Steve was to Alicia. Just curious, Wally was interested in a brotherly way, that was all. Sometimes Alicia went to the movies with Steve but she was always home at a decent hour. He couldn't help but notice, being on the ground floor and all, and his window right out onto the front porch, when he saw them kissing good night. He'd felt funny, angry, as if he had dibs on her. It turned out, however, that things had a way of taking care of themselves, in spite of his own reluctance to pursue her. She was too old for him.

Wally and Alicia were parked along the Tittabawassee River Road, about ten miles from Midland. It was about 6:00 p.m. in late May, and they had been shopping in Saginaw for a birthday present for Mrs. Buchanan. Wally'd turned down the bumpy lane toward the riverbank and shut off the engine of the Buick Special – it was his first car, second-hand, and he'd paid a lot for it. The hush of the evening surprised them, the absolute stillness of the air flattened even more by an overlay of a steady chirrup chirrup chirrup chirrup from the river bank.

"This is the place I was talking about. It's peaceful, isn't it?" he said.

"It sure is. How'd you find it?"

"I have to drive to Bay City sometimes. It's a nice place to stop off, break the ride."

Wally flung his arm casually across the top of the seat as he spoke, "Those crickets sure are loud."

"They're not crickets, they're tree toads."

"Really?"

"Yes, most people confuse them for crickets but they're toads. Tiny ones."

"Ya learn something every day." He removed his arm from the seat back and made a little self-deprecating laugh. What a jerk, he was saying to himself. Wally, a short, pudgy guy with horn rimmed glasses, wanted to kiss Alicia, but Alicia, a skinny Blondie, leaned forward to turn the radio dial and he lost his chance.

"It's Your Hit Parade, said the announcer. No. 1 on the charts." Jo Stafford started singing. "See the pyramids across the Nile…."

Alicia sat back, turned to him and with a little sound, reached over and removed Wallie's glasses and placed them on the dashboard. Wally looked at her for a moment with a sickly smile on his face. And then he lurched. It took her off guard and she said wait just a minute here and pushed him away. You need to learn to go slow, she said. It's better that way. She took his head in her hands and kissed him slowly on the mouth. After they'd kissed for awhile, she led his hand to her breasts; and arched her neck for him to kiss as well. The tree toads' chirping faded for Wally and he scrunched on his knees in the foot well of the big car so as to swing Alicia's body around on the car seat, light as a feather, positioning her so that her head lay under the steering wheel. He almost got a wrist burn from the woolly fabric. He carefully stretched himself over so he could lie on her, lightly lightly - don't crush, keeping one knee on the floor to take his weight. He could feel her heart beating through the chartreuse linen of her dress and he inched his right hand up under the hem of her dress toward her thigh. They tongue-wrestled, panting heavily. This was going to be easier than he dreamed. His

211

fingers found the nest of her pubic hair, moist and warm under her panties. Surprisingly lush.

Alicia suddenly opened her eyes as if coming out of a dream. She pushed him away and struggled to an upright position.

"No. We better go home, Wally. I don't think we should stay here any more."

He hesitated, then removed himself so she could sit up. Clambering back into the driver's seat, he looked in the rear view mirror and saw his own white, bland face, looking innocent without his glasses. He knew better. He wasn't innocent at all. He was trying to get sex. Sex without any suggestion of marriage. It took a moment to recover. He was glad in some way that she had principles after all.

"How much is that doggie in the window? [bark-bark]" sang Patti Page. Wally turned off the radio and picked up his glasses from the dashboard. "Why'd you stop?" he said as if he didn't know. No condoms with him, but after all, she'd been married once, she wasn't a virgin. "It's not as if you were doing it for the first time, or anything."

Alicia didn't answer right away. He immediately said, "I'm sorry. That was uncalled for."

She spoke slowly. "You're right - that was rude. Just because I've been married before doesn't mean I'm a slut." She took out a compact and her tube of Tangee and applied a thick swath of coral over her lips. Speaking into the little mirror, she said, "The truth is, I'm attracted to you but I have to think of my reputation."

"Not to be a wise guy, but who's going to see us out here? The tree toads and the crickets? I'll just bet they're planning to blab it all over town."

"No, Silly, not the frogs and the crickets. The neighbors. You'd be surprised how nosy they can be - even like when you get home at night.

And my mom is keeping an eye on the clock, don't think she's not, even if I'm old enough to be married."

"Well, how about one more kiss?" Wally put his hand on her breast.

"Wally!" Alicia slapped his hand away. "I said no and I mean it. Now take me home!"

Wally started the car, backed it around and bumped back toward the highway. They drove in silence. At the intersection of Eastman and Buttles Street, Alicia moved over to his side. He put his arm around her shoulders, forgiven. He really liked this girl. He decided he'd have to quit taking her for rides or she'd get ideas. He'd keep it on a strictly friends basis.

In June Wally received a bonus for his work in the new processes. He didn't work in the plastics division, but felt proud all the same when that same month he saw a commercial for Dow's new product, Saran Wrap, on TV. He started to have a social life. He went on a date with a girl Earl had fixed him up with named Janice Wackenreuter, a curvy redhead with buck teeth who worked in patents, but they hadn't clicked. He'd liked her enough but she seemed bored with him after trying to talk about ballet and the arts. She turned him down the third time he asked her out. He kept hanging around with Alicia. Alicia was always up for something. He and Alicia drove outside Midland one night after work. They thought vaguely of going to Bay City to see a movie but they ended up in a small café in Freeland.

From the edge of the road by the sugar beet field Wally could see all the way to the horizon. Those country highways. Straight lines running north / south set at every five miles intersected by straight lines coming from east / west.

"You can never really get lost in Michigan," said Alicia. "When it became a state, they laid out the roads in one-mile squares."

"It's not at all like in California. You can get lost fast. And in California you can always see the mountains. If you're on the coast, it's even prettier with the sea and the rocks and the temperate climate."

"I'd love to go to California some day," said Alicia, picking up a spoon and stirring her coffee. "It must be so beautiful." She looked particularly pretty tonight, Wally noticed, in a powder blue sheath dress, nylons and black heels. She had placed her black gloves on the table between them, leather sculptures of Alicia's small hands, fingers stiff, lying supine as if in a posture of supplication.

"It is, especially along the coast. They have a bunch of boulders in the bay near San Francisco called Seal Island and real seals come there and sun themselves. You can see them from the shore."

"Oh, that sounds fabulous! I'd love to see that. One of these days I'll have enough money and I'll get out of here. I want to travel."

"Why haven't you gone before now?"

"After Ron died, we had some debts that I had to pay off; the car and stuff. And I had an operation, you don't want to hear about that -" she laughed - "and well, by the time I got my finances in order, I just didn't have any desire to travel. Like I didn't care all that much about anything. It's been a long time, though, and I know I have to keep going with my life. But it's been hard."

"You loved him a lot?"

"He was my soul mate. And then he goes and gets himself killed in the war." She sighed and looked over Wally's shoulder into the distance. He finally thought of something to say.

"They were taking them so young then. I'm sorry."

After a pause Wally continued. "I have to tell you I peeked in your room and saw from your yearbook that you graduated in 1939. Did you get married right after?"

Alice froze. "You looked in my room? You trespassed?"

"Well, yes. I'm sorry." Wally blushed.

"We'd better go home now."

Once again they were driving in silence. Wally hoped he'd be forgiven but it would take time.

It was 10:30 when they parked in the driveway. They tiptoed in. Mrs. Buchanan appeared from the living room, her hair in curlers under a cloth shower cap, her face ghastly without her customary cherry pink lipstick. She'd been waiting for them.

"Mother, what's wrong?" asked Alicia.

"Where on earth have you been? I've been worried sick." She didn't wait for an answer. "Wally, you need to call your parents right away. There's been an accident. It's your brother."

"What?"

"That's all they said - just to get you to call home the minute you came in, no matter what time it was."

Wally heard his father's voice, the sound of his mother crying in the background. "Son. Bruce's car parked at a stop light. Another car. Rammed into it. Died instantly. Broken neck." It took a while to sink in, then, with the Buchanan family standing in a half circle looking at him with stricken faces. Wally said excuse me and walked into his room. He sat still for a long time and then broke down with big loud sobs that later evolved into quiet, steady, furtive crying. He got up and called his parents and went back to bed. Around 2:00 a.m. Alicia came downstairs. She didn't knock; she just went into the den and got into bed with him and held him. He cried again in her arms, and just before 6:00, she tiptoed away from his sleeping form and went back upstairs.

Alicia drove Wally to the airport the next morning.

"Alicia. I don't know what to say. Just thanks for being with me last night. It helped."

"There is nothing to say, Wally. I know what it's like to lose someone dear." She took his hand between her gloved ones and looked into his eyes. "Just remember that over time it hurts less. It never stops hurting altogether, but over time the hurt gets smaller." Her blue eyes had a turquoise intensity he'd never seen before.

So it was not long after that, in August, when they took another trip off the main road to sit by the Tittabawassee River. And they knew they were in love.

They married at Christmas time, moved into their own home and lived, childless, for many years in Midland. Alicia quit her job and went back to school and in 1957, got her elementary education teaching certificate. Many years later, they planned a trip to Europe and had to get passports. When Wally saw Alicia's passport, he did a double take. "Honey they made a mistake. It says here you were born in 1917. You were born in 1921."

Alicia came out of the kitchen where she'd been trying out a new recipe for something called pizza.

"No, there's no mistake."

"What?"

"I was born when it says. I just never told you."

"That makes you ten years older than me!..... But how could you have graduated four years later like it said in the yearbook? Remember when I snooped and you were so mad? That was the night I learned that Ron had died?"

Alice put down her pot holder and walked up to Wally who stood in the hallway, passports in hand. "Dear, the yearbook was right. I just had to take time away from school – I went back to school after my husband died for my final year. I was the oldest kid in the class but they let me do it, because of the war. I never told you because I was afraid you wouldn't love me."

Wally sat back in his chair, his face blank, absorbing the information.

"When you assumed I was only five years ahead of you, I just let you think it. I know I deceived you. I'm sorry." She looked like a kitten who had fallen into the bathroom sink and couldn't get out.

"Alicia." Wally sat down on the sofa. You come over here." He patted his lap. "You know what? Your age doesn't matter a whit to me. Except now I am going to be calling you the "old lady" for real.

The Mean Line

Charles pushed Sonja, hard. She hit the wall, dislodging some of the grass wallpaper Charles had insisted on having when they redid the house. Only grass paper conveyed the elegance Charles demanded for his role as headmaster of Dumbarton. Pushing was the closest he'd ever come to hitting Sonja, although he'd broken objects and hurt his own fist in prior rages, once, striking down a small hook she'd pasted onto the bathroom wall that was not to his liking, breaking the skin over his knuckles and requiring heavy bandages to stanch the bleeding.

He said, "Why the hell don't you just pack up your fucking things and move out?"

He walked over to the cherry bookcase near the door to his office. It held his graduate school history books from Princeton. He wanted everyone to see the dense volumes of historical analysis that he had struggled to understand to get his master's degree. When they had run out of money, he had started to teach at private schools, quickly moving up from teacher to housemaster and then into the Headmaster's slot. Sonja had been successful with her own doctorate, completing her dissertation "Pace in the Prose Fiction of Cervantes" in record time.

No question about it. Charles was angry. He pulled out Bill's novel, *White Grapes,* from the top shelf,. Its cover paper of a raspberry-and-gray design had reminded Sonja of the fabric of one of her mother's strapless gowns. The book was the signed copy of the privately printed edition Bill had given them when they had all been at Duke. Bill had been their French teacher while they both did a year of languages in preparation for graduate school and they'd become friends, spending many evenings at Bill and Eva's house. Charles opened Bill's pretty book and with a mighty grunt, tried to rip it in half. The stiff binding resisted. He tried again but still no luck, then he grabbed individual pages and started tearing them out in clumps, scattering them on the rug and yipping like Curly.

Sonja watched, feeling as if she had a role in a cheap melodrama. She didn't know her lines or how it would end but the play was unfolding at top speed. Charles flung the carcass of the book to join the pieces of raspberry cover paper strewn about the floor. Next he looked around for something else to tear apart, his eyes moist and piggy. The same eyes that once seduced her. In New York those sky-blue eyes had twinkled with mischief and masculine assurance. When they had their first martini together in his Madison Avenue apartment, Charles had described the process so meticulously as he mixed and shook that she had loved the strong concoction before she tasted it. Memories rushed in – how impressed she was when Charles once picked up the phone, winked at her, and talked the Pierre in New York into giving them a room during one sold-out Christmas week. She'd married him and been under his control ever since. She'd sincerely tried to make things work.

"There! That's what I think of that fucking phony. I told you to get out. Go now. But don't think you can just take Maida with you, oh no, you're not going anywhere with her."

Maida was their three-year old daughter who at the moment was upstairs in her room. Sonja prayed that Maida couldn't hear what was going on in the study downstairs. Sonja was baffled. She was operating on instinct, the rules of her ordered life no longer operable. She couldn't leave Charles without Maida. She wasn't even sure she wanted to leave him. Who ever mentioned leaving? She'd only wanted to save her self from drowning in Charles' control. Seventeen years younger than

Charles when they married, she hadn't known that she was a trophy wife; she only knew she'd lost all sense of herself after seven years of subservience to Charles. She was so in his thrall that even her point of view during an argument could not be respected. Sonja said, "Charles, I only wrote to Bill because you don't listen to me and I knew he would. Please understand." Charles interrupted. "You're making a mean line in your forehead, you're going to have a permanent line if you frown."

Sonja's mouth opened but nothing came out. Mean line? MEAN LINE?

She knew she had to be calm, to show Charles she was not afraid of him, even though her fear was threatening to derail her. But how to handle this? She couldn't find anything to latch on to. Her fear made her hollow as if it had scooped out her abdomen and left a skeleton covered with skin. She was not strong enough for this, not at all. If only she could find a measure of righteous anger to fight his fire with her own. No. All she felt was cowardice. And shame. Shame for both of them, shame that the frayed sack of their marriage had at last blown apart. It wasn't that she was ashamed of meeting Bill last night, or of betraying Charles. Her decision to meet Bill was a life-saving act. She had never thought beyond last night or the consequences of being caught. She'd just needed the idyllic couple of hours talking with Bill to be something she had created and executed on her own. They hadn't kissed. Just talked. But Charles perverted it into something ugly and sordid and Cynthia could find no way to justify herself

If only Charles hadn't noticed the tires this morning. She must have driven the car into some kind of field - the grass and sand must have stuck to the wheels. Now Charles knew everything. She didn't try to deny anything. She couldn't even get to the part about telling Charles she'd only talked with Bill. Once he had forced her to reveal that it had been Bill she'd met, he had a way of steamrollering her. She was exhausted. Sonja looked out the window at the little pond that ran behind the house. What a beautiful place, this campus she'd called home for three years. She'd been miserable here, but it was a beautiful place.

Charles was waiting for her to speak.

"You're being ridiculous. I can't help it if you've treated me like a doormat and I responded to a man who gave me kindness and attention!" Charles stood there, waiting, so she continued. "I just decided I needed a friend so I wrote him and suggested we meet." Why didn't Charles speak? Was he stunned like a bull who stands confused after the flourishes, unable to charge? Whatever the reason, she saw her moment. She sidled out of the study toward the stairs and said (a great exit line, she thought later), "When you're ready to discuss this sensibly, we'll talk. Until then, I'm going upstairs. And don't get in my way." She stalked out of the office.

The steps led straight up to their bedroom. She sat down on the bed, heart pounding as she saw that something had happened worse than just a temper tantrum involving a torn book. Charles would never understand why she had met Bill. Now he was angry. Fearless and decisive, Charles was a dangerous man to his enemies, a trait she'd always found attractive in him. And now she was the enemy. A movie scene crept into her head.

The camera follows Charles as he walks upstairs with heavy steps, kitchen knife held at his side revealed when the camera moves in for a close-up. Charles opens the bedroom door and searches around the room. A noise comes from the closet. He tears open the door and sees Sonja cowering behind her Saks robe. He roughly pulls her out. Maida runs from stage right and cries, "Daddy. Don't. Don't hurt Mommy!" He tells Maida to get out of the way and raises up the butcher knife — it's from their set of Sabatiers. He slashes down, plunging it into Sonja's chest, again and again. She staggers to the bed and collapses, the blood spreading in untidy blobs and patches. Charles shouts, "No, don't bleed on the bedspread!"

Sonja had to get out of the house.

She went to the walk-in closet and pulled out a backpack. She threw in a couple of pairs of panties, an extra bra, and went for her toiletries in the master bathroom. Once again she felt annoyed by the wallpaper. Why had she allowed the decorator to choose the outlandish green and white jungle print on shiny paper? It looked like a repurposed oilcloth tablecloth. She swept her toothbrush, her makeup base, eye liner and lipstick into the backpack.

Hurry. Where were the car keys? Purse, down on the entryway table. Now to pick up precious Maida. Sonja tiptoed into the hall and opened the door to her daughter's room, peeking in.

"Hi, Sweetheart! How's my little Sneaky? What are you doing?

Maida was sitting in the center of the green tufted rug holding a doll by one leg, trying to pull off the doll's underpants. Maida wore a pink and white-striped seersucker jumper, high top orthopedic leather shoes and socks, and a frilly pink Baby Gap cotton shirt. Her short auburn hair curled dark around her porcelain skin. She looked up and said, 'Mommy, this is Baby." She held out her doll, a Madame Alexander baby doll, whose hair was hopelessly matted but whose face had perfect ivory skin and unblemished features, not accidentally mirroring Maida's own features.

"Yes, Sweetheart, that's Baby! Are you playing with Baby?"

Maida looked back down at the doll and put her finger in the doll's ear.

"Baby's ear," she said.

"Yes, oh, yes, that's Baby's ear." Sonja moved fast, knelt and scooped up her daughter, hugging her.

"Guess what?" she whispered into Maida's ear. "We're going to go for a ride in the car. Would you like that?"

"No." Maida squirmed off Sonja's lap and climbed to the top of her Playschool wooden slide.

"Oh, I think maybe it could be fun!" She thought, Please, Maida, go along with me just this once.

Sonja grabbed a little nightgown and some panties and socks from the pale green dresser drawer and stuffed them into the backpack. She started to lift Maida off the top step of the little Playschool slide. "No! Mommy – watch me slide down."

Sonja said, her voice strained. "Okay. You slide down and I'll catch you." She crouched at the end of the slide. Maida looked anxiously from her perch. "Ready, Mommy?"

Sonja said, "Oh, yes, Honey, I'm ready. Come along and then we'll go in the car." Come along Daaaaarling!

Maida slide down the slide. "Do again!" Oh no you don't. Sonja took her by the hand and they started down the stairs.

Please let the keys be on the hall table, she was thinking as they descended. Please for once let the keys be there. She thought Charles was still in his study but she couldn't be sure. Just as she got to the hall, the study door opened and Charles loomed out at them like a funhouse ghoul.

"What do you think you are doing?" His eyes were still piggy but he spoke in a neutral tone so as not to upset Maida.

"We're just going to go out for a minute."

Sonja looked on the little table. No purse, no keys. She opened the outside door, Maida still firmly in one hand.

"Where are you going?" Charles asked in a strange voice.

"I don't know, Charles. We're just going out for awhile."

She led Maida through the front door, past their car parked at the curb in front of their house and to the sidewalk that wound around the campus connecting the four student houses and their attached housemaster dwellings. She walked toward Hathaway House. She heard the door close and steps close behind her.

"We're going to go for a walk, aren't we?" she said, smiling at Maida, stepping up the pace.

Maida looked at her mother, then turned around and looked behind at Charles.

Sonja heard the car door slam, then the roar of the engine. She was now past Phillips and just in front of Hathaway House. Hathaway was run by the head hockey coach. Jim and Janet were in their 50's and rumor had it that they would retire at the end of next season. Sonja remembered how cruel he and his wife had been to Sonja when she had first arrived on the campus. Janet was an Establishment snob who had lived all her married life on one private school grounds or another, following Jim around as he was hired and dumped by various private schools until he ended up at Charlton. She resented pretty newcomers. Janet assumed an amused manner whenever Sonja was in her presence, feigning interest, filing away information, and spreading vicious gossip about her and Charles at every opportunity.

The Volvo drew close. Damn! She looked around. Except for themselves executing this morality play on a peaceful Spring Saturday morning, nobody was in sight. The campus was deserted. The Dumbarton boys were all on Spring break and the few who remained at the school - the ones who lived in South America or California and couldn't go home - would sleep until noon. Sonja noted a squirrel on the common. Way over by the chapel the Johnson's black Labrador stood sniffing at something. Otherwise, no witnesses. Charles continued to drive slowly alongside her, keeping pace with her as she walked, his window down, silent. She kept walking. Absurd. A farce in the making. Now what?

She smiled down at Maida. Mustn't let Maida know what was going on. Maida looked up and said, "Why is Daddy driving next to us?"

Sonja didn't answer. She came to the next house: Burford House. Ginny was nice. On an impulse, she turned and walked up the little sidewalk to the front door. She knocked on the door and rang the bell at the same time. Charles had parked and was getting out of the car. She rang again. Come on! Come to the door. Save me!

Just as Sonja thought Charles would reach her, the door opened.

"Well, Hello Sonja. Hi Honey. Don't you look pretty today."

Ginny was wearing a head band and workout clothes. Ginny was married to George, another of the four housemasters. He taught math. Sonja liked Ginny, who had two kids of her own and was a little younger than Sonja.

"Hi, Ginny. Can we come in? Can we just come in for a little while and stay with you? " Sonja stared hard into Ginny's eyes as she spoke.

Ginny hesitated, spotted Charles advancing toward them and opened the door. 'Sure, come right on in."

Sonja and Maida whisked in through the door and Ginny closed and locked the screen door behind them. They stood in the dark hallway inside, staring out at the sunlit sidewalk. Ginny spoke through the screen door to Charles. "Charles, I don't think you should come in right now."

"I'd like to talk to my wife, Ginny. You're being a good neighbor but this doesn't concern you," he said, his voice stern.

Ginny said, "Well, no, Charles, I think that Sonja would like to sit down for a little while with us. Dick's not here right now but he'll be home soon. Why don't you go home and we'll call you later?" Sonja blessed Ginny a thousand times.

Charles gave Sonja a hard look, then turned and went back into the car.

Ginny closed the door and looked at Sonja.

"Hey Maida, you know what? Beth is upstairs – you wanta go play with her?' Maida ran upstairs to Beth's room as Ginny said to Sonja, "How about a cup of tea?"

It took Sonja about two hours to collect herself. She never told Ginny about the nature of the disagreement and Ginny never asked. When the phone rang, Sonja took Charles's call. They spoke a few words and after sincere apologies to Ginny, Sonja went home with Maida and cooked a nice dinner. She read a story to Maida and tucked her in. After an hour of reading her latest true crime novel, she prepared for bed.

That night after Charles had come to bed, she moved close to him, spooned for a while, then she moved her hand to his penis. Before long she had begun a series of activities that had him moaning with pleasure. She didn't know why she had initiated lovemaking. It was unusual for her, especially after this day. Was it because she had realized she was trapped and was trying to make amends, to lessen future strife? Or was it something else? When at long last she took him in her mouth, arching over him inside the soft sheet-cave she'd made for them, the question was still why? She herself experienced little physical pleasure that night. She didn't feel aroused at all and was pleased when Charles, pretty much worn out, began to snore.

Sonja pulled up the covers on her side of the bed and burrowed into her pillow. While years later she would understand the fact and nature of her denial of the reality of her marriage, controlling Charles for that night of lovemaking had made her feel powerful. As long as she kept him excited, Sonja was, for a short time and in a certain way, in charge of her life.

And that felt good.

The Burial of the Pájaro

The attendants had made us ready for lunch, putting our wheelchairs and walkers in a neat row. The woman on my left was talking to someone down the line, strings of burgundy hair hardly covering her bald head. ".... I could never go to Mexico because they would kidnap me and cut off my finger to get my diamond. They do that there don't you know? I always said to Arthur that we should only go to Florida, Palm Beach. Or Boca ...." Yap yap. I rolled my wheelchair out of the lineup toward the door at the end of the hallway. Anyone who tried to escape set off a blaring alarm of course. It happened a few times each week. But I wasn't interested in escaping. I was going for the patch of sun. Sunlight was one of my few pleasures. At ninety-four, arthritic and hard of hearing. I could no longer walk or do much for myself. My Episcopal minister husband of fifty-four years was gone and the kids were living their own lives, trying hard to be kind to me but waiting for me to die. They did need the money and I understood that.

A mote of dust floated by, twisting in a languid spiral. I wriggled in the warm sunshine that poured through the glass door.

Mexico. I had been twice to Mexico. Once, as a gangly girl with a group of high school kids, and once with my sister, Connie. When Connie had suggested the getaway to Mexico, my husband, dear thing, urged me to accept and soon I was flying away from our little town of Freeland, Wisconsin, escaping for a few days the righteous duties as minister's wife. I left them all behind - our family of two children, a dog, two cats and a lizard. I loved them all, even Boozy the lizard. But

I was wrung out. I had never bargained for the constant round of social and professional events that would demand my time and energy as the wife of a prominent spiritual leader. So many conservatives I had to manage to converse with during the dull dinner parties. "Oh Peter, you don't mean what you say about immigration," I'd say touching his arm, "but I will agree with you it's a complex problem." My role was that of exercising a false persona that I donned like a costume whenever we had dinner parties that were necessary to get money for the church from the big donors. I think it was when I refused to attend the Hebert's cocktail party – I could not take one more word against the immigrants - that my Paul saw I had reached a breaking point.

Connie and I stayed in Mexico City with a friend, Sissi Kilpatrick, a Physics professor and former congregant of Paul's church. She had moved to Mexico City for her sabbatical. After a few days of seeing the sights, we rented a van and the three of us, Connie, Sissi, and I, headed for the little silver mining town of Taxco, 108 miles away, for a relaxing weekend before going back.

My favorite nursing home attendant came toward me, a thin young African man with high cheekbones and skin the color of blacktop. "Time for lunch, Mrs. Roberts."

"Oh go away, Jomo, I'm not going to eat today."

He flashed me a brilliant smile and replied with his lilting Kenyan accent. "I'll come back in a few minutes. You know you got to eat, dear lady."

Oh. Why?

Jomo was the one who often picked me out of my wheelchair to set me on the toilet. He also took me into the shower with the help of another attendant who scrubbed me. I had long ago given over my dignity to these people. Jomo, more than most, seemed comfortable with his odious tasks and I loved him for it.

The sun probed the muscles in my neck and I stretched my feet.

Marco was a Mexican. So long ago. I had sinned with Marco on that trip and my guilt had taken up permanent residence in a little corner of my heart. But strangely, there was also in that tiny place a sweet sense of delight, a jolly intruder who was indifferent to censure and very sure of itself.

How had it happened? We three women first met Marco and his two friends – Jaime - and was it Pablo? - in Cuernavaca, a halfway point about sixty miles south of Mexico City. We six, in our two tables of three, were the only ones in the little restaurant that afternoon. The men apparently were also escaping the heat of the capital for the weekend. We were in our mid-thirties; they were in their twenties.

It happened so smoothly. First we fussed and lingered over our desserts, aware of the men but ignoring them, not sure how each other felt about the other's presence. The next thing, we were chatting with them like school girls. By that point we women must have become tired of each other's company for we entered into the conversation with gusto. Connie and Sissi, who were single, ordered piňa coladas all around. The Mexicans spoke little English and I was the only one with enough Spanish to actually converse. Marco knew some English, so he and I did all the translating of the jokes and stories that flowed in our attempts to communicate. The Mexicans were educated and of an age they were probably married but no one asked and no one cared. Marco was short and wiry, with black hair and skin the color and smoothness of a milk chocolate shake. He had an amused, aloof air about him. My own Paul back home had red hair and unlike Marco, was the epitome of friendliness. A real Midwesterner, trusting, generous, my pudgy Paul. No aloof air. No mystery about Paul.

We learned that the men had with them a little parakeet – a *pájaro* - who had died just as they had set out for their weekend, and Jaime, its owner, had brought it along in a box. After much humorous repartee that left *"pájaro"* a permanent part of our vocabulary, (along with *"exquisito"* a word picked up by Connie to use every time she found ways to interject it into the conversation, pronouncing it *ex-kwee-zeeto*), someone said we should have a funeral for the bird. Everyone thought it an excellent idea and we agreed to bury it en route to Taxco.

The men had used public transportation from Mexico City and planned to take a cab to Taxco. Sissi suggested wouldn't it be fun if they ditched the taxi and rode with us. Off we went through the winding green mountains, stopping at one point to bury the *pájaro* in a mock-funeral. Jaime took it out of its box so we could see it. It was emerald green with a little cone of a head, a coral beak hidden in its fluffy chest. I felt Jaime had loved this bird. Someone made a little cross for the tiny mound we left at the side of the road and we departed. As I drove along the winding road, I listened to the bantering. "Hey, what does "car-burr-a-door" mean?" but I drove alone, thinking about the spirit of the bird, knowing its soul had not died.

We dropped the guys off at their hotel and drove partway up one of the mountains to check in to our more expensive Hotel de la Borda – a place I had stayed during my high school excursion.

The sun in my end of the hallway was hot on my shoulders. I twisted the wheel of my chair toward the door to let the heat bathe the back of my head. The memories rushed back.

After my high school trip I had always wanted to return to Taxco and the De la Borda. Mexico had made a powerful impact on me. In fact, my will stipulated that my grandchildren use some of my money to fly to Mexico with my ashes and spread them over the ground near the hotel. It was a mean thing to do – to force the grandkids to use some of their inheritance for my own selfish ends - but I felt that they needed to experience the beauty of the place whether they wanted to or not. I had become querulous and demanding in my old age and not much mattered any more, even how they felt about me.

The sunlight penetrated my skin and I was back in Acapulco on my high school trip, lying on a beach. In the distance I could hear the wheelchair-and-walker brigade mumbling and stumbling toward the dining room. But I was soaking up the rays in Mexico.

Our middle-aged Mexican bus driver was a quiet, reserved man but as the week wore on, he surprised me by dancing with us at a beach in Acapulco one night, moving his hips to the soft sounds of the marimba in a way my own middle-aged father back home could scarcely have imagined doing. I loved that night. Then we were back in Mexico City to see the shabby gentleness of the floating gardens of Xochomilco with its flower-laden boats and smiling mariachi players who pumped out traditional songs. Ay yai yai yai-i-i-i-i-i. We floated around with other tourists and Mexican families – authentic Mexicans! I had loved the bright folk art at all the tourist stops, the shimmering beaches, the warm water. But there was so much poverty everywhere, as if the tourists had to pay for the enchantment with piercing views of misery, and I was badly shaken by seeing ragamuffins running alongside our car holding out their hands for pesos, or wrinkled women in filthy shawls crouching on the sidewalk while they cradled their babies. Such inequity. The eyes of the suffering women followed me into my dreams as our group moved around the country.

Yet when our bus had pulled into Taxco, a little silver mining town lying in the crevasse of steep mountains, my impressionable young self had been most stunned by its beauty. That night I had sat on the patio by the pool of aquamarine water while listening to the marimba band, the rest of the kids watching television somewhere, with the lightest breeze from somewhere out in the darkness touching my face and shoulders. Across the valley, the hillsides twinkled and the dogs barked.

I remember using my high school Spanish to decipher the de la Borda's family motto posted on the wall next to the front desk of our hotel: *Dios da a de la Borda; de la Borda da a Dios.* God gives to de la Borda; de la Borda gives to God. Apparently after taking riches from the mines on the backs of the peasants, the industrious French/Spanish interloper had given a lot of money to the Roman Catholic Church.

But this time in Mexico with Connie and Sissi, I was a hardened refugee from sentiment. I knew I'd soon return to hard work and responsibility. My husband seemed married to his calling and I was selfish then - the pleasure of serving others came much later – and I resented my life. Did I even really love Paul or had I settled into monotony that threatened to erase our original attraction to each other?

Our first night in Taxco we dined in town with our new pals and downed many glasses of wine in the tiny restaurant, the Cantarranas (the Singing Frogs. What a delightful name for a restaurant, I remember thinking.) Translations and misunderstandings became more and more hilarious as the night wore on, and Marco started catching my eye in a hidden kind of bond, as if we were different. I felt flattered to feel his attention, loving the mutual sense of superiority that bonded us. That night in bed I kept thinking of him, revved up for the excitement to come the next day.

Saturday morning we shopped in town for silver trinkets and Connie talked about Jaime. She was not sure what she would do about her attraction, if anything, but it was there. I listened without comment. By then I had recognized I was interested in Marco. It was a gut-hollow, queasy lust, and a thing that I tried to suppress. The more I denied my attraction, the stronger the urge grew. I knew Sissi, our professor friend, had her eye on Marco as well, and as the only married woman, I was assumed to be out of the running for romance, an assumption that only heightened my growing tension.

After shopping, I took a swim in the pool, had a nap, and met Connie and Sissi for dinner. We were to meet the men later. I felt hyped up, alert, and hollow with anticipation. Then we were all sitting around the pool drinking and talking. I lounged in a corner, merging in my mind with the velvety blackness of the evening, avoiding Marco's eyes and only half listening to the wisecracking of Sissi and Connie or the reciprocal comments from the others that sent everyone into laughter. Late into the night, it started to rain, but no one wanted to stop the party. We took our bottles and our glasses inside to the large lobby. The hotel was deserted; the night clerk had gone to bed. We became noisy, laughing at everything and nothing. We sang Beatles songs and during a lull, Marco whispered to ask me if I wanted to take a drive. I never stopped to considered my answer. Of course I did. Sissi looked hard at me as we hurried out through the foyer and into the storm but being drunk covered unpleasantness, I rationalized, and I had no intention of bowing to morality or kindness or the inevitable shame that would come later.

The rest is a cliché, a scene straight out of Nora Roberts: a deserted mountain road on the edge of a cliff overlooking twinkling lights in the valley, thunder crashing overhead, shards of electricity dividing the sky. As we groped and found positions and sweated, my body worked outside my mind. I remember wondering what it would be like if the van plunged over the cliff into the ravine.

The next day there were no probing questions— everybody acted with discretion. I slunk around getting packed, avoiding eye contact. Little stabs of glee kept pulling me back from self-hatred as I threw my bathing suit into the suitcase and folded my skirts. I had discovered a part of myself that felt authentic, mature, glad and ashamed at the same time. We returned to Mexico City, dropped off our men friends, Connie and I hugged Sissi, and we flew home. I decided never to tell Paul – just to live with my feelings. I tucked the experience away and we lived in harmony until he died.

So I sit out my days waiting. I am not suffering but I have no will to live either. I only have my memories. I read large-print books most of the time, or take naps. Time passes.

One night the red-headed yapper hobbled late into the dining room for the evening meal. She negotiated the tables with expertise, using her walker like the prow of a ship cutting through ice, bumping into others without apology. As the servers set down the food – the brown and green material looked pre-masticated to me but I ate it anyway – someone began a discussion of politics. How awful the politicians were, how unyielding, and how sinful they all were. The yapper condemned one of the politicians for being unfaithful to his wife. The two other women at the table nodded gravely as she prattled on. But I had tired of her opinions and blurted out, "Sometimes there are good reasons for infidelity, Shirley. Have you never had the joy of a lost weekend?"

"Of course not," she retorted. I caught in her look of disapproval just a hint of envy – she tried to hide it - before she turned to her red cubes of jello. I smiled at her, entirely without malice. I realized, in that instant, that she was lonely and as depressed as the rest of us at the table. I just said. "That's a shame." Nobody spoke for a moment, thinking about what I had just said.

"Would you like to hear about mine?"

Three heads swiveled as if one. "Yes, yes," came the response. I had to smile and something seemed to melt in my chest. A soothing sensation came over me about the possibility that these women, like me - old, decrepit, weakened and at the end of their long lives - might even share their own stories if we learned to trust each other enough.

"There was this *pájaro*," I began.